Balm

Also by Dolen Perkins-Valdez

Wench

Balm

A NOVEL

Dolen Perkins-Valdez

Amistad

An Imprint of HarperCollins*Publishers*

HarperCollins books may be purchased for educational, business, or sales promotional use. For information, please e-mail the Special Markets Department at SPsales@harpercollins.com.

FIRST EDITION

Designed by Suet Yee Chong

Library of Congress Cataloging-in-Publication Data

Perkins-Valdez, Dolen.

Balm : a novel / Dolen Perkins-Valdez.—First edition.

pages ; cm

Summary: "Set during the Civil War era and exploring the next chapter of history-the end of slavery-this powerful story of love and healing is about three people who struggle to overcome the pain of the past and define their own future"— Provided by publisher.

ISBN 978-0-06-231865-7 (hardcover)—ISBN 978-0-06-231866-4 (softcover)—ISBN 978-0-06-231867-1 (ebook) 1. United States—History—Civil War, 1861-1865—Fiction. I. Title.
PS3616.E7484B35 2015
813'.6—dc23
2014043635

15 16 17 18 19   OV/RRD   10 9 8 7 6 5 4 3 2 1

For David,
always

There is a balm in Gilead,
To make the wounded whole.
—*African American Spiritual, "There is a Balm in Gilead"*

See him at the seashore
Preaching to the people
Healing all the sick ones
Amen, Amen, Amen.
—*African American Spiritual, "Amen"*

For our trust in the healing root or in the strength of the
vine,—what is it else than a belief in thee, from whom all
that surrounds us derives its healing and restoring powers.
—The Sorrows of Young Werther, *Johann Wolfgang von Goethe*

With malice toward none; with charity for all; with firm-
ness in the right, as God gives us to see the right, let us
strive on to finish the work we are in; to bind up the nation's wounds; to care for him who shall have borne the
battle, and for his widow, and his orphan—to do all which
may achieve and cherish a just, and a lasting peace, among
ourselves, and with all nations.
—*Second Inaugural Address, Abraham Lincoln*

Part One

1

When Madge arrived in Chicago, it was an unusually windless summer day, and she could not take her eyes off the bluest water she had ever seen. She believed she was seeing the ocean for the first time, but she had heard from a woman who had heard from another woman that the ocean stirred waves as tall as trees, and this broad flatness looked like the floor of heaven itself. Surely it marked the end of the earth. Nothing could exist beyond that line where the sky reached down to kiss a shimmering edge.

She had only come from Tennessee, but she might as well have come from another country. It would take months to unpack this foreign land, months before she finally ventured out, walking through the retail district, a street along the lake, peering into plate-glass windows. Men behind wooden carts hawking fruits and vegetables in pitched voices. Hackneys, carriages, teams of horses flying madly by in all directions, leaving behind a cloud of dust so thick she could barely see. Signs advertising businesses whose names she could not read. The glance of a woman leaning out of a window. A grand building with wide stone steps leading up to some unimaginable heaven. A new word—*opera . . . opera . . . opera*—melting on her tongue. Tree-bordered boulevards. The South Side avenues. The soft glow of gas streetlights. Horsecars lined with narrow benches and shoving crowds, the bolts creaking so loudly she feared the animals would break free and leave the people in the contraption behind. Five flags waving grandly from the top of a building. The crunch of grit between her teeth, dust rising through her nostrils. She covered her nose and mouth, and as she drew the folded square of cloth from her face she saw the blood on it, and upon further hurried patting, understood that it came from her nose.

This city sure enough gone kill me, she thought.

Still, she relished every moment.

And the water: so many boats and ships like nothing she had ever seen. A city's lines etched by roads and waterways. Sweating Irish stevedores unloading lumber schooners while colored men huddled nearby, watching for injury or exhaustion or a skirmish loud enough to send the offenders home.

And Madge amidst it all, daringly alone, a freeborn woman hovering near the pier, watching as passenger pigeons descended by the dozens. She moved about unmolested, freely, wearing a bright orange neck scarf she'd found in the street two days before. Back in Tennessee, such a scarf might have been taken for hubris, but in the garish city, colors, even on a Negro woman, were just a quiet wink.

She turned, almost walking straight into the wheels of a carriage. The driver shouted at her, and she laughed. Reveling in the city's spirit, brimming with the effervescence of the newly baptized, she walked.

FOR A LONG TIME, Sadie felt like a visitor to another country.

The train had belched her onto the city's shores without so much as kith and kin to greet her, and she'd struggled to find her legs. The place was far enough removed from York to impress upon her the uncertainty of a future without a husband, but it would be some time before she understood that keeping alive the spirits of the lost sat in perfect order within that immortal city.

With its tall grain elevators, winding canal, and trestled bridges, it hummed. Draymen and horsecars and lake steamers. Dead rats lining ditches where sludge-filled water traveled on its way to the river. Its fragility—plank roads and leaning shanties, pine sidewalks and marble-faced buildings with wooden shake roofs—subsumed by an ever-increasing sense of its fortitude. Everything, it appeared, coexisted as an irresolvable contradiction, a trait Sadie would come to see in herself as well, long after she'd accepted the place as home.

The railroad and telegraph worked to adjust the people's sense of the clock, and perhaps because of this, she and the other mediums would be able to convince them that time was more fluid than they imagined, the other side just a ticking away from this one.

Death is not the end, she would tell them.

But hope withered in a city where cholera picked off entire families, men marched off to war never to return, and thousands of cattle were slaughtered in vast stockyards. She had heard that over three thousand miles of railroad touched the city like the arms of some mythical creature, but she did not enjoy knowing that number because it seemed to emphasize the distance between this lakefront city and the Pennsylvania town that birthed her.

Yet those awe-inspiring trains, slamming their brakes in a rush of steam, huffing like hulking shovers, reminded her of the impending sense of everything hurtling recklessly forward. It thrilled and frightened, entranced and repulsed. It was both a nascent Romish state and a virulent pesthole.

She'd journeyed to the city two weeks after he'd gone ahead to prepare their home, traveling on solemn boxcars filled with anxious faces dashing from one town to the next. Her hand shook the entire time, and she did not know if it was the rolling landscape outside the window or the train's constant rocking that made her feel ill.

It was March of 1863, which meant that her first impression of the city was not the height of winter's beauty but the dark, murky ruts of snow that had fallen for months. The river was frozen, the lake marbled with slices of water traveling between gray sheets of ice, the canal virtually impassable.

They did not send word ahead of her arrival, and it was only once she reached the city that she learned his train had derailed. The railroad company retrieved the bodies in the first-class cars first, then set to work accounting for its passenger list. She had not read a newspaper in some time and never saw the headline.

When she arrived at the house on Ontario Street, a silent group of servants hired by her husband waited for her: the butler, cook, housemaid, and coachman, all ready to greet the young widow and determine if she had the grit necessary to survive long in the city. The housemaid took the cape from Sadie's shoulders as she stepped inside.

The servants had kept the body in the house, and Sadie noticed two things: he looked exactly the same, down to the mustache-capped line that had been his mouth, and there was no odor. After clearing his throat, the butler recounted that her late husband had once met a certain gentleman in New York, an embalming surgeon, and after a long evening in which he sat riveted while the man explained the advancements of how one handles a body, preserves a face as if it were sleeping, injects an arsenious fluid into a man's arteries, Samuel had instructed his servant that should a calamitous fate befall him, he would like to be filled with this magical fluid, cast in an earthly monument to his living body. But Sadie was disturbed by the bluish cast of his face, so dull it glowed, hair so dark she was certain it had been blackened. The body achieved the odd illusion that he was younger in death than in life, certainly not the worldly man she'd accepted as her husband just two months ago.

The space above the fireplace was painted green, a barren field. She turned to face them, unsure what to say or do. She had no experience with servants. He was the one who was supposed to take care of these matters.

"Thank you," she said. One of the women, the cook perhaps, clearly outranked her in age. But they took it for the dismissal it was intended to be and left her alone.

Uncertain what was expected of her, she entered the drawing room, the mirror of the room across from it. He had proudly boasted that the two rooms were identical, stating it as if proof of his love that she would have a room dedicated to her evening pursuits as spacious as his. A lie. The house was not a monument of his love—he had not asked her opinion of a single yard of fabric, and she felt like any other mourner come to pay her respects.

Two years after this unexpected welcome by her husband's corpse she would see the house completely differently, a holy space where spirits convened and she, speaking in a voice unimaginable to anyone who'd ever known her, commanded reverence as the dead returned.

But at that moment, her only future had a corpse in it, and all she could do was stare at his grotesque face as she scrambled to pose the questions she'd planned to ask: What were his plans for the future? What was there for a wife to do? How did he like his breakfast prepared?

THE MISSIONARY HAD PROMISED to take him to a city where he could find work and where other coloreds might help him find his wife. But when the freedman arrived, the ceaseless noise silenced him. Waves broke against a pier. A train's whistle screeched. The plink of a piano skipped through a window. As wind rushed the street, a door slammed and a hat went sailing, the lady calling after it. Hemp turned and wiped a grain from his eye.

When he paused long enough to quiet the racket ringing about his head, the freedman was certain he looked upon a city where an unfettered man could swell into his new name. Wooden frame houses, pine cottages, swinging bridges, freighter smoke all stuffed together so tightly, he wondered how they had moved through the narrow lanes with the timber to build. He struggled to decipher among the smear of faces. On the other side of the street, one suit called to another, the accent so thick, Hemp wondered if it was another language. For a moment, he lost his missionary in a crowd. Relief when the man waved back at him. Hemp picked up his step, veering off the sidewalk as he circled a dozen bales of cloth lined up outside a store. The missionary stopped at a pump where the two men filled their canteens. Hemp spit out the water.

"They can help you here."

"Where?" Hemp said, alarmed.

Clearly, they had reached the end of their journey together, but Hemp was not ready. He wanted to clutch the white man's hand, express his gratitude.

"God bless you," the man said, slapping Hemp's arm, and the freedman struggled, once again, for words. He could not gather himself in time. The missionary was gone.

Hemp looked at the door to the church. A crude wooden cross hung from a nail. Built out of narrow, whitewashed boards, the balloon-frame building sat on a busy corner, and, aside from the occasional curious look, no one spoke to him. He sat on the edge of the porch. The preacher back home had expected something for his services, and this one would be no different. Hemp had nothing to offer but hands.

A meanly dressed white man walked by. Hemp scooted back, careful to keep his feet out of the way. He felt in his pocket for the freedom papers he'd received at Camp Nelson. The war was over, but Hemp was still gripped by the fear that at any moment, someone would chain his ankles, push him onto a wagon, and take him back to Kentucky.

The door opened behind him and he turned.

"You just arrived, son?"

Hemp nodded.

The man motioned for him to come inside. "You got water in that thing?"

"Yas, sir."

The man folded his hands in front of his chest, and Hemp thought he looked righteous in his stiff collar. He was a short man with thin curls picked out over a round head. Inside, Hemp could see the sky peeking through a hole in the ceiling over plain pine pews. Another man, thin and wiry with a shot of gray hair like a lightning bolt, descended a ladder.

"What's your name, son?" the preacher asked.

Hemp hesitated, wavering. Outside the city thrummed, sounding a beat in his ears.

"I goes by Hemp."

"Well, my name is Reverend Martin."

Reverend. Something about the very word felt like an embrace, and he allowed the exhaustion to pile softly behind his eyelids.

"Richard, take him on over to Mrs. Jenkins's house." He pointed to a basket in the corner. "It's some extra clothes in there though it's likely you can't fit none."

"I reckon a wash will do me just fine."

"Service here is on Sunday at nine. Come on by once you land on your feet."

"Yas, sir."

"Take some clothes anyhow. You need something decent to find work." He pointed to the basket again, but the freedman did not move.

"What is it?"

"I'm looking for my wife, go by the name Annie. She got a daughter, go by the name Herod. I'm wondering if you heard tell of them. We from Kentucky."

"Annie and Herod from Kentucky?"

"Yas, sir."

"Can't say I have. Once you settle, we can ask around."

Hemp nodded.

"How I'm supposed to know when it's nine in the morning?" he asked the gray-haired man when they were on their way.

"Courthouse bell. Count it."

Numbers meant little to Hemp. He could count his twelve knuckles, and that was it. There had been a class at the camp where they'd taught the men to apply those twelve numbers to the day, but he had not gone to class often enough to learn.

"What day is it?"

The man looked at Hemp as if he had just dropped from another world. "Tuesday. June fourteenth, 1865."

"This it?" he asked when they stopped in front of a row of tightly sandwiched houses.

"I be seeing you at church."

He offered his hand, and Hemp took it. There was no end to this new feeling of overwhelming gratitude. He wanted to ask the man to come inside, but he didn't. Hemp stared at the door. Behind it lay another threshold to be crossed. A fist of terror stuck in his throat. He lifted one leaden foot and then the other one.

He knocked and a woman in a dark dress opened the door, a broom propped between arm and body.

"You looking for a room?" She swept a glance from his tattered shoes to his harshly shaven face.

"Reverend Martin sent me."

"Where you from?" she asked.

"Kentucky."

She narrowed her eyes, wrinkling a scar across her face that had taken some of the bridge of her nose with it. "I don't allow no riffraff in my house. That include liars and cheats and no counts, the don't-want and the can't-do. My husband and me is God-fearing people."

"Yes, ma'am."

She stepped aside. The house looked clean, but an odor like rotting fruit hung in the air.

"Once you get work, you can pay my husband. He at work right now. I take care of things. I'm Mrs. Jenkins."

He saw a few repairs that needed to be made—a tilted floorboard, a gouged table—and he made up his mind to do things around the house until he found work.

She watched his eyes. "This ain't no fancy place. I provides a roof."

"Yes, ma'am." He wondered who had struck her.

A fly landed on his ear. He brushed off the tickle. She showed him the windowless room where he would sleep. Two narrow beds with just enough space to walk sideways between them. Rolled sleeping pallets lay against a wall. The walls were dark planks riddled with holes.

"I expect you hungry."

"Yes, ma'am."

"I cook once a day. In the morning before you go off to work, you and the mens sit down with my husband. You got to fend for your other eats."

"Yes, ma'am."

"Course I don't allow for no loafing. You can't sit round here all day."

"Yes, ma'am."

"Come on eat. It's some hoecakes left. You look hungry as a mule. Then get yourself on out in them streets and get some work."

"Yes, thank you, ma'am."

"You don't say much, do you? That's good. Ain't room but for one talker round here. Haw!"

When he was seated at the rough-hewn table, she set a plate and fork in front of him. He mopped the gravy with a finger, picked up the plate and licked it.

She chuckled as she took it from him. "Toilet and a well out back."

"Ma'am?"

"What you need now?"

"I ain't ate like that since my wife Annie was around."

She paused. "Well, God rest her soul. I suppose the good Lord taking care of her now."

"Fact is, she still living. I come up this way hoping to hear word of her."

"Annie, huh?"

"Got a daughter go by the name Herod. We from Kentucky, south of Danville, worked on a hemp farm owned by a Mr. Harrison."

"Well, I don't know nothing right off, but I sure will keep an ear on it. Everybody come through here looking for one person or another. Now. What's your name?"

"Hemp Harrison."

She paused, became serious. "I see. Now don't go getting lost, Mr. Hemp Harrison. If you do, just ask around for the Jenkins house."

"Yes, ma'am."

Hemp got work loading ships a week later and earned his first wages as a free man. He bought a sack, shoes, pants, but even his first paying job could not help him shake the sadness. He asked everyone he met, but no one knew of a woman fitting Annie's description. He decided it would be better for him to stay in one place. It did not make sense for both him and Annie to be moving around.

Before the month was out he knew that as nice as Mrs. Jenkins was, he could not go on sleeping in that tight, dark room. It reminded him too much of his cabin in the quarters. He began to think of where he could settle. He pooled his money with a group of men and they found a place. A two-room house with four men was sure better than a narrow sliver of a room with five.

2

FOR TWO YEARS SADIE TRIED TO PLAY THE ROLE of grieving widow. She was not familiar with the art, and without female friends to guide her she floundered. She skimmed an article on the subject, the pages of the magazine flat and smooth on her bedside table. Finally, she placed the burden in the hands of the finest couturier in the city.

When the boy delivered a package found in the storehouse containing the train's wreckage, she tore at the paper, expecting to see the likeness produced from the photograph taken on their wedding day. Instead, it was a portrait of her dead husband in a uniform.

"Is there another one?" she asked the courier.

"No, ma'am," he replied.

She peered at the space above the mantel and knew it was where Samuel had intended to hang his own image.

All of the things he had bought for the house had been imported: the set of wingback chairs, the Queen Anne table, longcase clock,

Oriental rugs. All from another world, even her. She sat beneath his portrait, knowing he'd desired a wife who would dwell amid his collection. She'd promised on their wedding day not to forsake him, so she left the house exactly as he'd furnished it, keeping the same coachman to tend the horses and the same cook to prepare the meals. She was still a wife.

At night, lying alone in the bed where she'd expected to perform her marital duty, Sadie tried to imagine what life would have been like had he lived. She pictured a stage with her on it: moving among society, entertaining, offering the demure smile and downcast eye as coyly as a trained actress. Invitations arrived, but she refused them all in a politely worded hand. She had no doubt many of the social calls were misguided attempts at matchmaking. She wrote lie-filled letters to her mother, astonishing herself with elaborate stories about parties she had never attended.

Had he lived, the city might have been more tolerable. But without him, the bitter cold was as unwelcoming as a house without walls. She was used to winter and the scratch of woolens, but this wind's force surprised her. Sometimes, it shoved her so brutally that she skipped a step. It was like being birthed all over again. She feared walking the streets where men stared at her unabashedly. She was unsure how she would get along without a husband in this dangerous place, and she was besieged by a sudden apprehension of empty things: carriages, doorways, alleys, rooms. The silence of the house when the servants retired startled her, and for the first time she understood what it meant to truly be alone. Despite the taste for solitude she'd craved in her youth, she now longed for someone with whom she could share her impressions. And she knew that, though he had not at all been her choice, the scent of his breath enough to elicit a shiver, she missed him, or at least, his companionship.

Each spring, she waited for the snow to melt, thinking over and over that once it was gone she would see the city anew. She could not go back to her parents, and, fortunately, the fortune left behind by Samuel afforded her a great deal of choice in that matter. Despite the brevity of the marriage, he had seen to it that a will was in place. A remote cousin in New York sent a threatening letter, but the lawyer, a faithful associate of the deceased, replied sternly enough to fend off the advances.

She sought companionship in books. A bookseller visited the house weekly, and she ordered from him in every subject—astronomy, horticulture, social reform—developing an obsession with the periodicals of the day. She perused *Harper's*, *Putnam's*, and *Graham's*, devouring news of the war. She imagined herself as part of a broad reading public, musing over the same ideas at the same time, and whenever she yearned for company, she thought of those other eyes, as eager as her own. She read until her back ached, took her meals in the upstairs library, napped in the chair with a book on her lap.

But the disapproving frowns of Olga, the cook, finally got to her, and she tried to get out of the house more. It was summer, and the heat rose like a vengeful guest finally arrived. She tried to make sense of the city's battery of noise—its squawking voices and the strident pealing of bells. Whores looked wall-eyed at her, and the sun hid behind a gown of dust that never cleared.

She left the carriage behind, ventured out alone. The hungry hunkered down into rubble, squatting in alleys. She passed a window, caught a glimpse of herself. She was no different from them: war widows. Cast-off dogs. No one to take her arm. No one to warn her before she stepped into a pile of something soft, the fetor rising. She was both newcomer and old settler. She could not go back to York, nor could she stay in her current state. Within that endless grid of city, horror engulfed, and her memory of recoil at Samuel's touch sifted into the benign. The death of her husband had freed her, but it had also imprisoned her within rows of up-slanted buildings that towered like iron bars.

She felt something open within her, a chill encircling her chest despite the day's heat. She turned to look for her carriage, whirling wildly. The noise rose, fell, sickened her. And she, lost, could not make it home, did not know north from south. A silly idea to tell the driver she would walk. This was, in the end, how Samuel had left her, alone in this teeming city. She stumbled, scanning the fronts of buildings for a safe place. A restaurant, perhaps. But she only saw warehouses, furniture stores, liveries. She fell off the sidewalk, caught herself before she hit the ground, wiped her forehead with the sleeve of her dress, and heard the soft rip of fine cotton. And then, amid it all, she heard him whisper, the sound of a man's throaty tones so close that only she could hear, and she was certain, from the very onset, that this voice was not an illusion. She shook her head. There was no one nearby, yet she clearly heard it again.

That way, he said. *That way is home.*

"CALL A DOCTOR," she told the cook.

"Something wrong? Are you sick?"

"Yes, yes, I am."

The doctor did not come until the next morning, and by that time Sadie's distress was pitch high.

"I'm Dr. Michael Heil," he said, handing her his card.

"There is a voice," she said before he could put down his bag. "In my head."

"Please, be seated." He pressed a palm to her forehead while Olga looked on.

"He speaks to me. He says he is a dead man."

"How long have you heard these voices?"

"There is just one. And I've been hearing him for two days now."

"The war has just ended, and many people are still recovering. You are without family? You lost someone in the war?" The doctor looked at her black dress, thinking of his own ghost.

"I have never had a history of problems. At least, I don't believe I have."

"Are you taking any medicines?"

"Can you make him stop talking to me?"

"I can give you something to help you sleep at night."

"He speaks during the day."

"You must rest," he said.

"Do you believe in such things?"

"Such things?"

"Yes. The dead speaking."

Olga coughed.

"I'm afraid I don't," he responded.

"Of course not. You are a man of science. Surely you have no fears."

"We all have our fears." He searched through his bag until he found a small glass bottle. He set it down beside her. "Put a drop in your tea when you are ready to sleep."

The doctor moved and she pinned his wrist with her thin fingers. He looked at her.

"Help me," she said.

"There isn't much I can do, I'm afraid."

Sadie turned as the doctor and Olga moved toward the door, their hushed whispers cornering her within certain madness. She heard him say: "Shall I visit in a week to see if there is anything more I can do?"

I won't hurt you. I told you so. It's just that it has been so long since I talked.

She sipped directly from the medicine bottle before rising to light all of the room's lamps. The faint scent of gas tickled her nostrils.

Listen.

The curtains puffed, and she shut the window. When she turned, Olga stood watching her.

I served in the Fourth Illinois Cavalry. We were mustered into service on the twenty-sixth of September in the year 1861. I died on April 6, 1862, after the battle at Shiloh.

"What's that, Mrs. Walker?"

General Grant was most capable. He earned our respect.

"That will be all, Olga."

"Do you need anything?"

It was a most gruesome battle. You would not believe.

"No. No, nothing."

"Well . . ."

Sadie nodded nervously. Good God. Am I going mad?

"Thank you, Olga."

The woman hesitated, then turned to leave.

EACH DAY, HE SPOKE TO SADIE more often, sometimes so rapidly she could not think. It became difficult to be around people, and she avoided them altogether, sending Olga out for the simplest errands. One day he was not there and the next he was, and it was impossible to remember what true solitude had felt like. The cook suggested that a ride around the neighborhood might do her some good.

The woman was right. When Sadie sank into the green cushions of the carriage, she could quiet him if she chose. He called her darling and she could have sworn he stroked her cheek. It was, in the end, easier if she did not fight. He did not silence her as her father had done or dismiss her as Samuel had. He listened patiently, delivering to her the rise of the mind she'd always craved.

And he did not come to her with judgment, his voice like a minister's call to the gospel, a merciful flood of acceptance. She had never been particularly religious, but her esteem for the spiritual increased. She fasted out of respect for this gift, refusing food for days. She caused the cook a great deal of worry when she appeared in the drawing room wearing only a chemise. Sadie had desired companionship, and it came in the form of this peculiar voice.

She sat—listening, receiving, awakening to the pleasure of unrivaled attention.

My wife passed a year ago. A heart condition. Now there are just my parents and a brother.

What is your name? she finally asked.

My name, he said, *is Private James Heil.*

The driver quietly tapped on the window. She was startled to discover that she had been sleeping in the back of the carriage. Her skin was warm, and she felt moisture in her undergarments. When she looked over at the seat beside her, she half-expected to see it compressed with the shape of his body. She believed she had done something unseemly in her stupor, and the thought frightened her.

3

THE DAY MADGE SPIED THE FANCY WHITE WOMAN watching her from across the street, she thought she'd come to expose her. Acts such as hers might be more well-known to strangers in the city. The trick was a good one, well worth the risk, taught to Madge by an itinerant white man back home. A tramp, the sisters had called him. Madge had just had to find the camphor, aqua vitae, quicksilver, and myrrh once she arrived north. Each morning, she washed the mixture over her palms and the flats of her fingers, allowing it to dry. If you rub this here potion on your feet, the tramp had claimed, you can walk right over the top of hot coals. Her face steadied as her hand hovered over the heat. First, the people in the crowd appeared afraid, and finally, a surge of smiles, her act bringing cheer to faces worn down by years of war.

The sisters had warned her about the dangers of the trick over and over, until finally Madge outlined the backwoods trail she would take if someone came after her, the quickest path between the feed store and their three-room house. Ever since the war began, the area around Brownsville had welcomed its share of don't-belongs: pale-faced ske-daddlers, the sick and wounded, the opportunistic. But Madge never once got into trouble. After she brought the trick north, the sisters' warnings dimmed as she quickly found a paying audience.

For months, she had been living in a rooming house in the sec-ond ward of the city, just south of the river, dreaming that someone would come along and rescue her, the idea of such an offer so fantasti-cal that when the white woman finally did arrive, it was as if an angel had swept down and granted her wish.

Across the street, Sadie followed the gathering crowd, leaving her driver behind. She pushed through the onlookers so she could bet-ter see the colored girl sitting in front of a fire coming out of a metal bucket resting on four feet. A dirty dress flared on the ground around her, its holes like spots on butterfly wings. The flames flicked up to a tidy point, their dark orange tips licking the air. The girl asked a volunteer to step closer, confirm the heat. Then she squared a hand over the fire, palm down, and began to lower it. Inch by inch, her hand descended into the fire until the flames hugged it, flaring out from its sides. She kept her hand there for five or six seconds, then lifted it, showing the crowd her unburned palm, even inviting the less timid to shake hands with her. They clapped, dropped coins into her basket, and Sadie caught a glimpse of a smile on the girl's lips.

Sadie squinted, wondered at the girl's story. She did not know exactly what she would say, but she had handled her late husband's money long enough to know the power it gave her. As the people dis-persed, the widow drew closer.

"Why you wear that dress?"

"What?" Sadie could not hide her surprise. She had not expected the girl to speak first. The woman lifted a hand to draw a hair from her face. It was the same hand that had rested over the fire, not just on its orange tips, but deeper into its blue glow. No visible burn marks. Not even a tinge of pink.

"No, I mean, your dress look awful hot."

A man in a tattered uniform walked by and gave the two women a curious look.

"Tell me. Can you do other tricks?"

The girl scratched her nose. Smooth, brown skin. The fire had not burned the skin, but it had singed the hair. Up close, Sadie could see she was older than she'd assumed, a young woman.

"Tricks?"

Sadie wanted to know more, but those steady eyes unnerved her.

"I'd like you to work for me."

"Work?"

"Yes. In my home. As a maid."

The woman shook her head, displaying an instinct to refuse before she had even processed the question. Sadie understood her suspicions. They were on a street corner, and Sadie had not asked for references. The proposition sounded odd, even to Sadie, but she'd been feeling unusually courageous since hearing the spirit's voice.

"I will pay you fairly," Sadie added. She did not know what kinds of wages free coloreds made, but she assumed that sitting on a corner performing tricks for a coin or two was a sign of need. She told the woman about the house, the room she could take.

"I got a name, you know."

Sadie nodded.

"What is it?"

"Madge."

"Very well. Come tomorrow, Madge. Ontario Street. There is a bird knocker on the door and an iron fence."

"You want to know how I did it, don't you."

"Did what?"

Madge held up her hands.

"See you tomorrow," Sadie said.

The widow's promise was just a beginning. She had not told Madge much of the position, only promised a fair wage, clean living quarters, an indoor toilet, a cookstove. So little to convince Madge: the black dress, a kind of eye-catching fancy she'd never known back home. The woman had appeared on that dust-soaked street like a ghost adrift in a column of smoke.

Madge accepted the widow's proposition, but she could not shake the feeling that she'd given up some of her independence by doing so. Two questions dogged her: How exactly does one go from being slightly free to being free free to being slightly free again? And what did these degrees of freedom have to do with this hurt that refused to pass?

DESPITE THE GLORIOUS DAYS of sunshine, the widow rarely left the house. Something about the woman unsettled Madge, and she discovered the answer in the pillows. They gave Madge the impression that the house on Ontario Street was not the home of a grieving woman. Certainly, the house contained semblances of sorrow: low lighting, stacks of condolence letters, an armoire of black dresses, measured sunlight filtering through barely cracked drapery. But the energy of the home spoke of something different. There was little . . . saintliness . . . in Sadie Walker's widowhood. Madge sensed, too, that the husband's spirit lingered though he had been dead two years. She had been assured he had not died in the house, yet she could not shake the feeling. She did not traffic in ghosts, but she was not a disbeliever either, and the occasional slamming door made Madge think the dead husband still wandered the house he had built but never enjoyed.

Ultimately, it was the pillows that convinced Madge the widow did not mourn her husband's departure. The stitching was too upbeat, too bright, loopy flowers and vines dangling like the arms of a dancer. In the gloomy house, the pillows were a rare bright touch. Squares roosted on beds, rectangles lounged in seats of chairs, circles lay cozily on the bench in the hall, all of them drawn in a neat hand. Even in the small servant's bedroom used by Madge there were two, an unexpected adornment in the otherwise plain space. Madge found them amusing, their beauty undeniable, and although others might have viewed their sheer quantity as a sign of the widow's loneliness, Madge thought they signaled something more hopeful than the black widow's garb, an unlikely contrast to the dead man's portrait. From the very beginning, she saw through the veil, knew before the widow ever uttered an insensitive thought of him that the woman had never loved her husband. It was the kind of early maturity that came from living in a house of women.

Clearly, Madge had moved into a desperate house. A maid and butler long departed. The cook, Olga, a terse woman of few words, left to do it all. Cook the widow's meals, iron anything that wrinkled, stoke fires, clear ashes, wipe lamps, trim wicks, beat rugs. Olga hired out the laundry and the coachman cared for the horses, tamed the run of yard, ran chores, but the house was large enough to cause the German to skip the smaller, less noticeable tasks. The widow did not entertain, and Olga took full advantage of this lack of scrutiny. When Madge arrived, the house was neat and orderly enough, but the cut crystal on the candelabras was coated in dust and balls of grime gathered in corners of rooms.

As the days went by, Madge started to think more and more about a woman she had never called Mama: smoking and chewing as she recounted stories of Madge's father, Frederick Kingsley, freed by his dead master's will only to find the document contested by an unscrupulous brother. The three-room house, the tree out back where the women strung up dead animals to bleed out, the last pair of shoes the youngest sister made for her, stored beneath the bed and forgotten during her hasty packing. Although she tried not to think of them, she could not help herself. The sisters' voices crowded her head. *Do it this-a-way, do it that-a-way. Girl, you act like you ain't never handled no rag.*

Still wrapped in the memories of the sisters, Madge did not flinch when the widow called her into the parlor and claimed that a dead man spoke to her.

4

*L*IVING AS FREE COLOREDS IN A PLACE LIKE TEN-
nessee put the sisters in a between-space. Their
free papers liberated them, but an indelible shadow
remained. The women lived at the mercy of the folks who patronized
them, forced to tend their paying customers as carefully as they did
the garden out back, while less than a mile away, slaves toiled in the
sun. It was the things the women were capable of—the rubbing out
of sore backs, careful excision of a bullet, sewing closed of a wound,
set of a broken bone, break of a fever, relief of an ache, puncture
of a gumboil—that kept them safe. Their teas and poultices, tonics
and ointments had value, and the sisters were treated like shamans
around town despite their refusal to tread more determinedly into
God's realm and declare themselves two-headed doctors. But when
somebody was sick and didn't seem to be getting better, it was the
sisters who came. Even the ones who supposedly did not believe in
their knowledge sent for them. They doctored on the high and low,

men and women, colored and white, slave and free. There were a number of people in the area who owed their lives to the sisters, and this proved to be no small debt.

The three—Polly Ann, Sarah Lou, and Berta Mae, for their mother had given each of her baby girls two names as a way to elevate them—were the second generation to walk about freely. Raised by a woman who had been jilted by a man she'd made the mistake of trusting, they grew up understanding the futility of forgiveness. Men, their mother taught them, would not allow them to do all the work they needed to do in the world, would do to them as the sisters' father had tried to do to her: rob them of the one thing that gave them standing feet. The story went that their father, a slave allowed to sleep with his free wife at night, never forgave the wife for not being able to save a frostbitten toe and ordered the healer to stop concocting.

"Woman, if you can't save me, you can't save nobody."

The wife refused, and the next she heard, he was back sleeping in his master's barn, leaving her to raise the three alone. So she taught the girls they had a choice between becoming a wife or a healer, and that the bond among them was stronger than anything. When one misbehaved, she beat all three with a hickory switch. When one fell ill, she forced the other two to stay up late tending the sick one. Three rows of plaits, three pairs of shoes, three dresses of homespun cloth. Only their looks differed: Polly Ann more like her father, short, round, with a belly that stuck out like a melon from a young age and never left; Berta Mae and Sarah Lou built up like the mother—tall, long-limbed, broad-shouldered, except Berta Mae got her father's dark-like-soil coloring, and Sarah Lou the red-tinged brown of her mother. When the mother died suddenly, the three sisters cut the wood for the coffin themselves and buried her beneath a dogwood tree, white blossoms shedding over the fresh hump of earth. They were all late into their teen years when they stood over the grave holding hands, the prospect of survival without their mother looking up their noses. Up until that time, the mother had led, directing the mixing, receiving the messages, carving out the morning's path through the woods while the girls acted as her capable assistants.

"We got to let 'em know she dead," said the oldest, Berta Mae.

What Berta meant was that now they would have to let folks know their mother was dead of something serious enough the daughters could not cure it, and that, despite that failing, they would be stepping into her healing shoes.

The first thing they did was take stock of all they had—what had already been picked and what was still shooting out of the ground. What could be eaten now and what could be eaten later, how much meat was salted, how much milk they could reliably draw from the goat, how many eggs the three hens marching around the yard might yield. None of the sisters could read, but they had been taught when they were young how to figure numbers in their heads. So they set about accounting with the desperation of orphans, and when they were done, they agreed that their mother's foresight had been considerable.

They could survive a year without healing a lick.

For months they floated lazily for the first time in their young lives, eating berries and steeping teas that were delightful just because they were delightful. Rather than sell the goat's milk as their mother had done, they drank it themselves, made cheese and sat on the porch eating it with fresh bread. Although they had calculated a year's store, they disregarded their numbers, and after six months, the youngest— Baby Sister—peered into an empty cabinet. In the meantime, the middle girl—Sarah Lou—chased the goat who, still thinking of her as a playmate, hid in a thicket of blueberry bushes. Nearby, the oldest, Berta Mae, cast two eyes upon a bug-ridden patch of cabbage.

The community had left them alone, partly because they did not fully believe the girls could do what their mother had done. But on the very day the sisters realized, one by one, that it was time to step into their mother's shoes, someone knocked at the door. A woman named Thea who lived on a farm just two miles west reported that the white woman who owned her had taken ill. Thea's wet hair brought news of a storm that had not yet reached the sisters' house.

"She ain't getting no better. She look near 'bout to die."

"Where her husband at?" asked Baby Sister.

"He gone off to see about his folks down near Somerville. I reckon when he get back he liable to say I done kilt her."

"You got something to pay us?" Berta Mae asked.

"He ain't leave nothing!"

"Lord strike you."

"You gone help or not?"

Berta studied the woman. "She don't even know you here, do she."

"Her husband kill me if she die. Besides, she a good woman. You help her get well, I pluck my eye out and give it to you."

"That old eye ain't no good and you know it."

Grayness descended upon the trees. The trunks cut through the mist, standing tall and straight like the dark legs of women. The sisters went back inside the house and closed the door behind them. Outside, rain began to hammer the ground, a pool of water filling the crater in the front yard. After gathering what they needed, they prepared as if they would not return for days. Baby Sister tucked scraps of men's pants around the windowsills to keep water from seeping inside. Sarah Lou put a bucket in the middle of the floor.

They walked in a line behind Thea, wide hats shielding their faces. At the farmhouse, they found the white woman lying in a pool of sour. All three sisters recognized her, remembering the time they had visited this very house with their mother some years before. The husband had been bitten by a mule, and they had come to tend a finger that dangled like a rotten tooth.

"I get the fresh bedclothes," Thea said, disappearing into another room.

Baby Sister helped the woman into a sitting position so they could pull her gown over her head. Sarah dipped a rag in a bowl of water on the table and cleaned her up. The woman did not resist, her eyes lidded.

When they had changed her gown and remade the bed, Sarah said, "I got some garlic in my pouch."

"Ain't enough."

"What about some sage."

"Ain't got none."

"Who was supposed to have brung it."

"Here, ma'am. Eat this bread."

"You the one been eating up all the store."

"Just heat the water for the tea and stop wagging your tongue."

"What we gone put in the tea, dogface."

"Shut up and get that water boiling before I slap the both of you."

The two older sisters settled upon a canker root tea to kill whatever was upsetting the woman's stomach while Baby Sister made her sit up and eat the bread. Despite their fighting, the sisters worked together, one on either side of the sick woman, the third holding the cup to her mouth.

"I can't hold nothing down," the woman said.

"Just eat one more bite of bread, ma'am. And drink," said Berta.

She drank. Visibly coloring, she avoided the sisters' eyes, saying only to Thea, "That's well enough. Pay 'em."

The sisters met Thea on the front porch. "Give her that tea every day. Put this leaf in it."

"What's wrong with her?"

The younger sisters looked at Berta Mae. This part had always been left to their mother, even when the girls were the ones to give the instructions on when and how to take the medicine. It was their first pronouncement.

"What you think? Throw that meat out you give her. Ain't fit for a dog."

The sisters looked uneasily at Berta, frightened her mouth would kill their business before it started.

"I could have made tea," said Thea.

"You already done cooked for her and look what happened. Now you heard what the woman said." Berta stuck a hand out.

Thea reached into a barrel sitting on the front porch and counted out six potatoes, four ears of corn. Later, Berta would say, "I knowed she was lying 'bout not having nothing to pay."

When the woman got better, she spread the word that the girls were their mother's daughters after all. The people sent for them, calling them into their sick rooms and paying for medicines with food, cloth, shoes. The daughters shed the idleness of the past months, and, before long, they had gained more confidence, Berta leading the way. Without their mother, the sisters stuck to their school of three, talking their way through the woods in order to remember all that the mother had taught them. They refused to marry, sticking by one another's side, rebuffing advances from men whose attentions they viewed as dangerous. They finished their second decade and began their third, marching faithfully toward the destiny carved out for them. It did not prove difficult, for their beauty was not such that men vowed to have them, and more than one frightened person whispered that the sisters danced in the woods at night.

Then Frederick Kingsley arrived, and Sarah Lou lost her mind for a brief time.

As Sarah's belly inched out the waist of her dress, the other two sisters shunned her. But by the time Madge was born and Kingsley had moved on, the sisters, satisfied with his departure, forgave the middle sister. Instead they blamed the baby, and as soon as she could walk and talk, Madge knew what it meant to be an unwanted child. She had been born into a community of women whose survival depended upon their loyalty to one another, and she upset the balance. Just as their neighbors working the nearby plantations had been born into slavery, Madge inherited a set of memories she had not chosen.

WHILE MADGE WAS STILL TRYING to claim some kind of love from the sisters, the armies fought in Tennessee near the Kentucky border. By April 1864, the war had reached within a hundred miles of the sisters. Folks nearby claimed there were thousands of men fighting on the banks of the Tennessee River. The sisters could hardly believe it, but they still bolted their door at night. Stories of slaughtered men left lying on the battlefield and tent hospitals stretching as far as the eye could see hinted to the women that a time would come when their healing services would be needed more than ever.

After the battle at Fort Pillow, groups of slaves with armfuls of belongings began to make their way through the woods. Folks were on the move, and Madge wanted to move, too. If she stayed in the same house of her mother and her mother's mother, continuing to serve the same folks they had, then the war meant nothing. She wanted to know what this newfound freedom had in store for a colored woman born with papers. She had seen and held the documents none of them could read, buried beneath the floor, declarations containing their names, complexions, heights, the dark pepper-shaped scar over Berta Mae's left eyebrow, the missing fingertip on Baby Sister's left hand. In return for removing a red hill off a white man's foot, he had read the words to them, precious pieces of paper that were more than paper, containing words worth more than scripture. In the meantime, Madge could not resist the restlessness that the word *freedom* created. She had shouted out loud when the first battle cry sounded, but the three sisters had merely shut the windows. Good news, they said, was usually followed by bad. Dark-eyed and uncertain, desperate for a life better than the last, the newly freed people boarded northbound boats and wagons, walking in groups or alone, trickling into contraband camps. Madge decided to join a group walking north to a city of ships and trains. She had no idea how many weeks of walking it would take to reach that land, but she was determined to go.

As she prepared to leave that hot summer morning, she carried a head full of noise: *This woman is my mama. Surely she feel something more than nem other women.* She had figured the two would not speak to her that morning as she put her free papers into a satchel. She had expected their silence.

Her mother stood in the yard washing clothes in a barrel, her hands moving up and down in the water. On the line, two dresses swayed, headless bodies.

"I be leaving soon," Madge called out.

Her mother did not swipe at the thicket of hair netting her face.

"I come to say my good-byes."

Hot water sloshed up Sarah's forearms, reddening them in the early light.

"Ain't got much time."

Sarah rose from the stool, wrung out a pair of drawers over the ground. She did not appear to notice the dirty water splattering onto the bottom of her dress. She turned away from Madge, hung the drawers on the line, carefully spreading them so the wind could pass through.

Madge had expected the two sisters to stick their lips out at her, but Sarah Lou was her mother, and with all the optimism of a young woman her age, the daughter had expected something more than the back Sarah had shown her.

5

IN LATE SUMMER 1865, SADIE'S FATHER WROTE TO say that her mother was ailing and to come at once. It would be the first time Sadie had returned home since her marriage, and she longed to see the familiar sights of her town: Market Street, George Street, the courthouse, Centre Square. No canal ran through York, carrying with it the stench of sewage and dull sight of barges. She was full of expectations, so when the conductor walked through the car yelling *York!* she stared through the window, signaling frantically for him.

"What happened to the station?"

"They burned it," he answered. "Didn't you know? But the people have built another one. A testament to their spirit, I'd say."

The old depot had been made of wood. The new one was brick. To steady herself, she recalled the feel of her mother's fingers in her hair, the tilt of bacon from pan to plate, the plain dress sewn each year. When she saw her, Sadie would admit the letters had been lies. She would tell her all about James.

But for the second time in her young life, Sadie arrived to the news of death. In front of her house, Sadie's trunk still on the seat of the hired carriage, a neighbor woman reported her mother had died of fever. Sadie ran inside, anticipating her father's face, but the rooms were empty. She sat in a chair, removed her hat, and placed it on her lap.

The fact that the house had been spruced failed to cheer her. Freshly laundered linens covered the bed in her old room. Fennel sprayed from a jar on the kitchen table. She waited for the old man, but when he arrived, they said little to each other. The bookbinder's hands were more curled than she remembered, fingers reaching toward palms. That night, he cooked supper for the two of them, dropped the spoon twice. She sat at the table watching and did not stoop to pick it up. He plated the food, and she tugged at the meat on her bone. Across from her, he studiously chewed. The kitchen was hot, close. He wiped his forehead. She remembered the small "mh" her mother would make as she ate, the soft grunts of satisfaction. Her father had cooked on occasion, her mother waiting patiently at the table, relieved of duty. Sadie put down her fork.

"You told me she was ailing. She's been dead for months."

He did not wait to take his last bite, rushing into the story as if he had been burning to tell it for the past two years. His voice surprised her. It had grown thin. He did not stop until he had told it all. How the city leaders gave up, surrendering to the invaders so quickly and unconditionally that the townspeople had little time to think. By then, free coloreds had scattered, hurrying out of town on the winds of rumors that they would be captured and sent south into slavery. Confederates were cutting telegraph wires, destroying railroad depots, tearing up track, burning bridges. Even the neighbors gave in to the fright, shuttering their windows, keeping the children inside. With the absence of their daughter, Margaret and Andrew felt safe, their most valuable possession put away in another place, far from the battlegrounds of war and the looting hands of men. But by the time hundreds of wounded soldiers poured into the hospital buildings set up on Penn Common, Margaret was restless and eager to help. Each morning, she walked down the road carrying a bag full of things she thought might give the men comfort: a Bible, ink and paper for letters, bound magazines from her husband's shop. After doing this for a little over a year, Margaret came home one day with a young woman on her dogcart. This woman, another volunteer from the hospital, had fallen ill, and Margaret was determined to move her out of that place of men. Andrew did not approve, but his wife could not be stopped. The volunteer nurse got better, and as soon as she was able, urged by a calling deeper than Andrew had seen in a woman so young, returned to the place that had sickened her. He begged his wife not to follow, but she did. Soon after that, Margaret became ill. Given her age, her fever proved calamitous.

Sadie looked down at the cold meat on her plate. It had all been such a pointless sacrifice. And for what? What god had taken the offering? It was not even likely the nurse had appreciated what her mother had given. Now her mother was dead. James was dead. Samuel, remembered by a loveless widow, had not fared much better. This war had destroyed families, and it was a shame, even for the imperfect ones like her own.

"I need to see the hospital for myself," she said.

"There is not much to see there now."

"I need to meet the nurse."

"She is no longer in the city."

"How do you know?"

"I looked for her."

"I need to go there."

"It will not bring her back, Sadie."

She turned from him, her hair brushing the wall. Sweat rode the groove of her nose and met her upper lip.

"Very well," he said. "We will go together."

The two of them ventured out on the dogcart the next morning. Her father allowed a man on a mule to pass, and he raised a hand in gratitude. Two others climbed down from their horses to help a boy who'd fallen. Even though the war was over, the pall of tragedy remained. Women walked arm in arm, eyes cast down. An empty sleeve dangled at a man's side. A waif begged for food. The town had awakened to an awareness of its mortality, and it moved with relief. But in her mind, the people of York needed a reminder of all that was wrong in the country. Their marked optimism struck her as false, a contrivance built up by minds eager to forget. Even her own mother. A casualty of war. These people could not see it. No rift this deep could heal. Sadie longed for simpler times, when her mother had rousted the embers of the fire to make bread and dusted the tools in the shop with a careful swipe of her rag, then woke up the next day to do the same thing all over again. This burgeoning web of sufferers, these people attempting to put their lives back together as quickly as they'd rebuilt the train station mystified her. She could barely see three feet ahead. Earlier that day, she'd tripped on a crack in the road, her shoe crushing a forgotten handkerchief.

The halting cart jolted her and she shook her head as her father extended a hand to help her down. They strode onto the grounds of Penn Common, her father's arm hooked through hers. *Mother, help me to understand. Did you want to take them all with you?* The corridors had recently been emptied and few patients remained, but Sadie imagined what her mother had seen: wasted faces like shriveled vegetables, thickets of beards, foul bedpans. She tried to understand the motivations of those women: cooking, washing, changing bandages as the men murmured gratitude through ruined faces. Her mother had rescued that sick nurse from a canyon of convalescents, an act for which she had given her life. A pain struck Sadie in her stomach. She needed to spit.

"Your mother was a new person when she was here," her father said, passing her a handkerchief.

"I've had enough," she told him.

Her mother was buried on a rise of land behind the Presbyterian church. Sadie stood quietly in the soft dirt, not praying but remembering.

For several nights, she could not sleep. To pluck out that ill nurse, save her, yet sacrifice her own life. Which was the greater need, one's own or another's? This question unraveled her. She sat in her mother's chair in the dark. Her foot grazed a stack of books, and it slid, tumbled. She reached down to straighten them, recognizing the bookbinder's signature gold leaf. The smell of calfskin. She touched a spine and brought it to her nose, thinking of the days she'd spent working with him in the bindery.

"Let me get them."

She had not known her father was awake. He kneeled beside her, handling the books gently as he squared them off and pushed them into a corner. The shelves were full. They lined the walls. He sat in the chair across from her. She considered going back to bed, but instead she lit a second candle. Even in the dim light, she could make out little half-moons of exhaustion puckering beneath his eyes. He looked intently at her. Once, that look would have withered her.

"I barely knew him."

"You were safer with him."

"You married me to the first soldier who came knocking."

"Not the first."

Something landed on the back of her hand.

"The wealthiest."

"His money had nothing to do with it."

"You sold me."

He laughed. "I thought marriage would strengthen you."

"I—" She coughed. He rose to touch her back. His shadow fell over her. She willed the coughing away. He sat back down.

"I hear a voice."

He stared.

"A spirit's voice. From the other side. I speak to the dead, Father."

"Dear God."

"I'm afraid of him. I'm afraid of everything." She began to cry.

"Sadie, Sadie." He rose up a little, sat again. "If you can't forgive me, then at least honor the memory of your mother. Don't try to punish me with this exaggerated talk."

"I barely knew the man, yet you married me to him."

"There was a war."

"So you washed your hands."

A ship passed over his face. "Sadie, you must marry again. You must come home."

For a moment, she was suspended, a spider extending its web to an object it can barely see. It was not just that she was an abandoned widow in a foreign city. It was more than that. The opposite, even. Within that space, a brightening, an assembling of desires. She did not say it, but she knew the sensation was simply this: she preferred her new life to her old one, a dead man over a living one.

She listened to the sounds of night, the whirr of nature's hum outside the window, and she found it easy to recall how large this house had once seemed, how vast even this chair had been. She held on to her arms, sitting in the dark long after her father had retired.

SADIE NO LONGER HAD to go on carriage rides to hear the voice. Now he visited her right there in the parlor beneath the portrait of her dead husband. One night, when she entered the room and sat at the small round table, he did the unthinkable. He brought forth her mother as she sat fixed in a spell.

Word spread that soldiers were pouring in. Lice-infested, bloody, malodorous, the men were deposited one after another in beds, and when there were no more beds, they lay on the floor, curled like snails beneath thin blankets. I volunteered three days after the battle at Gettysburg ended, virtually moving into the building for female nurses. At night, their haunted voices echoed as they called out the names of loved ones. My dear, it was something no mother should witness. So little of their youth remained. I was happy to do what I could to help: salving open wounds, holding down a man while his leg was sawed. Needless to say, it took its toll. Soon I found something I could do better than the others. I took men's halting words and transformed them. Your father always said a word, properly spoken, could save a life, but those men taught me the power of poetry. It felt so good to be useful. I even read your letters to them, my dear daughter, though I did not, for a second, believe you. But I hoped you were living a better life in Chicago, that your lies hid the joyous freedom of an eligible young widow in a large city. The war frightened us so, and Samuel had presented as a respectable man, eager to wed after having seen so much. What I now understand, and what you must know, is how much those men needed something to hold on to, something more than love of country.

Sadie drew a breath, afraid the spirit would end the message too soon. Her mother had been an accomplice in the decision to marry her off. A conspiracy between the two of them and no one had thought to ask Sadie's opinion. Her fury swelled, then flattened. She began to weep.

For days, she roamed the house, grief-stricken. It took weeks for her head to clear. If he could bring forth her mother, who else could he summon? He'd claimed he came to her because he wanted to help the families, and Chicago was full of widows. He suggested she could be a vehicle for them. She was still thinking of this when Olga delivered a newspaper along with her breakfast one morning.

"I don't subscribe to this one."

"We may as well keep it," said Olga.

Sadie leafed through the paper, scanning the columns. "Communications from the Inner Life." She turned to the back page, reading the advertisements. The breadth of them fascinated her: clairvoyant physicians and counsels, healing mediums, prophetic mediums, magnetic physicians, electropathists, spirit painters, psychometrics, telegraphic and inspirational mediums, business mediums, homeopathists. She could not believe there were others like her, people who could open doors to the other side. She had read of this spiritualist movement, but mostly the stories she'd heard told of men and women rapping on tables. She did not view her spirit as one of these; he was merely a voice in her head. But the sheer variety of people claiming to possess telepathic powers meant that there was more to the movement than she'd realized. She pored over the essays, poetry, and announcements.

Ultimately, it was the prospect of earnings that did it. The thought woke her up in the morning and kept her awake at night. Fifty cents per visitor was not much, but it wasn't the amount that convinced her. Earnings meant something else. With more than a little trepidation, and without telling anyone, she placed an advertisement in the spiritualist newspaper announcing that she would offer "spirit intercourse" between 9:00 a.m. and 12:00 p.m. for entranced communication with the dead.

6

ARLY, BEFORE THE HAIRS SPROUTED BENEATH HER arms like fungi, Madge understood the joy of the complaint. To ache was to long. To long was to be human. There was ecstasy even in the anguished telling of it. Unknowingly, folks were pleasured by a strained back, a rheumatic knee, a stiff neck, a burning pisshole, their suffering both comfort and grievance. Her task was not just to relieve them of it. First she had to listen, allow them to tell of it, so they could be, in that moment, fully alive. They needed her to acknowledge that this tale was not imagined. This pain that had not allowed them to work or have sex or hoist a musket or shell a pea mattered. And after her full acknowledgment of its power over them, she had to declare that they would be freed of it, and she would be the one to do it. Sometimes just this glimmer of hope was enough. The thought of relief proved relief itself. It was a mercy to allow the moment of diagnosis to linger as they weighed the news.

Finally, the pronouncement.

In the dark of a shed in the Tennessee countryside, she'd planned her decoctions. In the city, she worked to build a similar store in the widow's pantry: roots, herbs, powders, ointments, solutions, tonics. Working with plants, Madge knew exactly who she was. She was more than a woman who stuck her hand in fire for money. More than a Negro servant to a well-meaning white woman. She was a doctress, a healer. To relieve people of their pain was the greatest gift. What the widow did not understand was that this life reigned over the next. Madge had no need for a spirit guide to grant her authority. The Great Spirit itself anointed her with the knowledge tucked inside her head, bestowed upon her by the sisters. It lay in the hands that soaked crushed berries in alcohol, steeped veiny leaves in hot milk, wrapped a boil in a leaf, flushed out worms with purple bergamot tea. Even when the illness was feigned, Madge could pronounce. Malaria, dysentery, miasmatic or otherwise, she could pronounce.

But what she especially loved were the teas. The hunt in the woods for just the right leaf. Bark. Root. Scent of the brew. Shallow slurp of the sick. Knobby hands cradling the cup like a sacrament. Drying leaves, crumpling, mashing in a mortar. Roasting, grinding, stirring seeds into lard. The forest was a natural wonderland of spirit-growths.

She lined up her jars in the widow's kitchen, stacked bark, hung sacks of dried leaves from hooks, watered newborn stems in cups along the windowsill. She needed more herbs before she could start selling. A trip out to the Illinois country was in order, but Madge hadn't the faintest idea how to get there. It had to be far away because Chicago was too packed. One thing closed in on another, leaving little room for breath. She did not believe that anything with power could grow in such a place. She loved the city, but she loved it as one loves something that is so far removed from oneself as to stand outside all understanding. It was nothing less than the wonderment of it that besot her, the question of the divine's intent on those crowded, noisy streets. Surely the forest could not be far. She had been in Chicago for months, and she needed to go soon. The sisters had foraged year-round, picking through leaves, stabbing frozen ground, brushing back the occasional thin bed of flakes. Here, endless sheets of snow daunted Madge. She'd once been lost in a storm, only to find she was on the widow's street all along, just three doors down, had blindly walked the block twice in the implacable white haze.

A few days after Olga told the widow Madge knew how to doctor, the widow called the servant upstairs. Madge was not surprised by the summons. She had learned early on that they always wanted something—a hand to mix, two arms to lift, a fingertip pressed against a pulsing temple. To survive, she would just have to figure out what the widow wanted.

Seated in front of the mirror, the widow pulled down a sleeve, exposing a bony shoulder. The skin had puckered into a lump, red in the center and ringed white at the edges. Madge touched it, and the widow winced. Madge pressed a hand into Sadie's neck and thought of all she'd been taught. There was clearly a boil, yes. But what else was there? To be a healer was to see the invisible. The sisters had, in their own admission, not been as good at it as their mother. The sisters had not allowed Madge to pronounce, had never acknowledged how Madge could feel things with her hands. Pronouncing was reserved for the eldest. But Madge could feel, and sometimes hear, things the sisters could not. Like now. The soft wheeze of breath that signaled the beginnings of infection in the chest. A knot of gas in the stomach from last night's dinner. She pressed more deeply into the widow's neck. If she was going to be called on to heal the widow, she would need to feel it all. Something sparked and she drew back her hand.

"What are you doing?"

"That spirit."

"What did you bring to put on my boil?"

"That spirit man that talk to you. He hurt you?"

"Are you going to talk it away or are you going to put something on it?"

Back in the kitchen, Madge's hands shook as she ground a palmful of thimbleweed root with oil until it was paste. There was something wrong with the way that spirit occupied Sadie's body. She didn't know what it was, but there was no way that dead man could do the widow any good. She wondered what she could say. The woman would never listen to her. She carried the bowl up to the widow's room and set it on the table. She scraped the poultice onto a flat wooden handle and mashed it into the skin. When she had covered the boil in a thick green paste, she flattened a square of dry cloth over it and covered it with another dampened cloth.

"Just sit and rest a while."

"Where on earth did this thing come from? Is my dress too tight on my shoulders?"

"I don't know." Madge picked up her bowl, then paused. "Could I ask you a question, Mrs. Walker?"

"What is it?"

"What you know about this spirit?"

"Well, I believe in him, if that's what you're asking."

"He say why he choose you?"

"What?"

"What do he want from you?"

"You ask a lot of questions, don't you?" Sadie looked up at Madge. She had relaxed under the colored woman's touch, but then the woman had drawn her hand back as if she'd been burned. What skills did this healing woman possess? She had been putting her hand in fire without getting burned. What else could she do? Sadie's contact with the spirit had newly opened her to mysteries, but she was still not entirely comfortable with this newfound knowledge. "Well, he came to me about a year after his death. I suppose my needing him keeps him connected to this side. He wants to help."

The widow rushed her words when she talked, and Madge did not always catch everything.

"Ain't no good ever come from raising the dead," Madge said flatly.

The widow did not answer, and Madge did not speak further out of fear she would anger the spirit. She looked past the widow's shoulder, thinking it might be better to get out of this spirit's way, make her way back to Tennessee while she still had time to beg the sisters' forgiveness.

"You plan to tell me why you brung me here?"

"To be my maid."

"Is that right."

"Yes."

The widow's voice was high and reedy when she got excited, but in her calmer moments, it was as gentle as a girl's. Madge suspected it was the kind of voice that would not deepen with age, unlike her own, which had already gained its force. She stared at the widow's reflection in the mirror. Ringlets framed her face. Sometimes she appeared much younger than Madge, but other times she reminded Madge of someone wise and old.

"Since you asked, I'll tell you. I saw you putting your hand in that fire and I thought you were a believer."

"A believer in what?"

"I thought you'd understand me."

This the girl side of her, thought Madge. *Most days, I don't even understand my own self, let alone you.*

"Now I want to ask you something."

Madge held on to the bowl: *I done lived among women my whole life, and I still don't understand nem.*

"I want you to help me."

Here it was. The truth.

"Take their shawls, that sort of thing. I asked Olga, but she refused."

"Deliver me."

"I'm not asking, Madge."

"Yea though I walk."

She could hear the lowing, the sound of a cow dragging its feet as it was roped into a death pen, neck pinched. And as sure as she recognized she was that cow, the lowing sound in her own head, she knew she would do it: take capes in winter, store parasols in summer, cover the windows, pull back the portière to reveal a portrait and a table covered in black cloth. She would do it out of fear the widow would turn her out if she didn't.

Dead slaves had a tendency to come back hankering after unfinished business. Maybe white spirits were different, but Madge suspected many of those men who'd died on the battlefields had not left the earth singing hymns.

"I don't know why you came to Chicago, but I suspect you ran away from something. I know you were free down there, but something happened, didn't it?"

Free freedom, Madge wanted to say.

"You and I have something in common."

The woman was crazy. They had nothing in common. Madge placed her beliefs beside the widow's. To Madge, the spirits were in the flick of a flame. The ancestors inhabited whatever space they chose. The wrinkled bark of a tree. The bright anther of a flower. Core of a cabbage head. A baby's wormy tongue. When a pig was slaughtered, every part from tail to snout was filled with spirit. The Lord King was inseparable from the spirit world. Why, the widow did not even pray! How could this woman talk to spirits without recognizing the holiness of everything, the carefully and ingeniously drawn earth? If the two were not one, then where did bowels-of-Christ leaves and Adam-and-

Eve root come from? It was true that Madge believed in the widow's abilities, fully believed, as only a fellow person who respected life's mysteries could. What Madge did not agree with was the woman's understanding of it.

Madge wanted to turn and leave without answering. She didn't trust Sadie with her hurt. That's what the sisters had taught her, but alone in this new city, she did not know how she would keep it all bottled inside. She tried to think of what she could say that would make the widow understand.

"You ever wonder what heaven look like? You ever think it might be just 'round that corner only you can't see it none 'cause your steps too short to make it that far?"

"I'm afraid I'm not very religious," answered Sadie. "I think heaven is right here in this room."

"It ain't what I was running from. It's what I was running to. We all trying to get to the same place, Mrs. Walker."

"Where's that?"

"Blessed deliverance."

Sadie thought of her mother. Perhaps that was what she had been looking for in that hospital.

Madge paused. "Truth was, I didn't have no freedom with them women."

"What women?"

Madge rubbed her nose with her forearm, gesturing toward Sadie's shoulder with the bowl as she turned to leave the room. "You best stay out tight dresses till that thang heal."

"YOU'VE GONE AND GOTTEN RICH, have you? Funny thing. I thought you worked here same as me." Olga poked her head out of the back door, breathless. "She's calling for you again."

Madge did not hurry as she rose from her sitting position on the back step and made her way up the stairs to the widow's room. The boil had dried to a blemish, but the woman still insisted on a fresh poultice every other day.

"We can't be long because I have people coming this afternoon."

Madge slid the dress down. The good news was that when there weren't customers visiting the parlor, the widow let Madge be, preferring books over walking, talking company. On the second floor of the house a room was filled with them, the shelves packed with only the occasional slit of space like a missing tooth. Because she could not read, the room frightened Madge more than the darkened parlor ever had, and she imagined they contained a knowledge far more harmful than recipes for tonics and teas passed down through three reclusive sisters.

But she had done as she was told, because although she had never worked in someone's house, she found the work tolerable, relished the freedom allowed by the widow's distraction, and on those evenings when there were no visitors scheduled, Madge ceased her chores, sat on the back step, and chewed tobacco, streaming brown juice into the grass.

Every now and again, when the widow spoke at length in that strange accent, Madge struggled to understand as Sadie retold the story of a mother who died rescuing some nurse in a soldiers' hospital and a father, yet living, who had sold her off to a man she barely knew. Madge had the passing thought more than once that the widow might not be altogether right in the head. After all, a spirit guide was a far-fetched notion, no matter how sincere, and even the death of an unloved husband could do strange things to a woman.

"Madge," Sadie said after a few minutes, "don't you have anyone you'd like me to contact on the other side? Surely you do."

"No, ma'am." Madge dabbed at the mark with a wet cloth.

"Well, what about a letter to your people? Shall I send something for you? I hear the battles down in Tennessee were terrible. You should at least check on them."

"I don't write and they don't read."

Concern radiated from the widow, but Madge did not know what to do with it. She did not know how to receive what this white woman had to give. She could not forge something out of thin air where before none had existed. It had been hard enough to grow accustomed to the widow's odd indulgences: a sack of oranges, a scratched brooch for a gift. Madge frequently used the lessons she had been taught early on, staying low in the bushes, watching the widow from a height, seeing her in light of the things she owned: a fine house, a crepe-trimmed dress, ribboned shoes, strands of pearls. The things this white woman owned made it difficult for Madge to accept her kindnesses. But even more than that, if the sisters could not bring themselves to love her, then this woman surely couldn't either.

"Sometimes the healing is with the living," the widow murmured.

"You still got a daddy, don't you."

The widow looked at her intently, and Madge knew she'd spoken too much. She concentrated on her work, rubbing the darkened sore until the paste disappeared. Madge's hands were anointed, but healing took leaves and roots. Without God's bounty, she could do no more than place a warm palm against a forehead. It was the same with this affection Sadie dangled before her. Where was the plant, the tree, the bush that bound them? Such ties had not existed in Tennessee, and Madge doubted she could make them here, no matter how magical the city.

So as Sadie looked into Madge's face, clearly seeking the return of whatever warmth she was hoping for, Madge turned to leave.

7

BECAUSE HEMP KNEW RIGHTEOUSNESS WAS SOMEthing to be earned by the worthy, he sat in the same pew every Sunday morning. He had never heard a preacher like Daniel Martin. When the man thumbed the pages of his Bible, Hemp was certain he could read. Before freedom, Hemp worshipped under a tree. Now he crept along the boundary of a cleft, the new life perched on one side, the old one on the other, keeping in mind that the trick was to keep from falling in the gap, losing both old and new, for in that darkness lay something irretrievable, and when images and sounds landed on both sides, like the times he woke to the ring of a farm bell from somewhere inside his head, or saw Annie walking sure-footed through a crowded street, he slowed his step. Even now, as words tipped out of the reverend's mouth, words Hemp could not repeat even if God commanded it, he sat transfixed, feeling as though the words did not rightfully belong to him, stolen goods sliding from the man's mouth into Hemp's ears.

His loyal presence in the second row, the eagerness with which he pointed his finger to the ceiling, yelling "Yas, sir! Yas, sir!" when the spirit called, earned the preacher's respect, and Hemp became a deacon in a matter of weeks, ascended to that honored position just below the reverend who was just below the divine. He joined three other deacons, all refugees. The building that housed the churchgoers was not much of a building at all—the ceiling leaked in heavy rains, and every winter, ice damaged the roof. It was the offspring of a larger church, founded to meet the needs of newly arrived freedmen and -women, and like a new bud shooting from a stem, it was still seeking its direction. But the women wore respectable hand-me-down dresses and the preacher owned a robe adorned with the letter M sewn beneath his left shoulder. Hemp believed he had found something like a family in the city of strangers, and this comforted him even more than the sermons, for all his life Hemp had been creating a family where there was none. The deacons readily accepted him as one of them, and he did whatever was asked, so certain was he that this quiet work lay on the path to righteousness, this church the ship that would deliver him to glory.

But on the day they questioned him about Annie, he had his first doubts about joining the church so quickly. The men were patching a hole in the roof, taking turns holding the boards in place while another hammered. When the idle chatter turned to Hemp—*You ain't heard no news about your wife?*—he hammered more loudly. One of them stood looking, waiting. Hemp squinted, sunlight shooting memories into his eyes.

"Naw, nothing."

"You check with that colored association?"

"Yeah."

"Nothing from that notice we put in the paper?"

"Said I ain't heard nothing."

Reverend Martin climbed the ladder, a pail of water in his hand.

"It's some mighty pretty ladies in our congregation, Deacon Harrison. Several of 'em asked about you, too."

The men took turns plunging a dipper into the water.

"Friend of mine took up a new wife," said one of the deacons.

Hemp raised his hammer.

"You heard? Word is colored folks getting rightfully married all over the country."

In the sweep of a question, Hemp was alone again, learning to accept the charitable understanding of strangers, trying to open his shoulders. These were his friends, and they only wanted to help. *These men care about me.*

"I aims to find me a wife," Hemp said softly.

"Plenty of them 'round. Yes, sir, it is."

"No, I mean I still aims to find *my* wife."

"You and a million other freed niggers," said one of the deacons.

Hemp threw the tool, and it bounced off the roof, landing on the dirt with a thud.

"Son, don't," said the reverend. "He ain't mean no harm."

Hemp rolled the nail between his fingers. In the pause, the reverend gave Hemp a tender look that made him think of the day he put a flower in Annie's hair.

"You all right, son?"

Hemp shook his head, fought off a blue feeling. He remembered how, after word came of the recruitment camp for slaves looking to enlist, a few of the men vanished in the night. Others walked off the property in clear daylight. Hemp was the only husband who stayed behind, his face shocked and still. Annie, Annie, Annie, he'd prayed aloud. Once she heard news of freedom, surely she would come back. Harrison Hemp farm, south of Danville. Enough information for anyone. He was the one with no idea where to start. Two years after everyone else was gone, it dawned on Hemp that he would have to settle upon some other way of finding her. When he left the farm, he knew, even after traveling God knew how many miles, his love had not moved an inch.

The reverend gave a nod to the other deacons and led Hemp down the ladder propped beneath the hole in the middle of the sanctuary's ceiling. He sat, motioning for Hemp to sit in the row in front of him. The reverend spoke from behind, and what he said next nearly shocked the shoes off Hemp.

"Son, you believe in spirits?"

"What's that?"

"A spirit woman."

Hemp could not believe his ears. "What kind of woman?"

"A widow woman. Her husband died in the war, I believe. If your wife is dead, least you'll know."

Hemp was just as troubled by the reverend's suggestion they convene with spirits as he was that it involved a white woman.

"A time before, she sat right there in that back room and talked to us. Five colored folks paid good money to hear about their dead family."

"You think my Annie dead?"

"I ain't got the faintest idea, son. I wish I could tell you."

"What if she ain't. You reckon that widow can tell me where to find her?"

"Ain't you tried everything else? She might be your best chance."

Every day Hemp thought about the reverend's proposition, and when he returned to the row of tenements in the evening, he thought even more about it. He had not met many possibilities in his lifetime and knew well enough that hope was a slippery fish. If Annie did contact him, she might not reveal much. The reverend said a spirit spoke through the widow. Annie had always been a woman with little to say, and Hemp did not know if she would trust a white woman medium. Surely Annie was the same dead as she had been alive.

He saved his money and finally gave the reverend his consent. On the night of the sitting, Hemp combed his hair. He wanted to look presentable for his wife. The preacher had grouped the chairs into three lines of four with a single chair facing the others, but the room overflowed. They sat. They stood. They crouched and leaned, fretting, a keening in their backs. The faint stink of unwashed bodies hung over them, the men still in work clothes. Hemp's palms were so moist, they left damp spots on the fronts of his trousers. More people packed into the room. They ranged in age, but their cumulative years added up to more than a sum. He sensed a weariness among them. It was a room of believers and disbelievers. Yet they were all part of the same small flock. Their emotions had been hutted inside of them for too long. A deacon lit four candles and set them on a table. Someone accidentally knocked the cross off the wall. They shifted, fanning themselves, and their lace-ups, high buttons, russet-colored brogans, still covered in the dirt of the roads they had walked that day, scratched the floor as they prepared to harvest their memories and lay them out in untidy rows before the widow.

They all had names on their lips. Fanny. Jessie. Lydia. Herbert. Even the preacher claimed somebody on the other side. Behind Hemp, the grapevine worked:

Rhoda in Mississippi?

Naw. Harry on the Parker place down in Missouri?

Naw. Eleanora in Tennessee?

Eleanor or Eleanora, you say?

The room quieted and they turned. The widow's blue eyes did not appear to blink as she walked to the front. She looked much younger than Hemp had expected. A colored woman stood in the shadows against the wall, holding the widow's shawl. Hemp thought she might be a ghost.

The reverend moved her chair forward. "I appreciate you coming, Mrs. Walker."

The widow did not look at the people in the room. "The spirit comes and goes as it pleases," she murmured. She had barely seated herself before she closed her eyes.

Allow me to introduce myself. My name is James Heil and I was a soldier in the Fourth Illinois Cavalry of the United States Army. I died during a victorious battle at Shiloh led by General Grant, leaving behind all the sweet memories of my young life.

There is a girl. I am not sure who she belongs to. She says her sister is here.

A woman behind Hemp uttered, "Sweetness."

She says she hovers over you. She wants you to know she's peaceful over there. There's no pain or hunger. She's happy.

"Thank you, oh thank you, Jesus."

There is a man.

The room fell silent.

He says to tell his brother he sits with the angels.

Someone rocked in a chair. Its feet clicked on the wooden floor. The woman next to Hemp who had busily asked about relatives before the sitting did not make a sound.

There is a girl standing behind you.

Hemp turned with the others and saw nothing.

She wants to tell you something.

Mama ain't here . . . The voice wavered. *I can't find her. How come I can't find her? I looked for you at the farm, but you was gone. I don't believe Mama made it over here. Do you? She ain't with you, is she?*

Hemp had not known how much he needed to believe in this widow, how much her testimony would mean to him when it finally came. He fully believed he was hearing Herod's voice, and what the girl was saying nearly knocked him out of his chair: Herod was dead, but Annie was alive. With little embarrassment that he was in a room full of people, he did what he had not done when he last saw Annie, what he had not done in the camp or while traveling through the countryside. Hemp cried. Annie was alive, and although this was the news he'd hoped for, it somehow made him sadder than not knowing at all.

THE WIDOW'S HOUSE was surrounded by shrubbery, the foliage beginning to shed with fall's promise. But it was still a far cry from winter when everything was skinny and brown like her, so Madge did not see him until he was right in front of her. Her first thought was that she could all but smell the soil on him. Before he spoke a single word, she heard the music of his speech, knew how he would slide his letters together. When he announced himself as "Hemp" with a softer "Harrison" to follow, something grabbed her by the throat. He said he was looking for Richard, the widow's driver, and she remembered. The séance in the back room of that ramshackle church. The grouping of folks looking for relief on the other side. A dozen women at least, several men, and a gray-haired preacher who could not stop talking.

Madge tightened her squeeze on the plug in her jaw. "He 'round yonder," she said, and tilted her head.

She had not known any free men in Tennessee, but in Chicago she sensed a brashness among them. The way this one stood, this Hemp, the shaking in his hands, told her he had not been in the city long.

"Where you from?" she asked when he did not move. She tried to think of something she could give him from the kitchen.

"Kentucky."

She held back an urge to spit, but the juice collected and she let it fly. He looked at her strangely. Next time, she would hold it.

"Something hurting you?"

"Huh?" Hemp recognized her from the séance at church as the

woman holding the widow's shawl. She had not been a ghost, after all. He watched her taking in his physical measurements.

"You ain't got no aches? No pains?"

"Naw," he said, shaking his head. "I don't hurt much."

Richard came out of the carriage house, and Hemp was grateful for the rescue. He had never been so tongue-tied in all his life.

The two men walked off. Madge watched the stranger from her perch on the step. Even in pants, she could see the high outline of his behind, the cheeks. She spat again, went into the house, and wrapped her hair in a soft cloth.

There was a knock at the door. She opened it, and he stood there again looking at her. Richard was beside him.

"Miss Madge, he come to see the widow. You think she'll see him?"

She shrugged as if she did not care. She looked down at his shoes. "Maybe you had better take those off."

He followed her inside and she led him through the kitchen into a small corridor. She parted a thick curtain that blocked off a room in the front of the house, and he recognized the widow from the church. She was seated at a round table covered in black cloth.

A feeling rushed his head, the sinking dread that was becoming more frequent since freedom. Behind this curtain was another curtain and another, each leading to some new boundary. He looked behind him, but the colored woman was gone. Had she still been there to witness his fear, he might have fought harder to sober it. But with only the widow and those empty eyes before him, he allowed his aloneness to engulf him. His armpits dampened.

"Sit down," she said, unceremoniously.

It struck him that she did not startle at his appearance. His stockinged feet broomed the floor as he neared the chair. The band around his chest tightened. He sat. The soldier in the painting above her stared down at him. Hemp immediately did not like the man and sensed the surliness captured by the artist's brush to be a true likeness.

"I saw you at the church," he said, tightening his jawbone. "I'm looking for my wife."

Sadie held a flower beneath the table. Its juices slid between her fingers. She had not looked at it before the woman had pressed it into her hand just moments ago. A payment of something wild. Something picked from another's garden. Sometimes that was all they had to give—a hasty bargaining.

He was the first colored to come to her house, and the danger of it prickled her. But she recognized the desperation in his eyes and knew his intent was no different than any other visitor.

She closed her eyes. A bright light. Then darkness. The spirit did not come at once so she waited. The table did not begin to shake so much as tremble. The natural light in the room took a turn. Something troubling. The spirit took hold of her like a chill. He didn't speak to her, but she felt his uneasiness.

"A mother and daughter?" Her lips moved with the spirit's. Their voices were one. "Something happened. Something you don't speak about."

Her eyelids fluttered open. She stared at him. Sweat rolled freely down the side of his face. His nose flared wide. She mistook his expression for rage.

"Is . . . who . . ." He tried to speak but the words melted in his warm throat. The widow's eyes were clear like water. He had not seen eyes that blue since looking into Mr. Harrison's. She was Mr. Harrison.

He rose to his feet slowly, keeping his eyes on her. He felt if he turned, she might claw him. He backed up. She did not move, did not even appear to blink. The soft lip of curtain parted behind him.

8

WHEN SHE SAW HEMP WALKING ON THE SIDE of the house, Madge slipped out and followed. He did not walk as if he had somewhere to go, but it was not a casual stroll either, and it struck her as the pace of a man with awful things on his mind. She watched as he trawled the faces around him, worried he would look back and spy her, but he moved unwaveringly forward, heading south over the bridge into the city's heart. He kept to the edge of the street, lifted his pants around puddles, averted his face when a horse stopped to relieve itself. She thought of stories her mother had told her about her own father, his ability to appear carefree when he carried around the weight of his hatred, and for a moment the man walking in front of her was her father, the lover of the root woman on the outskirts of town who cracked his woman's toes and brought her handfuls of sweetspire.

Madge counted the tenth block. He had not avoided the filthier streets, and her shoes were soiled. They entered the ward where the city's colored lived, and he turned into the yard of a frame house next to a snug alley. A woman was hanging laundry in the side yard. Hemp barely spoke a hello. Madge stood near the corner and watched as he closed the door behind him. On the line hung a man's nightshirt. A pair of child's trousers. The laundress worked nimbly. She stretched the clothes over the line so the little bit of sun that peeked into the side yard could move through. The line sagged in the middle with the weight of the garments. A wagon shuffled by, its wheel making a ticking noise as if about to roll off. A one-armed boy rolled a cart, yelling "Peeee-cans!" The woman draped a piece of cloth to shield the yard from the dust kicking up from the street.

Madge thought of how his voice had hushed the clickety-clack inside her. Few things reminded her of home. The comfort of familiarity was that it lacked surprise—teeth biting into something that, whether bitter or sweet or both, made sense. His voice had sidled up to her like an old friend she had not even known she missed.

When she arrived back at the widow's house, she saw that Richard had washed down the steps, Olga had put out a salted triangle of ham on the table, and the sun was brightening the darkly painted parlor where Sadie held her sittings.

MADGE SAT ON THE STEPS, a fresh plug of tobacco in her jaw. The big man had visited Richard twice that week, and each time she had been inside working. She had determined that the only way to catch up with him was to wait outside. It meant she would have to endure Olga's sideways looks, but she did not care. She fingered a sack of dried soup herbs inside her dress pocket. She planned to give it to him even if she did feel foolish.

Thinking about him brought to mind the sisters, how they would disapprove of her waiting on a back step for some man. It was bad enough she cleaned up after a white woman. They had taught her about plants so she would never have to sweep a white woman's steps. It was a rare thing to feel within a person's depths and know when to use a poultice and when to make a tea. Each week, Madge tried to remain faithful to the gifts granted her, squirreling away what she could in the pantry: sacks of powder, jars of gelatinous muck, crocks of dried leaves, flowers strung together in necklaces. She had planted a garden in the back, and it was finally beginning to produce. The kitchen was like her own personal workroom, but she still needed to get out of the city, be in the presence of the Lord King, prod the earth with a stick. To take off her shoes, feel the cold earth beneath her toes, pick burrs out of her dress, scratch bites at her ankles came as natural as breathing. The city was not a place for a woman who had learned to walk by holding on to branches.

She'd managed to come by some pokeberry and arrowroot, but most of it wasn't any good. Picked too early or too late. Missing the roots or the caps. She had done what she could with it, but now the need to get out of the city was urgent. Madge touched her brow and kicked a rock toward the garden. Tomatoes a bright green. Cabbage leaves swollen and yellow. The patch of plantings would barely do for eating, and it would never do for working. She'd mixed in a few things the cook wouldn't notice, herbs that could pass for weeds.

When she saw him walking toward her, she quickly spit the tobacco into the grass behind her. She took out the bag of herbs from her pocket.

"I mixed up some soup for you." She handed him a bag, the crunch of dried leaves between her fingers.

"Deacon." Richard startled both of them, as he strode up clapping dust off his hands. Madge stood on the top step. Hemp stood on the ground, three steps below, his eyes even with hers.

"Deacon?" she repeated.

"Yes, Hemp is a deacon at my church."

"That surprise you?" Hemp asked.

"Should it?"

"Which church you belong to?"

"I don't belong to nobody."

Richard cleared his throat. "Deacon, Miss Madge been looking for somebody to take her out to the country to pick some plants. I figure, seeing as you got time on your hands and all, you could be the one."

"Time?"

"I tell you how to get there." Richard ran a hand over his gray streak.

Hemp turned to Madge. "What kind of plants?"

"I just need to get out there."

"You can take the train," said Richard.

"A train?" Hemp did not want to admit he had never been on one.

"I can use the widow's credit for the tickets," she said suddenly.

Hemp put a foot up on the step, leaned an elbow onto his thigh. He looked down at his hand, turned it over. Veins rose up like rope when he flexed his fingers. A needle of wind pricked his left eye. He put up a hand to block it as he looked up at her and said, "Sure, I might could take you."

SHE WAS HOPING THE RIDE would give them a chance to talk. But as the train took off, the poor man looked ready to vomit. She had felt the same queasiness when the widow first took her on a train ride, so she searched for a way to distract him.

Madge took her time looking him over again. Everything about the man was big. Even his head. And everything looked small on him. The shirt choked. The pants strangled the trunks of his thighs. The toes strained the tips of his shoes. He looked strong enough to protect the whole earth. Arms wide enough to shelter her. Being in Hemp's presence was like standing beneath something cool and shady. The man calmed.

"My ma died giving birth to me, so I don't know nothing about her," he said when she did not hide her rudeness. "The thing I most remember about my daddy was his hands, and they was sure enough big, too."

"Hands ain't no trifle. You lucky to know that. I don't know nothing about how my pa looked."

"That so?"

"My mama the only one of her sisters had a child. The sisters figure all they need is each other."

"That why you left?"

"What you care?" She immediately regretted the bite in her tone. She leaned back and tried to relax. Maybe talking wasn't the best idea.

The benches in the railcar were empty except for two men in the back wearing farmers' hats. Madge squeezed her rooting stick, but as they pulled away from the city, the sight out the window did not meet her measure. She had hoped to find woods like the bottomland forest full of old cypresses in the valley around the Hatchie River, but all she found was more of that flat Illinois prairie that had dominated the land when she'd come up from Tennessee. The desolate sight momentarily caused her to forget Hemp.

The two stepped off the train, the rail depot little more than a raised wooden platform.

"This where you taking me?"

"This where Richard tell us to go for you to find plants. Eighteen miles outside the city."

She walked to the edge of the platform, shaded her eyes, and looked. Even though it was already fall, the flowers stretched endlessly. Purple tips bent, angels rearing their lovely heads. A blackbird squawked, a long tail hanging from its beak. A sheet of sky covered them, the occasional cloud like a wrinkle. The scene whispered that knowledge was not just to be found in the knobby brush of a tangled forest floor but also in this flat sameness, this rambling underbelly of the Lord King's paradise.

Her stomach rolled. To right herself, she eyed an island of trees. A swarm of bees ignited, spread out like a fan, drifted, then disappeared.

"I can't do nothing with this," she whispered to Hemp who had moved to stand beside her.

"What kind of plants you say you need?"

Madge shook her head and took off her shoes. She stepped off the platform and walked into the grass. The ground was cold and wet beneath her feet. Her toes sank. She could barely see five feet in front of her. A bird that looked like a chicken hopped out of the high grass nearby. She jumped.

"Girl, that ain't nothing but a grouse," he called out, laughing.

She pulled at a purple flower. It stuck to the ground, its thick stem held fast by the root. She pushed her mouth into its face and bit off its head, chewing thoughtfully. She sensed the life that dwelled in the place and poked at the ground with her stick. Beetles scrambled beneath its tip.

Afterward, she waited with him for the train. They sat on a bench. Her bag held flowers, some grass. That was really all there was. Flowers and grass.

He spoke tenderly, drawing her out again. "You find something?"

She took some petals from her bag, held out her palm for him to sniff. He leaned. The muscle in his neck twitched, and she could not help but touch it with her other hand. For a moment, he allowed her hand to linger there, as most folks did. Not much to heal with this one. Everything sounded brisk and sharp inside him. But there was something else. A grievance down deep in his gut. She had never felt a sadness so thick. He suddenly drew back, and she mumbled an apology.

"Back home they call me Horse," he said, rubbing his neck where her hand had been. That hand had been so warm. She had soothed him with her touch, and now he felt split wide open.

The wind died; the grass ceased its rustling. Here it was again: the past reaching up to steal what little joy Madge could manage. Her tongue stuck to the roof of her mouth.

"Soon as I could, I pick a name for myself. Felt like being born again."

Her heart returned to its rightful place, and her voice arrived with it. "Horse ain't no kind of name."

"I was wanting to take a real name. I can't be called no Horse up here. But then I think, how she gone find me if I change it? What if she come looking?"

"What if who come looking."

"My wife."

She had hoped the laundress in his yard was not his wife, but it had not occurred to her there might have been a wife from before.

"You left a wife?"

"She left me. Sold off before we was freed. I'm aiming to find her."

"And the laundress?" She could not help herself, the first taste of jealousy on her lips. She had been taught to distrust men. Surely he could be no better than the rest. "Richard say a woman be washing in your yard."

He looked at her briefly, as if taking his first estimation of her, then looked away. "She just using the yard. Don't belong to us nohow."

The train's far-off whistle screeched. Coolness crept over her, and she pulled her cape around her shoulders.

"Why Hemp?"

"Hemp was what we grew. Man owned us by the name of Harrison. Harrison's Hemp. Be mighty nice if my new name help my wife find me."

The train appeared in the distance, and Madge looked at him, the drawn cheeks, the horn of a nose. The man's face was chiseled bone. She wanted to wrap her arms around his waist, but she had never done such a thing to a man in her life and did not even know where to start.

Hemp's eye flitted in and out of focus. One moment he was looking intently at her, the next he was elsewhere. He was like a half-person.

"I got to find her 'cause I got to confess."

"Confess what?"

The sound of the approaching train threatened to drown his words.

"Annie's girl, Herod. She try to do something with me that wasn't natural."

"Something like what?"

The train's wheels roared, the screech of metal on metal. They raised their voices.

"I hit her. I hit her to get her off of me."

"You hit her?"

"I was sleep! And I hit her to make her stop!"

She took his hands in hers and rubbed the backs of them. She did not believe he was telling her more than she could handle, but his eyes were wide with fear, his lips marked from the pressure of teeth. The train was upon them, and nothing either of them could say would be heard. Had the train not arrived at that moment, he might have caught the hushing sound coming from her lips. "Shhh. Shhh. Shhh."

When they got back to the house, he deposited her on the steps, his face back to its normal. "I hope you found what you went out there looking for."

She pulled the bonnet close, hiding her feelings as she stepped into the widow's kitchen, and shut the door softly behind her.

9

AFTER THEIR TRIP TO THE PRAIRIE, HE VIS-
ited her on Sundays after church, talking more
than he had ever talked to any woman. The
words tumbled out, and even though he felt it was unmanly to talk
so much, he could not stop. He talked mostly of himself, of Annie
and life on the Harrison farm. He spoke of the camp where thousands
of colored men and women sought sanctuary. In return, the Tennessee woman lent him a precious gift: the most patient ear he had ever
known. He learned the relief that comes from unleashed secrets, and
he was grateful. He knew what drew him to her, but he was not sure at
all of what she saw in him. They were as different as two people could
be. She was untouched by slavery, and he had been a slave all of his
life. The woman was a mystery.

As time went on, he began to think perhaps it was her freeborn status that made her a neutral audience of one, and he did not stop to think
she might have a pain of her own. She had never known what he knew:

the denial of everything that made him a man, the single, unmitigated belief that a man was born to work like an animal.

Madge kept something cooking on the stove for him, knowing he had been in church all morning and would be hungry when he arrived. Olga had Sundays off now, and Sadie stayed in her library most of the day, so it was easy for Madge to sneak food. On Sundays, Hemp ate whatever was on the widow's menu, and it was the best meal he had all week. They walked out to the carriage house and sat in chairs near the open doorway. She talked while he ate, and when he was finished, he talked while she rinsed their dishes in a tub of water. His constant stories about Annie inserted the pretense of innocence into the visits, but Madge was not fooled. When he didn't think she was watching, she caught him staring. The man came around for more than a hot meal.

And he brought her things. He knew that ever since their trip to the prairie, Madge had struggled to replenish her herb supply. Miraculously, Hemp got his hands on things that folks traveling from the South must have brought with them—snakeroot and collard leaves stashed in traveling sacks, seeds tucked into hair.

They spent those evenings together on the back steps of the widow's house, or in the carriage house where Richard stabled the horse. When Hemp got steady work at a palace hotel, she was the first person he told. He was hired to clean, but after a few weeks, the management took note of his bulk and he was appointed hostler. The wages changed his heart, but the uniform changed the way he thought of himself. It dignified. In that suit, there was no mistaking the difference between a horse and a man.

The hostlers were allowed a break to eat, and they sat cross-legged, their lunch in soggy bags, barely enough food to fuel them until their long shifts ended. Every one of them understood the good fortune of their positions, and they did what was asked without question, chewing leaves to stay on their feet, lifting trunks heavy enough to strain a back, carefully keeping their hands moving as they chatted, for the management was known to check on them unannounced.

Hemp shared all of this with the Tennessee woman.

"I expect you could say the day I got to Chicago was the day of my birth," he told her, the thought revealing itself to him as he spoke.

Eventually, he made his way up each of the back steps into the kitchen until he had seated himself at the table, their voices hushed but strong. Madge's kitchen was a doorway through which he could reach forward in time, and he did not think of the house as belonging to the widow. He thought of it as belonging to Madge, the room no less than Tennessee itself. That was no small feeling because he knew how hard it was to claim something of your own out of somebody else's things.

AS THEY WALKED AROUND the side of the house, Madge felt the widow's eyes. When she tilted her head up, she spied the woman standing in the second-story library window. Madge could have sworn she saw worry on the woman's face. The feeling shook her because she could not remember the sisters ever worrying about her. When she looked again, the widow was no longer there.

Hemp walked closely enough beside her that his jacket brushed her dress. He smelled of cedar, and she wanted to inhale him like a pocket of air. They turned a corner. A park lay on the east block, and the wind cut at her cheek. They crossed a swing bridge into the second district of the city. A tall-mast ship on the river moved silently by, and the moon lit their path.

"It's just a piece more."

She stumbled. He grabbed her arm to steady her. She slowed, turning an ear up to hear the syrup drip when his lips moved.

"You like working for that hotel?"

"Huh?"

"That hotel?"

"Guess so. Better than farm work."

"Well, I sure am glad to hear you don't mind it. I sure don't mind working for the widow. Finding a good house make all the difference in the world," she said, repeating something Olga had said to her, but Hemp looked puzzled by the statement.

"Your feet hurt? You need me to wave down a wagon?"

"You know they don't call it no wagon up here, Hemp. They call it a carriage."

He looked down at her and smiled. "What you know about carriages?"

"Not much."

Just then, a carriage pulled up in front of them, and a liveried colored driver emerged. He opened the door, and Hemp offered her his hand.

"What's this?"

"Since you know so much about carriages . . ."

She took Hemp's hand and climbed inside. The driver shut the door behind them. Madge looked out the window at the lake, whitecaps rippling along its dark surface.

"You sure are something. Where we going?"

"It's a nice night for a ride. Feel good, don't it."

"Surely do."

Madge squinted. She had never been out with a man before, and the realization quieted her for a few uncomfortable moments.

He cleared his throat. "So you say you like working for that widow?"

"She take good care of me, I guess," she said. "Better than them three women I live with down in Tennessee."

"Three women? You mean your aunts? The sisters?"

"All three. Not mine, though."

"It's something about your hands, ain't it. Something blessed."

"Tell me something. How you give birth to something and then turn your back on it?"

"I don't know. I never give birth to nobody."

"All I ask for was one good-bye. A be safe. A God keep you. I didn't get nothing, not even a kiss-my-foot."

"What you say to them? You bless them?"

"I don't understand family. We supposed to help each other, not tear each other up."

"Even a bad family a good one," he said.

"I ain't never done nothing to them women."

"Better than no family at all."

"Why I got to be born to them? Why I can't be born to a mama and a daddy?"

"Sound like you need to make peace with some folks."

She turned to him. "What are you talking about?"

"I'm saying this city is a dream, Madge. It ain't real."

"What's real then?"

"For you, Tennessee. For me, Kentucky. I had a life before this one even though I couldn't lay claim to it. Now all I got is this air biting at the back of my neck."

"You didn't have no life, Hemp. Everything you ever done while you was a slave was a wish. I ain't never known love and neither has you."

"You wrong, Miss Madge," he said quietly. "I known love and I known hate. I known a lot of things."

She looked through the window. Her eyes felt tight and small, as if they wanted to swell and shut. Why couldn't it be easy? Why couldn't they just lay it down and leave it all behind?

"I'm sorry. Hey, look at me." He touched her chin.

A squall of wind rocked the carriage. She leaned into him to steady herself, and when she looked back up at him, her lips touched his.

She felt his warm breath on her face as he whispered: "My wife."

"That woman is the past."

"Not nearly."

"Then why we here."

The voices of the sisters rose in her ears. *Just remember. Ain't no healing brew between your legs.*

Surely Hemp was different, even if he did have a wife lost somewhere in Kentucky, even if he did do something terrible with a daughter that wasn't even his own. All Madge's healing knowledge, all her gifts that seemed so powerful in the forest, failed to tell her what to do with this man. All her life she had been unlovable. He couldn't be any different. Couldn't be. Something moved in the street, a twist of leaves shuddering. She turned to look at him, but now it was his turn to stare through the window on his side. She tucked a loose hair back into her braid, her hand shaking as the carriage glided slowly over the lakefront street.

THE DAY THE HOTEL MANAGER told Hemp he was no longer needed, she was the first person who came to mind. There had been too little time to relish the bright little buttons of the uniform, the cap that barely fit his head. News of blacks campaigning for office. Talk of legislation that would right the wrongs against his people. He should have remembered. He had drunk too deeply from this newfound freedom, too easily forgetting the cracked pots he'd left behind.

We are one hostler too many.

Even in this free world, white men handled his fate as loosely as seeds thrown into a dirt row. He swallowed a desire to plead with the brown-eyed man, even though begging was not beneath him. He turned away, thought of running, turning south again to see if there were any pieces of a life to be salvaged.

"I got to look for work," he said to Madge once he had made it past the wilting flowers outside the back door. Madge nodded as she swept the kitchen. It was difficult for either one of them to wrestle with what it meant to be out of work.

The next day, Hemp went back to the docks, but a fight broke out between the white and colored men and Hemp left. He watched construction workers nail boards together, considered approaching them until he noticed there were no dark men among them. He was not yet desperate enough to go to the reverend, fearing the man would think he had done something unrighteous to lose his job. A sharp point jabbed him in the side, and he heard the hiss of a man demanding his coat. For a moment, he considered resisting, but the image of Annie alone in the world made him hand it over. As his coat walked off, he felt a weight settle into his shoulders, heavier than he'd felt since coming to the city. He smelled meat cooking and followed the scent. He dug in his pants for a coin and sat on a stool to wait for a sausage covered in wet strings. He bit into it, the taste burning his throat. Oil streamed down his hand. He sucked at his wrist bone. Heat warmed the counter, and he regretted eating so quickly. He jammed his hands in his trouser pockets. As men passed, he eyed them, thinking how easy it would be to twist their little necks. Taking another man's coat would do him no good. He was too large. But a hat might fit. Gloves might stretch. A tall-enough man walked by. The alley beckoned. Just one push and he could take hold of those arms thin as rabbit legs. Go see Tennessee wearing fur-lined boots and clutching a pocket of gifts. Here, woman. Would she ask or would she quietly accept his offerings, believing that the desperation of his circumstance permitted a breach or two?

His left ear rang as he crossed the bridge. The damp had frozen the stops of his hair. Now he stood in front of the widow's house again looking up at the windows. He circled around back, saw light shining in the kitchen. He peeped inside, hoping for something, unsure what. Madge stood over the table mixing. She sniffed the contents of a bowl, scooped into a jar. He had never seen her work before, and the sight of her moving about, a thin form of concentrated energy, silenced him. It occurred to him that there were still parts of her he did not know, and he wanted to know them. He tipped up to the back door and rapped. She unlatched the door and hustled him inside.

"Sit down," she commanded. Her look was forthright. He could tell that one discordant tone from him would unhinge her. She was different tonight. More of a woman. He rubbed his thighs together as she added wood to the firebox.

She pulled a jar from a shelf, poured water into a cup. Just the scent of the room lifted his spirits.

"Can you feel 'em?"

"Feel what?"

She pointed downward. "Your feet."

He tried to move his stiffened toes. How had she known? Before he could answer she had pulled off his shoes and wrapped his feet in a blanket. She placed a smooth stone on the fire. Moments later, she used tongs to lift it and place it on top of his wrapped feet. She draped a second blanket around his shoulders, stepped back.

"Mr. Walker was a little man or else I might find you some warm clothes. And what's wrong with you walking 'round with no coat?"

"My coat was took."

She leaned against the table. "You still ain't find no work?"

He shook his head, the heat lulling him into truth. He sipped. The floral-scented tea scalded his tongue. He glanced at the door, fearful that mean German woman would find him in the widow's kitchen wrapped in her blankets.

She poured more hot water into his cup. "Drink."

He drained his tea, unwrapped his feet, put his boots back on.

"Take that blanket with you. Bring it back when you able."

Not even four men could handle her. She might as well have been wearing pants. He could see this as clear as the moon was white.

"Who taught you how to heal?"

"My womenfolks."

"The sisters?"

"The widow my family now."

He laughed. "Ain't no white woman your family, girl."

"You done with that cup?"

He turned to face the door. "Least you know where your'n at."

"You the one with all the memories you can't let go," she said to his back.

"Memories all I got," he said to the air in front of him.

She faced his back and he faced the door.

"Not all."

Neither of them moved.

"If you don't get out that door, I'm gone take my blanket back."

Without looking around, he left, pulling the blanket around his shoulders. Only when he was back on the street did he allow himself to think of her. Madge was quiet, always letting him talk and wanting nothing in return. Annie had taken the ugly and stuffed it back down in the dark hole it'd come from. To those two women, he was something fine. And not no Horse neither. His nose an arrow. His lips a comfort. His eyes a pool. Annie had touched his ear with her tongue, washed the crevices of his neck while he leaned his head. Tennessee caused a rumbling in his stomach. Schooled in the root worker tradition, she surely held powers unknown to him. Hemp had heard of women like her, how they held power over the sick and well alike. But he'd never heard of a young pretty one. As he walked home, he tried to exhale his growing feelings.

He was a married man. *Married.*

10

WHEN RICHARD SHOWED UP AT THE BACK DOOR with the news that Hemp was sick, Madge immediately moved toward her pantry. She called over her shoulder, "What's wrong with him?"

"Could be the flux."

Madge came out of the pantry with her hands full, a sack wedged in an armpit. "How long he been down?"

"Near about three days."

Madge wrapped her cape around her and pulled a hat over her ears. She followed him outside. He opened the door to the carriage. Shards of snow whipped her face as she climbed inside. Richard turned the horses and they headed south. The carriage tilted, and Madge thought they might slip off the icy road. Two horses pulling a sleigh slid by them, the people bundled in dark coats like lumps of coal. The trip was taking twice as long as it usually did. Madge pulled the beaver skin over her legs. Whenever her mind began to envision the worst, she reeled the thoughts back in.

They had just crossed the bridge when the carriage stopped. Richard climbed out of his seat, walked around to the side of the carriage, and disappeared out of sight. Madge tapped on the glass.

"It's stuck!" he yelled.

Madge pushed the blanket away and climbed out. "I can walk from here."

Richard pointed down the street. "Just go on around that block there. House next to the alley."

She knew exactly where Hemp's house was, but she was grateful for the directions because the snow had whitened everything and it would not do to get lost. Outside Hemp's house, a gathering of men milled about, stamping to keep warm. Hemp had friends. And they had not assumed her services would be free. One of the men pressed a stack of wood into her arms.

"Around here, Hemp fix things. He make my grandbaby a crib like you wouldn't believe."

"Hemp a deacon at the church. A fine man," said another, giving her two warm potatoes.

Another handed her a tiny comb with a row of sparkling beads on it. "From my wife."

One of them followed her inside where Hemp lay on rumpled bedcovers.

"How long he been like this you say?"

"Three days."

"Three days? Why ain't y'all come get me sooner?"

"He say he fine."

"Put the wood on that fire."

The man closed the door behind him when he left. On the table, as if someone had fetched Madge in the middle of something, an island of ice floated in water. She put an ear to Hemp's mouth. His breath was clear. She placed a hand on his cheek. Then she opened her pouch and lifted out a piece of bark. She carried a pot outside and filled it with snow, brought it back in, and put it on the fire to melt. She gently scraped green powder off a crusty loaf.

The house had two rooms. The smaller room held two beds, a dresser. The living area, where Hemp lay sleeping, was crammed with furniture, a sea of junk. It was clear the men prepared their meals under the room's only window. She organized the kitchen area, put everything in a logical place. She was surprised to find an old, rusted tub in the corner. She scooted it into the center of the room.

He lay there watching her, not wanting to alert her just yet that he had awakened. When he walked away from the army camp, every exposed part of him had been bitten as he walked through the Kentucky countryside looking for Annie. Nothing he would ever experience could compare to that hurt. How little he'd known. How small his world had been. Now he knew there were more trains than he could count, more roads, more waters. Maybe if he took a train from city to city all over the country, he could find her. But with what money? He thought of Reverend Martin and his church. Surely they could help. But everyone Hemp knew was looking for someone, and the city's pile of grief buried his own. Madge turned around and he shut his eyes. He could not do right by this woman. He could not do right by anyone, not in this country. Claiming righteousness was not possible for a colored man, and he wasted his time fighting it. Down with the traitor, up with the star. Those were the words of the song, but who was the traitor and where was the star?

She put the potatoes in the embers to keep them warm, then perched on the bed beside him and placed a hand on his cheek. A little warm, but not too much. She listened as she pressed his chest, moving her hand down to massage the meat of his hip. When he turned again, she rubbed the other side. Even dead things wake up to loving hands, Sarah Lou used to say. She grazed his nose with the side of her thumb. She was too watchful not to notice the change in his breathing, but at first she did not say anything.

Finally, she whispered, "You up?"

"Hungry," he said. He needed to get out of bed and go look for work. He wanted to ask her to mix up a tea or something that would bring him around, but his swollen tongue refused to move. A sour gas erupted in his throat. "How you come here?"

"Richard brung me." She pulled the cover up to his chin.

"What you ate today?" she asked, but he did not answer. She felt his stomach, and he began to shake.

"Hemp? Hemp."

He dropped into another slumber, and she went outside to relieve herself, staying close to the wall of the house. At night, her fascination with the city turned to fear, and she did not venture to the flap of door over the privy. She lifted her dress and relieved herself against the wall in the shadows of the alley.

Inside, she poked the fire to kick it up. She was afraid to look at him. Once the water boiled, she poured it into a cup over the strip of bark. At first, the bark floated, then it sank, leaving flakes on the surface. She strained the liquid through a piece of cloth. She sat beside him, cupping his head with the palm of her hand as she lifted him. He opened red-streaked eyes.

"Drink," she said.

Tennessee's speech was slow and sure. Annie was frugal with words, and when she did speak, she spoke in short phrases. Bring me that. Co'mere. Be rain soon. Annie's voice was a well-worn doorknob. And when she smiled, it was with her voice rather than her face. This one was completely different. When he had finished drinking, she put the cup on the floor beside the bed.

"How long I been down?"

"Three days."

"Three days?"

She nodded.

"Somebody need to run tell the hotel."

"The wha—? Listen. Don't worry about none of that."

"I done lost her, ain't I?"

"Ain't your body what ails you, is it."

"What kind of life I got?"

A life, she wanted to say. "Maybe you just needs to start over."

"I start over every morning."

"And today a new day."

"How?"

"That ain't the question. You know how. The question is why. 'Cause ain't no other choice. Unlessen you ready to die," she said.

The force of her words surprised her. She could not believe they were coming out of her mouth. She should have been hushing him, urging him to rest.

He turned toward the wall. The cup hit the floor. He heard the liquid seep through the floorboard and drip onto the ground below.

"Annie heal me."

"Time for you to heal your own wounds," she said, mopping up the mess. "Can't nobody else fix you."

"God give up on me."

"You give up on yourself."

"What you come here for?"

He heard her prod the fire. The corners of the room rounded, and the face was Annie's. Her thick shoulder, the flap of dog-bitten ear, the glistening eyes. Arms wrapped around him. He trembled.

"Hemp? Hemp."

A whistle in his ear. The high whine of an insect. At first, it was just a ticklish feeling. Then it rose, until the note of it was like steel grinding against steel. The sound of a train. Annie was coming. As soon as the train stopped, she would get off and he would be waiting.

"Hemp?"

Darkness.

HE TRIED TO LIFT HIMSELF UP. He peered down at his feet, the end of the coverlet resting just below his knee. He did not recognize the socks. Beside him a bug traced the rim of a bowl of uneaten soup. He knew he had lain in the same covers too long, and he did not care. A pot rubbed against him. He fingered his penis, tilted the pot up, and relieved himself into it.

The door to the house opened.

"You alive."

She had put pot after pot of snow on the fire until it melted. Then she'd poured the hot water into the tub. The water barely filled the tub halfway, but it would have to do.

"You strong enough to get in this tub?" She began to unbutton his shirt.

He placed a hand over hers. "I'm a man. Can't you see that?"

She shook his hand from hers. "You smell like one, too." She turned, and while he removed his clothes, she judged the distance to the tub. Might be easier to drag the tub than to move him.

"I can make it," he said.

He tried to hide his embarrassment by thinking of her as an old healing woman. Annie had worked him with her hands, but this girl's touch was different. Annie—with her missing tooth and graying hair and firm touch; Madge—pretty with hands as soft as cotton. He slipped out of his clothes and walked over to the tub, easing into the water.

She busied herself changing the bedclothes. His knees pushed twin hills out of the water's surface. She rolled up his dirty shirt, placed it beneath his neck. Just as she thought it would, the water calmed him. He closed his eyes. She picked up a rag, wrung it, and placed it against his cheek. Then she cleared the crust from his lashes, stretching an ear to wipe behind it, running the rag around his neck. Oil puddled on the surface of the water. After she had cleaned him, she lay the rag on his chest.

She woke him and told him it was time to get out. When he was back in the bed, she stretched the cover up to his neck. The embers ticked. She had used all of the wood melting snow for the bath. His breathing was even, not as steady as sleeping, but not quite awake. She thought again of what he had told her about Annie's daughter. What had really happened that night? Had he done something dishonorable? More than dishonorable? As much as they had talked, sometimes she suspected there was a part of him she did not know. He said he was trying to respect his marriage vows. Madge wanted to believe that. If it was true, she was the temptation that stood between him and honor, not that Herod girl.

Slowly, she climbed into bed beside him, rested her arm across his mountain of chest. If anyone entered the door, Madge would be hard-pressed for an explanation. No doctoring required her to lay with him, but his heat warmed her and the room had cooled.

Hemp cracked open an eye. "Annie?"

She kissed him, and he did not move. She pushed her body onto his.

The sisters stood at the end of the bed watching. Madge had never been one of them, had always known they shared a bond she could not sever. Three was a good, solid number. Disputes settled with one vote. A fourth created dangerous alliances, one in which ties were possible. And what if mother and daughter sided against the others? Where was the peace in that?

"Annie?" he whispered, groaning. His hands were sore where he'd gripped the hackle. In his younger days, he could thrash much more. Annie took his hands in hers and rubbed the hurt out of them. He felt a finger on his lips, and he reached out to her, pulling her to him. She mounted him, and he crushed his face into her neck. She smelled of the hyacinth that grew in the yard. *Annie Annie Annie.*

He thought she was his wife, and she did not care. This was her chance, the first one that would really cut her ties with the sisters. He could be hers if he would just let that wife go. There was no cure for his body. This illness was in his mind. She had never deceived anyone, yet when the time came she made the choice easily.

In that briefest of moments, she decided to give herself to him because, at least with Hemp and Annie, she was part of the three.

Part Two

11

BOTH SADIE AND MICHAEL WERE TRYING TO FIG-
ure out how it all started, what took them from ac-
quaintances to companions to a marriage proposal.
She recalled his second visit to her house, when he'd interrupted a call
from her late husband's lawyer just a few months after she'd begun
delivering séances in her home.

"Some women mediums," the lawyer had claimed, "have been sub-
jected to authenticity tests."

"Authenticity tests?"

"And there is talk."

"What kind of talk?"

"Please forgive me if this sounds impertinent, but there are some
who would like for you to cease your séances."

She waved her hand dismissively.

"Mrs. Walker, have you received many proposals? Surely there is
a suitor. I believe it would be best—"

A knock interrupted just as Sadie was pushing her chin into her chest to tamp down her anger.

Madge announced a doctor. The lawyer bowed, looking pointedly at the other man as he left.

"Mrs. Walker, please forgive the intrusion."

"It is quite all right, although I don't believe I called for a doctor. The voice—I—"

She was smaller than he remembered, and though she was not wearing the veil she had become known for, he detected a guardedness, an odd sense that something still obscured her face. He did not know if he believed, but he was open to the possibility. If she truly possessed a gift, he would soon be speaking with his brother. He raised a hand. "I am not here to cure you of that remarkable voice."

"I don't think I'm following you."

He rested against the back of an armchair. He tried to form his words, but he was stricken by thoughts of what it would be like if his brother's voice were to overtake the widow's, if the movements of her body morphed until she took on the crooked way James had held his mouth, the nervous foot tap. Michael looked through the window at the black iron gate. He tried to speak again. The only way he could explain his behavior was to admit that his lack of courage was some kind of defect. He had no doubt. He was in need of saving.

"Mrs. Walker, I am here to engage your services. You see, my brother died in the war, and I . . . I'm wondering if you might help him speak to me."

She smoothed out the skirts of her dress, looked toward the other parlor. She started to say, *Now I remember you. I thought you didn't believe.* But a noise rushed her ears like waves. Faraway, her father sat down to dinner each evening in a quiet house. Beneath him, the book-bindery was closed, long emptied of its tools. Once, they'd worked together in that little room.

Michael nervously began to fill the silence, telling her about his brother, how he'd died in the war. Finally, she appeared to understand. She led him to a room across the hall. A round table covered in black cloth sat between two chairs. He could smell the remains of a meal, and it calmed him to know she ate, that she was human. He looked up at a large painting of a man with a thick face and trim mustache. The man's eyes penetrated. Bloodred wallpaper, a wooden cabinet in the corner as tall as a coffin, a pair of porcelain urns on the mantel. He pictured the widow projecting a voice, casting spectral shadows with a lantern.

"Pardon me?"

"Please sit."

He lowered himself into the chair opposite her. Minutes passed as she gave him time to collect himself.

"You lost your brother in the war?"

"Yes."

"So many lost." She closed her eyes. "I make no promises, Doctor."

She placed her palms on the table. He did not know what else to do, so he followed her lead. She closed her eyes. He watched her, afraid that if he, too, closed his eyes, he would miss James, and he wanted to see everything. He had heard a woman recount at a party how her deceased husband rapped messages on a table. He wanted more than a rap, but he would take even that.

He waited. There was no clap of thunder, no darkening of the room as clouds hovered above the house, only the soft sound of the two of them breathing. Her body shrank, and he feared she might slip out of her chair. She was so slight. The lips moved, and though it was her voice—the same girlish vocal—there was something else.

He waited, strung between his need to know and the scientific skepticism of his training. On either side, two lights summoned. He smelled something, detected an odor coming from his clothes. It was the same scent that had been with him the day he read the letter from his brother, the day he entered the enlistment office and paid money in exchange for his freedom. He opened his mouth and the scent slipped inside, moved over his tongue, passed a flap of skin into his nasal passage.

A light shook on its string, its flame weak, but steady. He reached for it.

JUST AS THE SPIRIT OVERTOOK HER, her own thoughts nothing more than a background whisper, she remembered the doctor's name: *Heil.*

I figured you'd make your way back to me.

The widow's eyes were empty, and Michael knew he was speaking to the spirit. His doubts slipped down a chute. He cleared his throat. Was he supposed to speak back?

"I beg your pardon?" he uttered softly.

No one has told you my name? You don't know who I am?

Michael shook his head. Laughter erupted from the widow's mouth and Michael went cold. The sound was as familiar to him as any he'd ever heard. It pitched into high notes, went on for longer than natural. He focused on it, trying to fathom what his brain could not imagine. The laughter trickled into silence.

Then, a whisper: *I have missed you, Michael.*

Michael leaped up from the table, almost knocking it over. He reached over and shook the widow's shoulders. She lay limp in his hands, her cheeks jiggling as he arrested her. "Wake up!"

Her lips moved. *Please sit down, brother. Control yourself before you hurt her.*

Michael released her and sat down. Though it was still the widow's face, he could not look at her. The room went out of focus.

"James . . . ?" he asked, but he did not need proof. Suddenly there was no need to verify.

I know why you came.

Michael still did not look up. "You do?"

You want to hear how it was. Well, not actually. It is not war you want to know about, but the things that go along with war. Where did we go? How did we carry on? You want to know about the mettle of a soldier. You want to know how we rose from the smoke of battle, not how we fell. You, of all people, know how one falls—the tearing of muscle and tissue. You want to know why one soldier banged his head on a tree until it bloodied. Why another talked to himself. The reasons behind the empty eyes in a soldier's photograph. The nostalgia, not just for home, but for a more innocent time. After war, a man walks and talks differently. You want to know why. You want to know everything.

We joined out of duty. We owed it to this land that had embraced our fathers and our fathers' fathers. We owed a debt. Our country was ripped apart and we needed to set things right. These were the things we told ourselves before battles, in those hopeful spaces when we imagined we would survive it. And to survive it, we did everything we could. We set up tables and threw cards. We danced, caroused, and then prayed for forgiveness the next morning. We dressed each other's wounds when there were none around to help. If provisions did not reach our camps, we ate grass and emptied long strings of it in the woods. We dreamed of women and spilled seed onto barren ground. We sang patriotic songs through bleeding, cracked lips, slept packed together on cold nights, gummed rotten hardtack. We walked until we could not pick up our knees. We gambled. We cursed. We cried. We prayed. We left precious little pieces of ourselves behind on each battlefield.

His brother plunged right into Michael's heartsickness with little warning and it went on for hours. As James talked, Michael absorbed it all. He pictured the sixteen-gun concentrations. Picket detachments. Mistaken siege tactics. When his brother discussed the first time he was shot, Michael touched the spot on his own back where the bullet would have entered. And the same leap of imagination he used to hear the voice that came from Sadie's mouth was the same leap that allowed him to inhabit James's body. Gone was the paunchy middle. Gone was the straight hair. When the woolen uniforms did not arrive in time for winter's first frost and the provisions of camp had run out, Michael shivered on the forest floor. Michael who poured powder into the barrel. Michael who thrust the bayonet. Michael who heard the chilling yell of rebel soldiers as they charged.

When Sadie awakened him, he looked at her strangely. He had just returned from battle, had witnessed flesh burned from a man's face, and, for a moment, he did not know who she was. She looked as exhausted as he felt. The darkened light in the room told of an entire day passed in her parlor.

"It's over," she said, as solemnly as if she were telling him the war had ended.

He nodded stiffly.

"Would you like to stay and rest a while?"

"No, I couldn't. I mean, yes, I could. But I should go." He needed sleep, time to mull over what had just happened. But he was afraid he would never meet his brother again. There was still so much to say.

She touched his shoulder and he felt a spark pass between them. Both jumped from the jolt. She looked down at her hand as if it were the offender.

"He is the spirit. He is the one who speaks through me. He will be here when you return."

"What do you mean?"

"Your brother is the spirit who is my intermediary to the other side. I'm sorry that I didn't connect your name to his before."

"I don't understand."

"Neither do I."

"Why is he doing this? Why did he come back?"

"Madge will bring your coat."

He shook his head, unsure whether he meant to clear it or to deny the end of the visit.

"Dr. Heil?"

"Yes?"

"I didn't know it was him. Had I known, I would have told you." She seemed as if she were trying to apologize, but she stopped before saying anything further. Then she disappeared through the curtain.

He leaned back and stared at the ceiling in disbelief.

12

*I*N 1859, MICHAEL'S BROTHER MARRIED KATHER-
ine Schneider in a ceremony at her family home in
Halifax County, Virginia. The bride wore a simple
lace sheath sewn by her mother, and slaves attended every detail of
the occasion, cooking and serving the food, cleaning the rooms, while
others worked in fields down the hill from the house. The high-spirited
command of their servants by the Schneider family created a ripple in
the weekend's merriment, prompting the Illinoisans to muse over the
allure of such a system. The mildest of them found it intoxicating; the
more principled took offense.

At dinner, the guests turned to less controversial talk, the Great
West, namely Chicago. The Virginians did not know much about the
city, only that it was reported that the population was increasing rapidly, the city growing at a feverish pace.

The night before the wedding, they passed out dishes for the Pol-
terabend. The guests threw the plates one by one at the brick patio,

afterward declaring the noise loud enough to scare off malevolent spirits. The bride and groom cleaned up, exchanging smiles as they swept. The next morning the guests assembled on the front lawn where the couple was united. Later, Michael would think of the Virginia cousins he'd met, men who had, undoubtedly, donned gray uniforms and gone off to fight against regiments like those containing his brother. The memory of that day, the hopeful promise of James's union—the sound of breaking dishes, a marriage blessed—spoiled by a nation determined to sever itself.

Two weeks after the wedding, Michael traveled back to Chicago. He had finished his medical training at Rush Medical College, and he was eager to set up his practice right away, distribute a fee table, advertise. He had apprenticed with a surgeon for several months, and he stated in his literature that he was equipped to handle everything from dressing wounds to applying leeches.

When the war started, Michael was not surprised to hear his younger brother announce his decision to enlist. The family expected him to return in a matter of months, so Michael did not travel to Cairo to see his brother off as a newly minted corporal in the Twelfth Regiment. He told himself he was too busy being a man of affairs—working to earn a reputation, courting eligible women.

All over Chicago, men volunteered, the words of Stephen Douglas in their ears, *There can be no neutrals in this war: only patriots—or traitors*. Enlistment rallies sprang up in parks and public meeting halls, the sounds of brass bands ringing in the streets. The North's call for loyalty troubled Michael, and he did not know how to respond when James wrote asking if he planned to join the fight. The day after receiving the letter, Michael walked to the recruitment office and stood outside it, watching man after man enter to get his papers.

Inside, two soldiers sat at adjacent desks, surrounded by a disorderly queue of men holding hats in their hands. In the corner, a woman waited in a chair with two shabbily dressed children on her lap. Along the opposite wall, a tall counter held paper and lead. Above, a fat-bellied pigeon cooed from an open rafter. Michael looked up at the bird before stepping forward. A boy called out to him.

"I suppose you are here to enlist," said the boy. He wore a poorly mended soldier's jacket. Cording hung from the shoulder of each sleeve. A small flag decorated his lapel.

"I am a doctor."

"Excellent, excellent," the boy piped. "I'm sure the men could use you."

The child spoke as if he had been to battle himself. Michael blinked at the boy's precocity before fleeing the building. Behind him, he heard the boy cry out *Sir? Sir?*

In the days after, he closely followed the movements of his brother's regiment in the paper. For a while, James was safe. His company stayed in Paducah, Kentucky, for six months before moving south to Tennessee to engage in its first battle. After fighting at Fort Henry, the Twelfth moved on to Fort Donelson. The Union celebrated the capture of the fort, but the paper reported the names of the dead, wounded, and missing. James's name was not on that list, and Michael rejoiced.

He struggled to make up his mind. As a surgeon, he might be insulated from the worst. Surgeons received the rank of officer, shielding them from direct conflict, but there was still the dreaded march, the threat of disease. Reports of German American regiments lit up barside conversations. A *Tribune* article told of the heroic efforts of the all-German Thirty-second Infantry from Indiana fighting with valor at Rowlett's Station in Kentucky. Michael was both German and American, yet he felt zeal for neither. He was paralyzed by inaction, by the fear that his brother possessed something he did not.

Briefly, he considered the issue of slavery. At the Schneider plantation in Virginia, he had looked upon the treatment of slaves with disgust. He found the system horrific, but it was a subject he would rather ignore. After all, there was nothing to be done. Surely, the slaves would not be freed, even if the North were victorious in the war. If pressed, he did not believe his reaction would be: *Leave the Southerners to their culture, and us to ours.* Yet this was exactly where his neutrality left him, his desire to keep his hands clean of it resulting in a clear position nonetheless.

He buried himself in his practice, spending an inordinate amount of time on patient letters, writing out six, seven, eight pages of advice on how to treat a headache. Spring came, and he enjoyed the outdoors, walking the streets, peering through windows. The city was a bustling hub of progress, and men eagerly sought their fortune. He pictured himself among them: a man of industry, a pioneer. One day, someone grabbed his shoulders, a wild look in his eye: *What is the status of your soul?* the stranger demanded to know.

When the telegraph arrived, he was pacing in his parlor, thinking of the latest study on smallpox he'd read. More vaccinations were needed. Outbreaks of smallpox among soldiers were high. Surely there was some way to be of service without enlisting.

"This is just arrived?" he asked the messenger.

"I ran all the way here, sir."

Michael thanked the boy. He sat down before reading the message:

> Springfield, Ill. May 1862.
> MICHAEL HEIL, Chicago, Ill.
> We must travel to Corinth, MS at once. It is grave.
> S. HEIL

A week later, the two remaining Heil men stood over a coffin that appeared to have been made for a child. It contained only an arm.

"I suppose we should take him back to his mother," the elder said.

As the men traveled north to Springfield, the youngest Heil's arm in a box, they said little. There had been a time when all three Heil men were close, but by the time the boys' voices deepened, the three had succumbed to their differences. More than years separated Michael from a father who had immigrated as a teen, been raised by parents whose English never fully matured, then made his fortune in property. The mother, third-generation American, did not teach her sons to speak the language proficiently, and the subtler aspects of the culture eluded them. Michael imagined that his father's feelings at that moment were inexpressible in his second language.

"I don't want to lose all three of you," his mother told them after she had inspected her son's remains. In the days to follow, she tried more than once to bridge the gap between the two men. After the arm was buried and the condolence givers had departed, Michael returned to Chicago.

EVEN THOUGH HIS BROTHER WAS DEAD, Michael obsessed over the war, scanning the paper for notices of the wounded. At the station, he spied upon families waiting for railcars carrying the corpses of officers, watched guns and artillery packed into cars and sent off to be delivered into the hands of soldiers. He listened as men discussed the news in the lobby of the Tremont House. The mood turned somber as someone read the list of dead aloud, each name a slice into the heart of the city. Thousands of men in Chicago had risen to meet the call for troops. Along with war, German men—particularly the socialists—spoke of fires, taxes, steel. The war was impossible to ignore, but in this state, the home of Lincoln, the hope of westward expansion flourished.

Michael considered his aversion to battle. As a child, his cowardice

had been pure. Now, as a man, it migrated into something else, mir-
ing itself in a formless politics. As he walked the city streets, he dwelt
calmly in this no-man's-land where neither the narratives he rejected
nor the ones he might be willing to embrace could reach him. What he
really wanted to do was to disappear into his old life, but the war would
not allow that.

In early 1863 the president freed slaves in the rebellious states.
Congress signed the Draft Act. Michael weighed his chances. He
landed solidly in the age range of eligible draftees, and he was unmarried. Surely Chicago's men would not be drafted. Men were still vol-
untarily enlisting all over Cook County. That summer, Michael read a
disturbing opinion in the paper.

Thursday, June 25, 1863
Chicago Tribune

CONSCRIPTION FOR THE WHOLE WAR
Let the law be equal, and the Federal army a conscripted
army. We have, as we lately pointed out, three millions
of men yet to draw upon to do our fighting. Let them be
conscripted; every man needed.

Calls for a draft disrupted his sleep. He could not stand it. The
second time he entered the enlistment office, it was empty, and Michael
walked directly to the desk of the recruitment officer, withdrawing the
money from his pocket. He was glad the boy was nowhere in sight. He
did not believe he could have done it before those watchful eyes. He
filled out the necessary paperwork and sealed it. It was done. Surrogate
insurance. He left that day, relieved. Whatever happened, he would
not go to war.

March 27, 1866
Chicago Tribune

LOSSES OF ILLINOIS TROOPS
DURING THE REBELLION

Total Number of Deaths: 28,842.

As is known, Illinois furnished for the war, under all the
calls, two hundred and fifty-eight thousand, two hundred
and seventeen men.

He put the newspaper on the table and looked up: an accordion
player whose foot tapping did little to correct his poor time, a skinny
barmaid who inflated prices according to the customer's appearance,
the German barkeep with the arrow-shaped scar across his cheek. Michael sat at a long table near a fire pit, a couple dancing nearby. The
crowd clapped as the woman danced around her partner. Michael's father had succeeded in raising two American sons, but German culture
still ignited something within him. He would have liked to believe his
own dispassionate brew of American patriotism connected to some
far-off affection for his father's home, but truthfully he could claim no
such thing. The oom-pah pounded in his chest, the yodel rose and fell
in his leg, the polka did a quick step in his knee. And yet he remained
outside of it. When he entered Nord Seite, they viewed him as a visitor,
a masquerader. His accent was passable, but it was a broken German at
best. A bratwurst sandwich did the job, satisfied the empty belly. His
last name spoke of his heritage, but his tailored American style of dress
marked him as something else. Perhaps his German-ness lay in the fact
that it was Sunday, and he did not feel the least compunction about sitting in a beer garden.

Just the sound of the widow's voice was a companionship he had not known he yearned. Only the driver knew where he went on those late afternoons. Then the driver took ill, and Michael was unable to save him. A bad leg left unattended. Michael had not even known the man was in pain, let alone near death. The widow's driver had recommended a friend from his church, a man with a strange name. Michael had hired the man without even checking a reference. He did not care.

He visited her regularly. Over two months, he saw her six times. Each visit, a little more added to the story here, a bit more there, the words coming quicker than he could hear them. If Michael closed his eyes, he could make it appear: the squint against dust, the prayer for victory, the walk into the woods to relieve himself. He had come to her hoping to be connected to his brother, not knowing that his brother was the great spirit itself.

The couple before him moved naturally to the music, and the audience clapped good-naturedly. He stood and walked through a pair of trees. He opened his pants and a hot stream flowed into a hole. He fastened up and turned around. As he walked through the crowd, he stepped on someone's toe. The man cursed him. Sometimes Michael hated this city. Surely there were other cities he could have settled upon after leaving Springfield. The hardscrabble winters. The sewer stench. Gambling houses on Hairtrigger Block, where men wagered at games of faro, keno, poker, and bunko. Dance houses where women requested twenty-five cents a dance.

He sat down again, picked up a nearly empty glass of beer, and brought it to his lips, clanging his teeth against the glass. The noise vibrated in his head as if a bell had been struck. In his mouth, the taste of ale bubbled, rising. A woman at the bar eyed him. He looked the other way. One of the two people dancing had begun to emit an objectionable odor, and as they whirled near him, he edged the scent from his nose with a final suck of beer. He licked his lips, the taste of wheat on his tongue.

He thought of entering local politics. If blacksmiths, bakers, butchers, and tailors could declare themselves involved in the city's future, surely he could. The war had been over almost a year, and men of all ranks were running for elected office. He had strolled past the Arbeiter-Halle on Twelfth Street, counted groups of German workers streaming through its doors. He'd considered joining a social organization: the Turnverein or Freimannerverein or Arbeiterverein, but his cowardly burden cast a screen between him and most plebeian causes. The *Staadts Zeitung* had never interested him with its strident views. He thought he believed in this "new Fatherland" but he was unsure. Caught in a web, fluttering his wings back and forth in a trap of indecision, he sulked. He had come of age in a city shaped by war politics, but when thousands had gathered in the wigwam on the city's waterfront in 1860 for the Republican convention, he had stayed out of it, refused to vote. Easily, he'd worn his well-cultivated indifference, and now that the war was over, he found it difficult to shed. He reached for his coat, slung over the back of a chair like a black streak.

"Ist everything *Ordnung?"*

The barkeep extended a hand. Michael took it, the man's cool skin inching back and forth, reptilian. His hairline formed a crooked M.

Why had Michael come to this place? For relief. But he'd found none.

"Ja," he clipped.

He put on his coat, walked outside. A hand on his arm. A woman. He wrenched himself from her grasp. She lost her balance and stumbled. He suspected the barkeep had sent her out after him. The street was empty. Earlier, he'd sent his driver home. Somewhere beyond the buildings stretched that impenetrable dark lake.

He squatted in the alley. His feet planted on the dirt floor, he leaned into the wall, succumbing to the fog of alcohol in his head.

13

I T WAS MICHAEL'S SUGGESTION THAT HE ACCOM-
pany Sadie during her entranced talks. He had been
faithfully visiting the parlor for several months, and
she'd grown to trust him. At least he was respectful, avoiding her eyes
when he could. Besides, the spirit was his brother. If anyone could
help her, Michael could.

While Michael spoke with the audience, Sadie peeked out from
a side room, blowing at her upper lip to cool her face behind the veil.
Madge stood beside her.

"It sure is a lot of them," Madge whispered.

"I think I'm going to be sick."

"I'd be scared, too."

Michael spoke over a din of noise. "Is there anyone here who would
like to select the topic for tonight's lecture?"

The doctor paced back and forth, picking man after man. One,
two, three. You there. Gentleman in the brown hat. You with the red

beard. You. You. In the back there. Down they came, settling into two rows of chairs set out front. Ten men conferred, murmuring. Their words floated in the air. Politics? Religion? Literature? Finally, the botanist among them convinced them to settle upon his specialty for a topic. The man would confirm the veracity of her facts. He'd taught at Oberlin. His books were well known. The others assented, clapping each other's backs as they anticipated victory. It struck Sadie that none of them cared about speaking to loved ones on the other side. They only wished to celebrate her demise, prove her fraudulence. She was an actress, and they would be the ones to expose her. The selection of a jury ensured that her speech was not prepared.

Sadie's business had flourished. Her residence just north of the river allowed those who lived south or west to seek her out. They need only cross a bridge. Many paid her. Others kissed her hands, blessing her, fingering wooden rosaries around their necks as they prayed their gratitude. Others left gifts: fruit, coffee, potatoes. They came to hear a word from the fallen, widows hoping anxiously to hear from dead husbands, mothers bringing children to hear a father's voice. Although spiritualists had existed before the war, Sadie discovered that the time generated an even greater thirst for her services. They had marched into her parlor, searching uncertainly for the right words, the right memories to uphold their families, the widows carefully appraising their prospects, this new, untested autonomy like an ill-fitting dress. Within the vast city, the manlessness of wartime had lain them bare. Thousands of casualties meant that death had become more than a personal grievance: it required an entirely new way of thinking. Scores of mediums claimed to physically manifest spirits: pale faces, arms appearing from cabinets in dark corners. Others used planchettes. Some rapped out messages. Sadie gained prominence as a trance speaker, her voice offering something more than the others. The bereaved hungered for the specificity of words, assurances from the mouths of loved ones. A succession of the aggrieved stumbled out of their nests and answered her call. Many came to her parlor in widow's attire, relaxing at the sight of her own dress, the central portrait of Samuel in his uniform. At first the women told her little, sat erect in the chair as if to say: *Prove it. Prove to me you are what you say.* And Sadie responded, first with a hesitancy of her own, and then with more successes. One woman lamented upon sitting at the table that she had lost four sons to the war. Another woman lost her first husband to cholera in '54 and the second to the war. Before she spoke, Sadie saw the woman's fate plainly written on her threadbare clothing. Impoverished by the second husband's death, destitution was imminent.

Go talk to the landlord. He will allow you more time.

Although she still thought of herself as Sadie, she became known as the Widow. She rotated her black mourning dresses and was never seen in public without a veil. While walking down Booksellers' Row or shopping on State Street, it was not uncommon for people to stare. The city was constantly regenerating, but newcomers quickly learned of her reputation. "Why, that's the Widow!" a seasoned city dweller might knowingly declare. Even those who swore never to pay her a visit, loudly proclaiming she did the work of demons, stepped out of her path. Some even compared her to that famous medium, Cora Hatch.

Yet while her presence drew respect in public settings, the social invitations ceased. She was ostracized from the society her wealth had previously afforded. In her own neighborhood, women refused to greet her or look her in the eye. Dozens of people visited her parlor each week, but Sadie was lonely. She missed home, especially her mother, and she often wondered how a city with over a hundred thousand people could feel so empty.

"When I can't figure what's wrong with somebody, I just go all quiet inside," Madge whispered.

"Then what?"

"Then I wait. Sometimes you got to wait on it."

The room quieted. Michael's voice echoed. "I introduce to you—the Widow."

He held her hand as she emerged, guiding her to the lone chair on a platform at the front of the room. He whispered he would be right there if she needed him. Her veil cast the room in a haze. She pulled it back to see them better, this room of skeptics. When he left her side, she turned, thinking they should end it right then. She could see Madge's face in the shadows. The sight comforted her, and the strange noise coming from her stomach slowly settled down.

"I—I . . ." It was Sadie speaking, but they wanted James. She thought of her mother, the daily walk into that place of sickness, her tools tucked into a bag. The men in this hall did not want to be healed with letters. This was a tour of conversion. First, they required a glimpse of the miraculous, a painless proof. To bring forth the dead was to remind them of something dark, so instead they chose the natural world.

Her eyelids fluttered within her reddened face. She tapped her feet, shaking. Her movements slowed. *Wait on it*, Madge had said. Sadie breathed slowly, in and out.

Allow me to introduce myself. My name is Private James Heil and I was a soldier in the Fourth Illinois Cavalry of the United States Army. I died during a victorious battle at Shiloh led by General Grant, leaving behind all the sweet memories of my young life.

The widow's eyes remained closed, hands cupped in her lap. She was so perfectly motionless, seeming to take only the occasional breath, that it was quite easy for them to imagine another speaking through her—the mouth moving of its own accord, the face impassive even as the voice inflected.

When I was a boy, I spent many a spring afternoon with my brother climbing the horse chestnut tree behind our house. My father, tired of the scatter of spiked fruits in the yard, the animals sickened from eating them, decided to cut it down. When my brother and I saw the ax dangling from his hand, we begged him not to do it. We loved that tree, its broad leafy branches, its delicate white flowers.

The crowd murmured.

So when my father lifted his arm to deliver the blow, my brother grabbed him. The ax fell, hitting the trunk and sticking there, but the angle was off, not strong enough to bring it down. My brother and I were sent to bed without supper that night, but we rejoiced, having saved the tree. The next morning, we went out to say hello to our old friend, and we saw the ax had chipped away a large piece of the tree's trunk at the base. Now as you know, the epidermis of a tree can be quite delicate. It can develop infections or suffer a parasitical invasion. Each day we checked on it, watching as suberous tissue developed over the wound. The blow had not reached the tree's medulla, so it healed by closing up, a corklike substance growing over it. Those botanists among you will understand that this tissue consists of parenchyma cells. They are tabular, compactly organized, and they form a kind of callus. It is not unlike a scab that grows over a human wound.

The widow licked her lips. A door slammed as a latecomer entered.

Even then, I found it interesting how plants repair themselves differently than animals. If a lizard loses its tail, it grows back. A plant, however, creates something entirely new. It is not regenerative. When a tree's leaves die and fall in autumn, new ones return. My father did not destroy the tree, but he did damage it. The cut was done and, though it healed, the scar remained. It remains, I presume, if the tree still stands, to this very day.

A pause, and James continued.

You want to speak of botany so you can avoid talk of the terrible conflict that consumed this country, but there is no escape. This war did not just make a superficial gash in our skin. How are you making sense of the sacrifices we have made? I see you. I see you all. A room of men struggling for the sense to make sense.

The widow quieted. The crowd sat mute and frightened. She was, indeed, a woman possessed. How else could this woman, so young, dressed in a color so dark and unnatural for one her age, face framed by schoolgirl ringlets, speak to them in such a way? Some whispered she sounded like both man and woman. The next night, she impressed another crowd, spoke of yet another botanical subject. And on the third and final evening the crowd overflowed into the street. Inside, the room erupted into shouts after she discussed the effects of fire on some trees. She's a fraud! That's no spirit! They stomped, the noise thundering like a stampede. A man ran toward her before she'd fully awakened. Michael burst from the side room, reaching for her. The stranger had her by the wrist and was pulling up her sleeve to prove his presumption of hidden writing on her arms. Madge pulled at her other arm while Michael restrained the man.

That night, even Madge's tea did not help Sadie sleep.

WHENEVER SADIE LEFT THE HOUSE built by the cold mind of her husband and warmed by the healing hands of Madge, it was as if she were being set adrift at sea. The house would never feel like it belonged to her, but when she traveled it sounded a siren calling her back. She believed it was the soul of the building—its joists and posts and girts— that strengthened her. Outside of it, she looked to Michael for support. He had become a fixture, always waiting patiently in the carriage, doing everything he could to lessen the inevitable obstacles she encountered as a traveling medium. When she stepped into the carriage to sit beside him, she entered another world.

Despite this unmooring, she continued to board train after uncomfortable train, rarely sleeping in those well-worn cars. Their attempts to resemble a home were woeful: dreary landscape paintings, stained carpet, cramped washrooms. Amid the worrying noise of itinerant salesmen, shouting newsboys, buzzing flies, she tried to learn to welcome the call of the next station, the blast of wind when the doors opened; before long, passes over unsteady bridges did not unsettle her as they once had. Soon, she looked forward to the arrival in each new city: the momentary disorientation as Michael sought the driver who was to meet them. While he sorted things out, she read the faces: we are all Americans, for better or for worse. She couldn't help but romanticize those town centers, picturing fair merchants and robust families, her deepest affection lying with the rugged, the faith-filled, their dusty shirts as wrinkled as elephant skin.

It was in those towns where Sadie fully understood the gravity of her mission. She traveled through a nation mourning. The country's thirty million souls pulled at her, and she could feel the tug of hands at her throat. A Texas of lament. Her father had produced hardbound copies of his handiwork. She bound oral messages. Fully maturing out of her shyness, she moved into a recognition of her purpose. When she entered the cleared saloon, the swept parlor, the dusty storehouse, the cold barn, she saw only the chair, a seat waiting to transport, and she sensed the tension of the people: their foreheads creased like paper, their doubtful rumblings.

The conductor walked through the car, announcing they were two hours from Chicago. He stopped at their seats.

"Are you comfortable, sir?" He addressed the question to Michael who turned to her. She nodded.

She studied his square face as he read his book. When he entered a crowded hall, he revealed an expression meant to inspire trust, the one he must have once used at a sick patient's bedside. On trains and in lodging houses, that face focused on her, saw to her comfort. Who was he? She knew the death of his brother troubled him. He never talked at all about patients, and she wondered more than once about the size of his wealth. She did not pay him, and he did not ask.

He squinted. After days of travel, his face grew a more wearied shadow. At least she had grown accustomed to his moods and inflections. At that moment, his skin was gray. He did not look well. She wished Madge were there to tell her what was the matter with him.

"How are you feeling?"

He kept his eyes on his book. "As well as can be expected. Thank you for asking."

She thought of what would make her father happy, what would bring about peace. And as she pressed her palm to Michael's, watching as his eyes jumped to the front of the car and back to hers again, the book slipping into the cushion, she considered a life with him, the ins and outs.

"You know you have been a great friend to me," she said.

All the times he had taken her arm, the meals they'd shared, the late evenings sitting together going over the night's lecture had been so comfortably normal. She reached to touch his cheek.

As they left the rail depot, she thought of what her father would think. There was no denying it: she was no longer dutiful nor dignified. She was not the daughter he'd married off. Then again, maybe she should just give in and do what everyone expected of her.

An oval hearse stopped beside them, topped by six carved wooden urns. Black and white curtains hung at the windows, framed by gold fringe and tassels. She ran her eyes over its glass front, the gleaming steel tires. Had she been born with hands like her father, she might have built hearses, she thought, poring over the details. The clarence fronts. The fluted moldings and swollen sides. On top, it read: "The house appointed for all living."

He moved closer as they rode into the North Division. She looked up at his face again, saw that he had momentarily lost his pale color and taken on the slightly flushed look of a man captured by a woman. His hand rested on hers. How different this would be from her marriage to

Samuel. Here was a man who would never curtail her freedom, who inspired her to follow her own mind.

Yet when he looked over at her, wearing the expression she easily recognized as his most genuine, she had an uneasy feeling that she was making a terrible mistake.

14

SADIE COVERED HER MOUTH WITH A HANDKERCHIEF, looked upward at a slice of sky between the buildings, stepped down and then up and then down again on the uneven boards. A man burned trash in a barrel, and the heat passed over his face in a wet bath. A dray rumbled by carrying stacks of freshly sawed lumber. A red-haired dog, its dark tongue hanging like a piece of rotten flesh, sat beside its owner. Somewhere, she believed, were the wives of these men, waiting for the pittance that would allow them to buy one more bag of meal, a sack of potatoes, an extra bolt of cloth.

At one time, she believed black protected her from the worst of the place, the stares of the indecent driven off by the color's solemnity. But now that her father had written to say that he was coming for a visit, she would shed the black dress, wear fanciful hats, puffed sleeves, gauntlet cuffs. She would order an entirely new wardrobe. She would indulge, wear color again, order a dress in a brilliant shade of orange.

She was ready to move on from this illusion of grief. She marched the block, searching for Michael's apartment. There was a relief, she realized, that came with clarity of vision, an assured certitude. Spiritualism had nurtured her, opened up a new way of thinking. Once, she had lived as a bird who does not know what wings can do. Now she would do things her way. The thought propelled her.

She had no idea what the doctor would think of her proposition. Obviously, he was captivated by her, but marriage was a much more serious topic. Her opinions of most men had been formed during her travels. Men proved themselves to be just as fanciful as women. Hopefully, the doctor would understand that she proposed rationality over romance.

His apartment sat just above a smoking lounge. An open door revealed a steep set of stairs. She climbed them, her skirts brushing both walls of the narrow corridor. He opened the door for her with a surprised look on his face. The rooms smelled of smoke. He had prepared hot water for tea, and the thought of him taking tea alone saddened her.

He did not look at her as he poured for the two of them. She studied the apartment. For a man who lived alone, the place was comfortable. There was even a piano. Of course, he played. He was the kind of man with hidden talents. She sat in a faded armchair, its coils digging into her backside.

"It isn't mine. The rooms came furnished."

"What?"

"The piano."

"Oh." She sipped, stalling. "I want to be honest with you, Dr. Heil. Surely you agree that honesty is the best course."

"Yes. There is never a bad time for sincerity."

He was speaking in that measured way she found maddening. For a moment, she met his serious tone with a similar humorlessness. "We live in an era where the call for earnestness is most urgent. The war has reminded us of the brevity of our time."

"As a doctor, I was not trained to believe in the broadness of truth," he said.

"And you think differently now, yes?"

He paused. "I would say, yes. You have taught me otherwise."

"I realize this visit is unorthodox." She cleared her throat, hardly believing what she was about to say. "I apologize for intruding upon you."

"Your company is never an intrusion, Mrs. Walker." He looked at her expectantly.

"Please call me Sadie."

"Very well."

"You see, I want to be completely clear with you."

"Of course," he said.

He was so earnest. It struck her that the man never smiled. He walked the streets as if doomed. Still, he was one of the few people she trusted. She needed him.

"I have something to say," she said.

"It would seem so."

Her cup clattered into her plate, tea spilling over its sides.

"Forgive me," she whispered.

"I'll get something to clean it up," he said, hurrying out of the room.

When he returned with a cloth, his hand shook as he wiped up the tea. Their partnership had subverted more than one societal rule, and she was aware how much the subterranean quality of their dealings simulated the thrill of criminality. Perhaps she had momentarily confused that feeling with fondness. The truth was that the doctor barely seemed to feel anything outside of his love for his brother. He was more corpse than man.

Say it. Say it.

He tilted his head down, the light catching the red in his hair.

When he looked up, there was a pained seriousness in the way he looked at her.

"Please know, Mrs. Walker, that by bringing my brother's voice to me, you have provided so much. I am forever grate—"

"I wish you'd call me Sadie."

"Oh yes. Then call me Michael."

"I came here to propose marriage, Dr. Heil. A marriage of convenience, of course. An arrangement between you and me. We could just draw up the necessary documents."

She heard the desperation in her tone, and it shamed her. "You don't have to answer right away," she whispered as she stood up. She looked around for the door.

"Marriage?"

The sound of her skirts muffled his voice.

She moved down the narrow stairwell so quickly that she nearly tripped and tumbled.

MICHAEL HEIL LAY IN BED, missing his brother. The widow had announced her strange marriage proposal just the day before, but before he could seriously consider it, the gloom had returned. So he searched, as he did each morning, for a way to shake it. Get out of bed, that was first. Pull on trousers, that was second. A shirt. Adjust the socks until they were level. Shoes. Put on the frock coat before leaving the bedroom. He clasped his hands together and shook his head to clear it. After he'd straightened his necktie, he picked up the empty medical bag.

Outside, he walked past the open door of a butcher where the carcasses of lambs hung by their feet, past buildings covered in signboards, a closed saloon, a lawyer's office, a furniture factory with the name E. P. Huntington painted directly above the entrance. It was the time between breakfast and the midday meal, when work still carried its cheerful notes, and he, a doctor without a single patient, dusty medical satchel at his side, walked one direction and then the next. He paused to take a small cigar from his pocket, lit it with a match, continuing on, smoking and walking, exhaling the smoke until the foot of it burned his finger. He threw the stub into the street, a glowing eye. He came upon a row of women selling fruit out of wooden carts. Behind them, a gang of dogs awaited an opportunity, eyed a hill of plums. One of the women had a large growth on her cheek—darker than a birthmark, fleshy as a mole. Michael squeezed a tomato, threw it up and caught it, drawing a frown from the marked woman. He turned from her, shaded his eyes with the side of his hand.

Farther on, another woman, frail, leaning on a wooden cane, beckoned to him. He sat at a table near her stall. She cooked over an open fire, her cane in one hand, long metal pincers in the other. Grease sizzled in a large skillet set over a fiery pit in a circle of mud bricks. She dropped four white circles into the pan and opened the lid of a deep pot resting on the fire beside it. He waited, listening to the jocularity around him. Three men sitting nearby exploded with laughter. He looked out at them from a dark hole. Everything bright appeared on a horizon. She served him a boneless piece of meat in a watery broth. The meat broke up at the first onslaught of his spoon. The smell of salt stung his eyes. He was as tender as the meat. She placed two biscuits on his plate and pointed. He bit into one, frowned, turned it over, exposing the blackened bottom.

"Do you have more?"

She did not answer.

"Haben sie mehrere dieser?" he said.

She squinted at his mouth. She was German, but she was also deaf, he realized. She smiled, and he saw beauty in her wrinkled cheeks, a goodness in the way she pointed at the food again, urging him to eat.

He obeyed, thinking gratefully that his eyes had not lost the ability to see such things. He dipped the burned biscuits into the soup and took a bite. He could not taste. He reached for the meat with his spoon, but it swam away from him. When he was finished, he paid her and she patted him on the arm.

He strolled down Franklin Street. It was an unusually warm spring day, and the air shimmered. Trash stirred into funnels. He walked through a hazy underworld, his lashes brushed with dirt, his sweat-moistened neck rubbing a stain into the collar of his shirt. Men walked past, stalwart backs in wrinkled pants, whitened dickeys under soiled jackets. One exited a coupe and hurried through the door of a building where, upstairs, two women on a balcony waved at any man who happened to look up, their breasts heaving over the tight necklines of their dresses as they fanned the air in tiny desperate motions with paper fans. He stopped to buy a newspaper before turning back to the street, a city drunk with profit, industry, the dizzying rise of lumber, grain, cattle, while faraway, men had died and their corpses lay rotted in fields.

A touter approached with a bill stretched in a wooden frame, selling tickets to the theater. Michael ignored him, taking off in a different direction.

Without so much as a glance, he passed the hospital on Clark and Randolph Streets, the swinging bridges, lorry men calling out to one another. He thought of what it would be like if he accepted the widow's proposal. He would have access to his brother any time he chose. It would be as if his brother had never died. What if . . . what if . . . she were able to . . . eventually . . . make his brother materialize? If he married her, he could cultivate her talents. Then he could be with his brother all the time!

He stepped off a wooden walkway into a hole. The ankle twisted, and he went down with the newspaper still tucked beneath his arm.

"Are you all right, sir?"

A stranger extended a hand. Michael stood, looking back at the offending hole as he cursed the rapid changes in the city, the incessant building and rebuilding.

"I'm fine." He brushed the dirt from his pants. One step and he knew he could not make it. He dragged his leg into the street, summoned a hack. The twisted ankle slowed him, and he viewed it as a sign. He would accept the widow's proposal, but first he had to admit everything to his brother. There was no going forward without truth.

An omnibus passed, the driver's whip crying in the air. A hawk dipped into the street and landed on an electric telegraph wire. A wagon loaded with dirty children, a stern-faced woman among them, pulled up beside him, and the children stared at him with knowing eyes. He saw a horse race by chasing another, glittering Spanish spurs on high jackboots, a pistol, a lean frame suspended over a saddle. The chase thrilled him, and he felt bound to this great city and its promises of the miracular.

15

As Madge organized the kitchen closet, running her fingers over all that she had put together, she found herself wishing that there was a tonic for memory. The city rang with possibility, yet Madge's feet were still weighed down by two men who'd left a trail of hurt behind, a trio of sisters who refused to believe in anything outside the narrow pocket of their own lives, a mother who turned her back. She could not outrun the past, so she pressed it down instead, concentrating with all her might on making up a valerian tea to help the widow sleep. She heard a knock at the kitchen door and opened it to find an unfamiliar face.

"I'm here to call on Mrs. Walker, see if she needs any medicines or healing aids."

He passed a card to her, and Madge nodded before closing the door. She climbed the back stairs to the widow's room, silently handing over the visitor's card.

"Ah," the widow said. "The apothecarist. There is nothing I need at the moment."

"Yes, ma'am."

Madge walked back down to the kitchen, thinking of him all at once—the wooden box, derby hat, impossible-to-repeat word. She asked him inside and pointed to a chair at the pockmarked kitchen table.

"What you got in that box?"

He looked around, as if waiting for the widow to emerge. "Does Mrs. Walker need something specific?"

"She tell me to look and see what you got."

"Is the cook here?" he asked.

"No, she ain't come today. You want some tea?"

She did not wait for a response. The water was already heated. She shook dried lavender leaves into a cup. The aroma sweetened the air, and after the first sip his face relaxed.

"You got some medicines and such?" she asked quietly.

He opened his case, clearly weighing the possibility of a sale with a colored servant as he took out several glass bottles, lining them up on the table. They were filled with white, brown, and black pills that looked like seeds. She picked up one of the tall, thin bottles and opened it. He continued to present things from his bag as she inspected. She poured a drop of something into her palm, touched the tip of her tongue to it, listening carefully as he explained: this one cured cough, that one stopped a toothache, this one cleared a rash, that one moved the bowels, this one cooled a fever. Encouraged by her interest and becoming anxious at the prospect of a sale, the man brought out everything. When he finished, Madge sat quietly. The door to a new world stood wide open.

"Is there something Mrs. Walker needs? Is she ill?"

"No, but come here. Give me your hand."

"What?"

She took the man's hand in hers, roughly turning it over and squeezing. He pulled it back from her, but it only took a few seconds to feel something. The man's toe pained him. The nail would fall off soon. Madge disappeared into her closet.

"What is it?" he asked, turning over the glass container of oil she'd placed before him.

"Turn a brown nail white." The results would take a while, but she assured him the pungent oil would heal his left toenail.

He looked down at his shoes. "How did you know about my toe? Have I met you somewhere before?"

"Use some and sell the rest. Your people gone be hollering for it." She sat at the end of the table and waited. He carefully placed the offering in his bag along with the rest of his things.

Weeks later, the apothecarist returned and confirmed that the liquid had performed as promised, asking if she could do it again.

"Do what again?"

"Take my hand."

She did it, lingering over his fingers this time. She touched each one, then lifted her eyes to his. "You been having some mighty bad headaches. I got some tea for you. I can't stop them, but I can help you feel better."

"Remarkable," he whispered.

"First, give me what you owe me."

"Owe?"

"Pony up," she said.

He glanced around the well-stocked kitchen: the clean floor, the hanging pots. Finally, he placed two medicine bottles on the table. She fished a pouch from behind the stove.

"What's that?"

"Your tea."

"You're some kind of southern root doctor, aren't you?" He paused before taking the pouch from her.

"Now why on earth would you say that."

She went to the closet and returned with three bottles.

"This," she said, pointing to a small jar filled with black paste, "open up the chest." She pointed to the second jar. "This right here keep a cut from leaving its mark. And this right here is for a mouth sore."

He stared. "You made these?"

She didn't answer.

"They're all, more or less, the same color. How will I tell them apart?"

She stared at him, more closely than she had before, the gaunt cheeks beneath an uneven beard. It did not take healing hands to read the greed in his eyes.

"Don't you label them?" he asked.

"I label with my eyes."

"Once I sell these, I'll bring you more."

She hesitated, then nodded.

After he left, she had a rush of thoughts. This apothecarist could offer her something. She picked up the bottle he'd left. It glinted in the light. In that bottle she saw a life of her own making. Real freedom from the sisters. She had already been developing her reputation in the city selling her potions. The steady flow of women visiting the widow's parlor had provided a ready customer base. When she took their coats, she touched their hands, seeing if she could pick up something. During the sittings, she prepared potions and offered them as they were leaving out the door. That first time was free, but they always came back for more. Between her herbs and the apothecarist's funny-smelling mixtures, she would be able to attend to most anything. The widow would not like it if she knew, but Madge didn't care. She fingered the jar between her fingers. It contained some kind of root she had never seen. Next time, she would demand more from the apothecarist, building and building, until, before he knew it, the man was in business with her.

THE DOCTOR LEANED FORWARD as Madge took his coat, his stance so off balance she thought his cane might slip right out from under him.

She waved her fingers toward the kitchen. "She ain't here yet. Come on back and let me take a look at that leg."

In the kitchen, she pointed to a chair close to her stool so he could lift his foot onto her lap. She rubbed along the anklebone, feeling for the doughy softness that should have been there. She pulled off the sock, examined the coloring. She paused, looking at the doctor curiously.

Once the water had warmed in the reservoir on the back of the stove, she mixed red pepper in a bowl. She unscrewed the cap of a bottle, put it to her nose, and recapped it before placing it in the middle of the pot. After a few minutes, she took it out and poured its oily contents into the pepper liquid. The doctor sneezed. While she waited for it to dissolve, she poured the remaining hot water from the pot into a mug and dropped a piece of willow bark in it. She sat down and returned the foot to her lap.

He watched as she rubbed the pepper oil onto his foot, her hands moving from the ends of his crooked toes, down the bones onto the meat and hair of his leg. Although his mind reacted against him sitting in the kitchen with his foot in a colored woman's lap, he felt an overwhelming sense of relief. He was so taken by the pleasure of her touch that he did not ask what she used. His medical mind faded beneath her hands. The woman's superstitious remedy would do nothing to heal him, but her touch left him with little will to protest.

Her finger bumped a knot and the pronouncement came to her:

this pain was not physical. The ankle was barely injured, but the man limped like a shot dog. She could see how stiffly he held his neck. This was a man who did not speak about what went on inside, and the evidence was written in his body. If she could move her hands across his shoulders, she knew she would find more of the unspoken.

Madge wiped off the excess oil with a rag and patted him to signal she was finished.

"Can you wrap some of that up for me to take?"

"You pay me."

She could tell what he was thinking: if he told the widow, Madge would lose her place in the house. She sensed the threat in his eyes.

He looked around the kitchen for signs of commerce, suddenly convinced she was selling these homemade remedies out of Sadie's kitchen. He had been around Madge long enough to sense the woman's ambition. She could not hide the intelligence in her eyes. He wondered if Sadie knew about this little kitchen enterprise.

But he was there to accept the widow's marriage proposal, and he did not want to make enemies with her favored maid. He held out a coin.

"Tell me something," he said as she pocketed the money. "Has the widow ever spoken to my . . . to the dead for you?"

She did not let him see her surprise. The widow's business was not her business. Besides, there were no dead people she wished to reach.

"No, sir."

He settled into the chair again. The musky scent of herbs had a relaxing effect, and she had seen this reaction before. If she approached a subject with just the right amount of quiet, the perfect tone, absent presumption, she might be able to get something out of him. Like pulling a root holding steadfastly to the ground without damaging it. The right yank and it emerged intact.

"But your driver Hemp Harrison is looking for a wife."

"What's that? My driver lost his wife?" He remembered how the other driver's leg had escaped his notice. He was still ashamed of that.

"He ain't lose her in the way you thinking. He believe she living. The widow look for her, but can't find her. He think it's 'cause she still alive."

The house shifted. The stove warmed the kitchen too much. The colored woman smelled ripe, but it was a changing smell. One moment it was earthy, the next, acrid. Emotion struggled beneath the maid's face; he wondered about her motives.

"Did you know her?"

"Know who?"

"His wife."

"Naw, I didn't know her. I wasn't no slave." She could not keep the annoyance out of her voice. All northern white folks thought all southern colored folks came from the same plantation. She slowed. If she was not careful, she would anger him.

That explained the imperious manner. She was a freeborn. He thought of this new driver, a face so blank as if the man had no emotions whatsoever, though surely an entire life lurked behind those dark eyes. Michael's mind snapped to this: I had an arm. A finger with a ring. That colored coachman had none of that, had even less than families whose sons never returned from the battlefield. At least those grieving families had the comfort of likelihood. The driver had no corpse, letter, news of where his wife might have ended up. Michael thought of the detached look of him, the dark hands that calmed the flanks of horses.

"Kentucky, you say?"

She nodded.

Here was his chance. He would reach across the country, pick through masses of coloreds to find the man's wife. Some of them had ventured to Chicago, but there were millions, by God. The Schneider plantation had claimed over a hundred, though Katie's father reported that not a single one remained. From a hill on the eve of his brother's wedding, Michael had seen their dark bodies moving in the distance. He had never dreamed one of those people would offer him a chance like this. His brother had sacrificed first, and Michael would finish the work. He would participate in the war effort without ever firing a weapon. Michael thought of something he had read about in the news on the eve of the war: the trial of John Hossack, a white man who'd been audacious enough to rescue an escaped slave from a federal courtroom and successfully sneak him off to Canada. Michael would be like this Hossack fellow. All of his turmoil of the past four years distilled into a single, undeniably just cause: reuniting a man with his wife. Momentarily, he forgot the purpose of his visit. Madge brought him his overcoat, and he slipped his arms into it.

She saw it in his eyes. She had overheard his conversations with the widow, and she knew about his brother. The sisters had always taught her to seek out the valuable, and she knew she had offered the doctor something he could use: redemption. In return, this would be the thing to cleanse Madge of her stain. If the doctor found Annie, Hemp would be healed, restored to his rightful state, and she would be able to relieve herself of the guilt of taking advantage of a sick man. She never should have lain with him that night. It was wrong. Beyond wrong. But Annie and Hemp's reunion would settle everything, and Madge could finally rid herself of these useless feelings.

Michael looked into the dark empty parlor, the small round table. His fingers trembled as he buttoned his coat. White crowded the edges of his eyes. Someone placed a hat on his head. His shoes squeezed his toes and turned his feet toward the door.

"Kentucky, you say?"

Hemp waited atop the open driver's seat. Michael saw the man tuck a bottle under the seat.

"Take me home, Mr. Harrison," he whispered.

The carriage lurched through the street. Michael stared straight ahead, his eyes lit anew. Here was his opportunity. The man had lost a wife, yet he did not complain. He still worked and made a life for himself. Michael was the stuck one, the one who had lost hope. But if he could help this man he would finally be able to redeem himself.

16

FIVE ROUGHLY BUILT SHACKS HOUSED SEVEN-
teen slaves—twelve men, four women, and a
child delivered by Annie long before Horse took
her as his wife. At the time of the birth, thrilled at the prospect of
expanding his brood, Mr. Harrison insisted on naming Annie's baby,
writing down *Herodias* in his ledger and sending a message to the
quarters that this was what they were to call her. The slaves would
blame it all on the name when, at just three years old, the trouble
with the girl started: words that cut to the quick, a thrown cup that
whipped up a knot on the back of Annie's head, bites that turned
a brown arm purple. Annie became convinced that the girl was
touched by something other than childlike innocence, and she in-
terrogated the literate house slave about the name who reported she
heard it came from some book. When the child's father dropped dead
in the field that spring, the preacher performing the rites told Annie
about Herodias in the Bible, and while Annie knew nothing of Gus-

tave Flaubert, she knew something about what Herodias had done to John the Baptist and made a decision to call her girl Lily. Too late. The name Herod stuck, and even Annie found herself forgetting to call out the name of a flower. She even hung a sack around the girl's neck to rid her of the curse.

Later, after Herod slipped up beside him on the straw tick, after her two points of womanhood touched his chest and he responded, kissing her with a fever that would bring years of regret, after he hit her full in the face, hard enough that he was too ashamed to share the encounter with Annie, leaving the bloom on her cheek, after he'd forgotten whether he struck her with an open hand or a fist, after all of that, Horse would remember the meaning of her name.

With more men than women on the farm, it was no easy thing to lay claim to one of the women. After the death of Herod's father, Annie let it be known that she would not couple again. When Horse turned and caught her watching him work, he knew she was ready to go back on her word. It had taken twelve years after the man's death, but when Horse boiled a pot of water to wash her hair, she threw her head back and let him rake his fingers through her tight curls. Annie and Herod lived alone, and because he shared a shack with four other men, Horse spent his evenings in Annie's place, sending the girl out into the dirt yard. Over the course of his manhood, Horse had never impregnated a woman, so he did not believe he could. At first, he tried to claim Herod as his own, told the girl she could call him Pa, but her quiet watchfulness kept him ill at ease. He decided to step back. He felt safe enough in the knowledge that Annie's love for him was steadfast, but after the night Herod attempted an abomination, he kept away. The girl was cursed, just like they said. He pressed down the memory: the feeling of sweet nestling against curled hairs. Herod told her mother Mr. Harrison hit her when she spilled hot milk on him, and Annie did not think once to cast an eye toward Horse.

The day after Herod tried what she tried, and Horse did what he did, he lay with Annie, holding her tightly.

"You all right?" she asked.

"We ain't living right."

"What you talking 'bout?"

"You know what I'm talking about."

"I reckon Mister don't care. George and Dinah done it. Henry and Jess. They all been declared by the preacher. I reckon he allow the same for us."

"Yeah."

"You already live here. Make a heap of sense."

"Make more than sense."

She rubbed his neck. "Herod ought to be fine with it."

He pulled away. "Annie, that girl growing up. She need to find her own man. Plenty of 'em 'round here."

"She a child."

"No, she ain't."

Annie lifted onto an elbow, a cloud of hair ringing her face. "The last fool try to break up me and Herod got run out of here."

"Fool? The last?"

"She my blood."

Horse tried to slow his breathing so he could hear what was behind the words. Thirteen years she'd spent praying off the spirit that claimed the girl by name and he knew he would not penetrate it. If Herod told Annie what happened, he had no illusions whose side the mother would take.

"I guess they is plenty room enough in this cabin for the three of us," he said slowly.

Annie took his hand in hers. "You know I wants to marry you, Horse. Ain't no question."

Later that week, Horse knocked on the back door of the farmhouse, standing with his bare feet sunk in the mud while somebody went to fetch Mr. Harrison.

"Who is that out there?" The old man's vision had begun to fail him, and he refused to wear spectacles.

"It's Horse, sir. I come up here to ask you something."

"Well, spit it out. I know you ain't sick."

"Naw, sir. I'm good and strong. Never felt better." Horse and Annie had deliberately chosen to ask the old man before the hemp harvest, when the promise of work lay just around the bend, weeks ahead of the time the men were due to head out to the fields and cut it all down. "You know I can beat more shocks in a day than any hand down in that yard."

"Go on and spit out what you come up here to ask me. Hurry up while I'm still of a mind to listen."

Horse could not help but notice how disheveled the man's clothes were, as if he'd just awakened from a nap.

"The thing is, sir, me and Annie wants to get married."

Behind the old man, a sand-colored woman peeked out.

"You and who?"

The woman shouted over the old man's shoulder. "The one fell and broke her toe couple years back."

"Which one?"

"The one with half a ear!"

"Which?"

"The one with the girl Herodias!"

"Ah."

In earlier days, the old man had cast himself as preacher, gathering his small group of slaves on the edge of the orchard to talk about morality and sinning and God's laws for them. He had never been much of a churchgoer himself, so he did not take up the Bible when he spoke. Instead, he used his own life as an example—how he treated them, for instance, or, later, how he remained faithful to his dead wife, refusing to remarry. In years past, when he'd taken a more vigorous interest in the workings of the farm, he'd voiced his pride over the young boy whose handle of a brake and hackle was well beyond his years, calling him Horse, and even then, like most things that came from his mouth, the name stuck. Everyone on the farm knew the old man's son was a disappointment, a dandy, so when Harrison saw the slave child working and said he was "as strong as a horse," it was clear he did so out of what he perceived to be a high compliment.

"You realize that I cannot allow you and that woman to call yourselves married. I'mo tell you the same thing what I tell the others. You can do whatever you want in terms of ceremony down there. But as far as the law is concerned, you are not and never will be married. You unnerstand?"

"Yas, sir."

"I do not control the laws of this great state. But if I did, I wouldn't mind you all getting married every now and again, unnerstand? Now I have heard from others, honorable white men, that is, that slave marriages don't do a farm any good. Old Betty who used to work in the house once told me she had enough masters between me and God and didn't need another man to wipe up after."

"Yas, sir."

"But I believe in God's commandments, and I have always preached morality to your kind. This here farm is mine, and I intend to maintain it the way I see fit. Now other things, the cost of wheat, for instance, don't have nothing to do with me." He placed a hand on the doorjamb. "I'm afraid with this country's growing demand for grain, wheat might outgrow the cost of cotton, and if cotton fail, won't be much need for hemp. Wheat is necessary, I suppose. We must have our bread. The Irish come running over here once there wasn't no more potatoes. The thing one has got to do to be rich in this country is to outrun the poor. Get there first. These days, everybody is running to the cities. Not me. I prefer life on a farm, waking up to the sound of a rooster, unnerstand?"

Horse glanced back down the hill where Annie waited, fighting an urge to step back. Mr. Harrison smelled of old things, like when the cobbler came around with discards for the slaves. Patched shoes that reeked of feet. Pants that smelled like ass.

"Yas, sir."

"They won't be satisfied until we are a nation of cities. God, how I hate the men that drive those blasphemed rails. What the hell do we need with all these railroads for? Men need to do like my daddy did, and his daddy before him. That's the problem with that son of mine. That boy need to come on back, settle on this here land, and plow it!"

"Yas, sir."

Harrison waved a hand and turned around. "I don't give a damn what you do. Long as it don't affect your work. This whole country is going to hell anyway. Maybe you and the old hag can save yourselves from damnation."

Horse waited outside for the housemaid to come back out. Once she'd delivered the old man to his chair, she would offer something. A pilfered gift like the bag of apples for George and Dinah or the cake for Henry and Jess. Marriages on the farm were a simple affair. A preacher usually came around, blessed the union.

She pressed a handkerchief into Horse's hand. "It belonged to the missus. I reckon she don't need it none now."

Horse took it, grateful she had given him something for Annie.

THE RIGHTEOUS BUT GREEDY-EYED PREACHER would not come, and Horse had nothing to give. He tried to think of what he could make. Horse and Annie wanted to marry before the harvest, and he did not have much time. He thought of asking somebody else to bless them. Just being blessed by one of the other men might be enough in God's eyes, but Annie insisted they needed an anointed preacher. George and Dinah had given the preacher George's shoes. Henry and Jess had wrapped up cloth for him. Horse had nothing to spare, and he lost sleep over it. A week after asking the master for Annie's hand, Horse made her stand, then turned her chair over in his hands and ran a palm across the back of it. It was a crude chair, its maker an unseasoned craftsman. But the seat was made of a good block of wood, and it did not show a single crack.

"I make you another one," he told her.

Horse sat on the step of the cabin with the upturned chair between his legs. Everyone said he could scratch a piece of wood until it sang, a skill taught him by a white farmer who'd taken an interest in him as a boy. For six years, the man hired Horse every summer to help around his farm, and when the work was done for the day, Horse watched the man carve scrolls into the arms of chairs, feet into the legs of sofas. Back in the quarters, Horse sketched designs with sticks in the dirt, and when the woman who worked in the house saw a bird he'd drawn, she sneaked him paper and lead.

Before the farmer died, he surprised Horse with a gift: his stash of tools. And Horse had kept the cherished instruments ever since. Now he carefully unrolled the leather pouch, exposing the rough assortment of gouges and chisels. The mallet propped against his leg, he took up his lead, sketching onto the underside of the chair, his hand moving quickly.

He picked up a gouge, pushed it against the wood with both hands, and leaned into the end of its handle with his chest. The tool cut into the wood; he blew the flakes clear, chipping and cutting, changing tools and angles as he worked his way around the bottom of the seat.

Annie found him humming in the dark.

"What's it gone be?" she asked.

"You see," he said.

One night, while he sat carving, she scratched the itch out of his scalp with her fingernails, the ecstasy of her touch enough to make him drop the chair and take her right there. But they were running short on time and he could not stop working. A week later, when the chair was finished, he asked her to sit on it. She sat, and he lifted her skirt, wrapping his fingers around one of her ankles. He dipped a knife into a bowl of dirty water and scraped the skin from her heel. It fell in yellowed chips. He took care not to slice too deeply and cause a bleed in the softer spots. Once he could feel the new skin, he coaxed the soreness out with his thumbs.

The preacher arrived the next day, and while Annie dressed for the ceremony, Horse presented the chair to him. The man took a quick look at it, muttered he did not need a rickety old chair that his mule was too old to carry. Horse offered to tie the chair to the back of the animal himself, promising that when he was finished the animal would not even know it was there.

Horse turned the chair over. The preacher bent down, rested his palms on his knees. Pine tree points, peaks of hills cresting into a ridged sky, blades of grass reaching upward, a fawn in mid-step. The chair explained what Horse had known from the very beginning, that the greatest irony of their condition was the beauty of the country in which they toiled, and the heartbreak of their lives was the fogged lens through which they gazed upon God's country. The wide-eyed surprise of the young deer, the tweet of nestlings, the banks of a river that curved into hills. This land around them was both the site of their darkness and the source of their light. The relief of casting a rod into the Dix, his feet resting on the river's banks, had saved Horse's life on more than one occasion, and beneath the seat of the chair, Horse had tried to capture that feeling and draw the earth as God intended, perfection before man's spoiling, untainted by the sin of bondage. And he had risked that the preacher would not get it, could not see the Eden before him, for there were some, hopeless ones, who found no comfort in the satisfied nicker rising from a horse's throat. The preacher stared, speechless, and Horse guessed that later on, the man would look upon it, turn the chair over and rest beside it, not in it, for the preacher's wife had long been dead, and Horse knew he lived alone in a shack beside his master's house. *By God, this chair got the power to love me*, Horse had thought when he finished, and with just one look into the preacher's eye, Horse knew the man felt the same.

Horse had hidden the carving on its underside, knowing it was a dangerous thing for a Negro to own something of value. When upright, people would see a plain chair, worn, nicked. Only the preacher would know to turn it over and set an eye upon its preciousness.

He cleared his throat. "A few ears of corn would have sufficed."

"Corn still in the fields," Horse said.

"Tie it up."

That afternoon, the preacher pronounced them husband and wife. The bride wiped her eyes with the dead mistress's handkerchief, her toothless grin like a child's, and Horse tucked a dandelion in her hair as they stood in the cool of a hackberry's shade. Herod did not speak, and it was not lost upon Horse that had she not tried that nighttime trick, he would have placed a flower in her hair, too.

Bone of my bones, flesh of my flesh.

After the preacher pronounced them married, Horse and Annie walked hand in hand through the quarters, slaves calling out to them, shouting blessings and wishes for protection. In the cabin, a bowl of water and a freshly washed coverlet awaited. He held his bride, trying not to think of the next morning's work. In the coming Resurrection, the trees would be greener, the sky bluer. A man of lesser faith might have thought this moment itself was heaven. But Horse, even with his un-Christian name, was thinking of an even better time. Lying with Annie led him to believe not in the existence of a heaven but in the possibility that he would get there.

17

IN THE FIRST YEARS OF THEIR MARRIAGE, HORSE revealed his loyalty to Annie piece by piece, and she thrived beneath the attention. She was his holy woman, his Hagar, his Sarah. And he was her Horse. She opened up and talked more, even kissed him on the cheek when he was not expecting it. By the time news of an attack on Fort Sumter reached the farm, Horse had settled comfortably into married life.

A year later, it shocked them all when a bespectacled boy knocked on the door with the news that Mr. Harrison's son had died in a battle down in Tennessee. Months earlier, when they learned the younger Harrison had volunteered with a Kentucky regiment, they feared for him, but none anticipated what happened next. It was April 1862, and the word *Shiloh* passed between them. They looked for news, hoping for abolition but more concerned with who would inherit all of them should the old man die. Once Harrison learned he would not even have a body to bury, he sat in his chair staring out at the stand of maples in his front yard. Nothing could rouse him. Every now and then the housemaid summoned Horse to the house for a repair and whispered what she had gleaned from the occasional newspaper that reached them. River transport was disrupted. So was cotton production. The war was affecting everything, and the demand for hemp would be considerably less that year.

The men were cutting timothy hay when Horse relayed the information.

"What do it mean for us?" Jess coughed and wiped the sweat from his face before straightening up to look at Horse.

"I don't rightly know," Horse answered.

Off in the distance, Horse saw two hats astride horses. He shaded his eyes with his hands. The Harrison farm was not on the way to anywhere else, the trail ending at the house, so it was a rare sight to see passersby. He squinted. A slow, dark line snaked behind the horses. The other men were looking now, too. A muffled yell rang out, and though none of the husbands knew whose voice it was, each one of them sprang to life, certain he had heard his own name. Among them, Horse's feet beat through the grass, and he tried to say *Annie!* As he neared them, he saw the shadow of a white man raising his gun, but Horse could not stop running, even when he heard the shot, because there was the unmistakable figure of Annie crouching at the back of the coffle. Now the women were screaming, and it took a moment for Horse to understand that they were yelling for the men to stop. Horse slowed, glancing around at the husbands. They had halted, but their necks were strung tightly. Horse had to act or they would all get hurt. He searched his head for the words that would save them and opened his mouth, knowing, before he'd uttered a sound, how little he could salvage.

"Sir, we don't aim to cause no trouble. We just want to say a word to the women."

The man spat. "Women? I don't see no women."

Horse did not look beneath the hat's brim. "Just a word. That's all we ask."

The hat aimed his pistol at each man, silently counting the three of them and, perhaps, counting his bullets and measuring his speed against six arms and six legs. He spoke from behind the gun: "Make it quick. I ain't no Christian, neither is you, and hell ain't no happy place."

Horse approached Annie, but he could not look at her. She raised her hands to touch his face and he heard the tinkle of chains. He could see the back of the girl Herod who did not turn around to see this farewell between the only two parents she could remember. Horse wished he had something to give Annie, but he had nothing, not even a drop of water in his can. He heard her sniffle and knew she was crying. He and Annie had lived on the same farm for years, and he could not ever remember her shedding a tear.

"I thought God didn't make mens like you no more," she said.

Horse looked at the ground. Annie's voice was low, but it rose through his ears like a message coming from the grave. He knew his face was streaked with dirt and sweat, and he could smell himself. He faced her open heart feeling soiled. He had asked for a word, and now he had none to share. He closed his eyes. When he opened them, her feet had disappeared. He lifted his chin and saw her skirt thin until it vanished.

"You give me a piece of myself back."

"My scalp." It was all he could say as he lifted his eyes, watching her disappear right in front of him. Nothing was left but her head, her dark eyes. She reached into the back of her hair and pulled something out—the comb he had made her.

"My scalp," he said as she pressed it into his hand.

Later, Horse would remember how he'd stood in the dust left behind by the coffle, thinking: *So this how it feel.* There had been too little time with her, and it baffled him how he let her and Herod live on the farm as long as they had without him seeing that she was the one who would bring him back to life.

He should have said more. What he'd wanted to say was, *Joy, woman. That's what you give me. You my joy.* Instead of *My scalp.*

Maybe he was the dumb horse Mister thought he was.

The next day, Horse cut his finger badly with a knife. At night, the three husbands spoke quietly about their chances of escape. Harrison brought in men with guns who took turns on night patrol around the property. Horse held on to a faint hope that the women would remain close by, their skills with hemp rope keeping them from being sold down the river. The husbands begged the housemaid to find out where the women had been sold. To them, her reading skill was akin to magical powers, but her searches turned up nothing. She had no way of finding out the information every husband on the place was after.

By fall of that year, Mr. Harrison was bedridden, and the men had ceased working. The hemp was not yet hackled and the fibers full of hurd when the first two of them ran off. The rest of them, save Horse and the housemaid, marched off the farm in clear daylight. While the woman continued to empty the old man's bedpan and cook up the meat that remained in the smokehouse, Horse slept alone in the loft he'd shared with Annie, hopeful that his wife would return.

He stayed on for two more years, until one morning the housemaid delivered his breakfast with the news that the old man had passed in his sleep. She wanted to go to the camp where some of the men had gone to enlist, up near Nicholasville, and she begged Horse to travel with her as her husband so she could seek refuge. They were promising free papers if he joined the army. Besides, she did not think they would survive the winter. There was no food left. Horse looked at her, noting that somewhere along the way she had lost her beauty. Her eyes sank into her face, and the skin peeled from her cheeks. He did not want to leave, but she needed his help and he had already failed a coffle of women. He marked the moment: first, he would bury the old man; second, he would take the woman to this camp. He had not cared for Harrison at all, but being righteous was a step toward becoming a man.

THEY KEPT CLOSE TO THE ROADS, staying just out of sight until they reached the cantilevered bridge over the river. Beneath them, the river swelled into white peaks, then dove forward in a relentless march south. He took her hand as they crossed a bridge. They came upon a village of white tents, neatly arranged in eight rows of four. At the head, a band of men sat around a fire. Horse approached, but one of them waved his arm and pointed in another direction. Horse took the shivering woman's hand. *Come on.* Positioned at the foot of a river, the land drew up into steep, stone gorges. On one end, the river palisades protected the camp; on the other a stretch of forest ended at Hickman Creek. In front of a gable-roofed building, a group of colored men drilled in a neat military step. Horse stopped to watch, openmouthed. A white officer barked an order, and the men turned, their feet perfectly aligned.

My land, he whispered.

Horse sent the woman off to look for his wife while he waited for a turn to enter headquarters. A lit stove in the corner warmed the room, but Horse rubbed his hands together anyway. At the sound, the white officer looked up from where he was sitting at a table. Horse froze.

"Name?"

"Horse, sir."

The officer put down his pencil.

The soldier standing behind him spoke. "Sir, this is not the first one. We have been asking some of them to think of suitable names."

"Horse? You got another name you go by?"

"Ain't never been called nothing else, sir."

"Well, is there something you'd like to be called? You are enlisting as a soldier in the federal army. We cannot call you Horse. That would be . . . unpatriotic." He paused. "Do you understand me?"

The officer behind him snickered.

Horse hesitated. He believed his wife, Annie, and her daughter, Herod, might be somewhere out in that sea of huts and shanties. If he changed his name and people called him anything but Horse, Annie would never be able to find him. He hesitated.

"But Horse is my name, sir."

The men glanced at one another.

"How about George? That's a fine American name. Or how about your master's name? Most of the slaves are taking their masters' names."

Horse thought of the soldier's suggestion. Whenever any of them were away from the farm, they knew they belonged to the Harrison Hemp farm. Surely that would leave enough of a clue for Annie to find. Still, the thought of taking his master's name saddened him. Already, he could sense the inescapable reach of the old man's arm, a hand on his back that would follow him into his new life.

"I reckon Hemp Harrison'll do," he said, twisting the clues just enough to make the name his own.

"Hemp? Why don't we just call him cotton?"

Another snicker.

"Hemp ain't much better than Horse," the officer seated at the table said, but he wrote the name anyway.

He was ordered to live in the colored soldiers' barracks, while the woman was sent down to the tents with the other women and children. In exchange for his service, he would receive his certificate of freedom. As he walked to the barracks, he hopped over a puddle, the reality of freedom almost too much to believe. He stood outside the building, watching as colored men joked with one another. Laughing! This place was no place at all. It was some cruel trick, like the first touch of crazy when the stomach had been empty too long. He could not describe what he felt. He tossed the images he witnessed back and forth in his mind like pinecones as he sought to put a feeling to it—it was not a word, but a melody. It was like . . . a push of air beneath a wing, a twitch of muscle in the breast.

He began to think of all he would do once he found Annie. Build her a house. Plant her a garden. Suddenly, his feet stuck to the ground as he realized that without Annie, freedom meant nothing. Nothing at all.

Rather than enter the barracks, he made his way down to where the women camped. A girl directed him to a shanty where two old women stood throwing wood onto a fire. They took his hands from him, rubbed them until they were warm. Their dry touch soothed him and he never wanted them to let go. What's your name, baby? God bless you, they said. They told him they knew nothing of Annie and Herod, but he should feel free to take a look around. He walked slowly back up the hill, still mulling over the word *free*.

In the day, he drilled. In the evening, he checked for new arrivals. When nothing came of his search, he joined the men sitting around the stove in the mess hall. Their talk shifted between high and low. They spoke of the sickness raging through the camp, one man recounting the day's death tally. When they spoke of the children, a few cried openly. The families of the enlisted men had not been granted freedom, but they came to the camp anyway. To the dismay of the white officers, thousands of women and children had arrived seeking shelter, and just months before, hundreds of families had been forced off the grounds in freezing temperatures. Many of them had died, and Horse knew that even this long-awaited freedom was not enough to ease their pain.

The men were still eager to march, however, boasting of the Fifth U.S. Colored Cavalry trained at Camp Nelson that had gone off to fight at the Battle of Saltville in Virginia. Even Horse could not help but share in their patriotism. The sight of men who had been enslaved their entire lives dressed in uniform made him draw up his chest.

He continued to ask around for Annie, fearing that they would call upon him to fight before he found her. The flow of families in and out of the camp dwindled, and he no longer anticipated the new arrivals. He met a man who had passed through the Harrison farm and reported that the quarters were deserted. Horse was glad to know Annie had not returned there, but he did not know where else to look. Still, he made up his mind to leave and go look for her.

After saying farewell to the housemaid, he moved north through the palisades, alone, carrying only a canteen, a tin spoon, and his leather roll of carving tools in his sack. His supply dwindled. He downed birds and possum with rocks, using his drawknife to slice them open. He walked nearly fourteen hours a day, staying close to the river, tracing its snaky outline through the state, and when the sun reached its highest notch in the sky, he whispered his thanks that it was not the middle of winter or summer, the spring temperatures mild enough for foot travel.

At the end of the week, it began to rain and did not stop for three days. He looked for shelter as he wrapped his shirt around his head, tying it into a knot at his neck. Once the rain let up, he carried on. A sticky humidity soaked him all over again. He hung his clothes from a tree to dry and squatted naked on a rocky riverbank, warming his backside in the sun. He stumbled as he dipped a toe into the water's cool. He stepped back onto dry land and put a palm against his brow. North of him, he thought he saw the chimney of a cabin. He followed the sight until he found it. Deserted. He rummaged inside the house, finding nothing of value save a dull little knife to add to his pack. Out back, he discovered a footpath, and he took it, making sure to keep the river in his view, climbing the hillier parts until he was walking along a cliff so steep that he dared not look below.

He began to come upon other travelers, colored men and women, children. He asked everyone he met about her. He knew he was traveling north, but he was still confused. The names of towns he did not recognize made him feel he was out of Kentucky and in some other country. Each day, he did not stop searching until the setting sun had turned the hues of flowers and the final shadowing of their blossoms was lost in the black of night. He learned to appreciate a fuller moon, the cover of its whitish glow.

One night, he camped with another man who was also looking for family. The man had a fishing pole, and the two of them leaned against a rock, each man silent in his thoughts. Horse noticed that the fish upriver were the same he'd fished down near the Harrison farm— silvery trout and perch and the little goggle-eyed ones that changed color with the angle of light. They dried the meat in the sun, stored slithers of chewy flesh in their pockets. Corncrakes swooped as Horse filled his canteen from a brook before eyeing the land for a suitable spot to sleep by nightfall. His stomach troubled him, so he climbed up into the neck of a tree, its rooted trunk rising into a spray of arms that cradled him. As he napped, he dreamed of Annie. Soft arms and thighs and the loose folds of a belly that warmed him.

In the morning, the two men parted ways.

He gained another footpath and followed it until it thinned and the land rose up before him in a tangle of brush. He used a stick to trudge through it, his fear of snakes turning the wind's whistle into a rattle. He liked it most when the land opened up before him, trees stacked against hills. He was not ready to give up, but he had been walking for weeks and was beginning to despair that he could not find her. Furthermore, he was lost. He did not know the geography of the state, and if it weren't for the river, he would swear he had been walking in circles. Wandering slaves, lost just the same as he, peppered him with questions: Where was he headed? What was up ahead? He met a man who told him he had reached a town called Carrollton and would need to jump a ferry to cross the river. Furthermore, the war was over and the president was dead. Had he heard? Horse felt the same confusion he'd felt at the camp. Joy and uncertainty rolled into a phlegmy ball in his chest. Lord, where is my earthly chariot? Ain't it due?

Weeks later, when the white missionary found him sprawled semiconscious beneath a tree, the missionary who would eventually lead him to Chicago, Horse's beard and hair had grown into matted flaps. By then, he was deep into Indiana.

18

MADGE AND OLGA HUDDLED IN THE kitchen. Upstairs, the widow slept. It was so early, the sun had not risen yet. Madge had been surprised to find Olga already in the kitchen, chopping onions in the dark. The bitter scent of them hovered over the room. Madge rubbed her eyes.

"She's changed," Olga declared.

It was true. Three lines drew across Sadie's forehead. She hunched over when she walked. Her hair had begun to darken. When she spoke, she'd lost the slightly flat sound of Pennsylvania and taken on the nasal *ah* of Illinois. She walked stiffly, her hips straight. She ate more at each meal, and her waist had begun to fill out so much that Madge had to order new dresses. Even her habits were changing. She no longer picked at her eyebrows when she was thinking. She belched freely.

But there was something more. It wasn't in her face, not in the eyes or skin. It was not a stretch to the two servants to believe a spirit could come into the physical world, one layer at a time. Soon James Heil might fill the air, and it struck Madge that they should warn her somehow.

The German woman usually kept her distance from everyone in the household, including Madge, but now they stood together near the heat of the stove, united in worry.

"What you make of it?" Madge asked.

"He's using her to stay here. And I think it's wearing her down."

Both had felt the presence of the spirit in the house. For Olga, she thought she could sense him looking over her shoulder when she was boiling a stew, as if waiting to taste it. And she did not blame her own ailing memory when a pot appeared where a bowl should be or when a dish cracked while sitting on a shelf. When Madge touched the widow, she felt his presence. She tried not to minister too much to the woman because she hoped to avoid him. Lately, even a whiff of the woman's odor carried a note of the spirit in it.

"Who can stop it?" Olga refused to utter his name. Like Madge, she feared this spirit, but not enough to give up her job working in the widow's house.

The closest person to the widow, Dr. Heil, was not even to be trusted. He visited the house more than anyone. Not only did he serve as her escort, but he called upon the spirit every chance he got.

"What can we do?"

Olga used the term *we* and Madge took note of it. Even when they spoke of their common household duties—such as answering the door or taking meals up to the widow—Olga never grouped them together. In truth, the woman seldom even referred to her own family in that way—the husband who worked laying bricks, the son who came to walk her home in the evenings. Even the teamwork of family did not lesson the woman's misanthropy.

So when she asked Madge what *we* should do, the healer felt obligated to come up with a ready answer.

"What about her daddy? He her only family, right?"

Olga stroked the single dark hair on her chin. "The boy can read and write."

"What boy?"

"Who else? My son."

"You mean sign her name? That won't work."

Olga looked at Madge as if she were a fool. "He works at the telegraph office."

"Ah," Madge said. "Tell you what. You get that telegraph and I can get the train ticket. You remember the name? York something? I can get the man to charge it to the widow's bill. She don't half look at her accounting no way. When her daddy get here and see for himself what's happening, he'll know what to do."

"Yes," Olga said. "It might just take a man to run that ghost off." Olga pursed her lips and turned back to the onions. She swiped a handful of them into a bowl. The juices released again and Madge was close enough to feel the sting.

WHEN MADGE RETURNED HOME, she saw Hemp outside the stable sipping from a canteen. It was not the first time she had seen him. He visited Richard every now and then. She had been careful to stay out of his line of sight since that terrible night she'd lain with him. She nodded at him and he looked off distantly as if he did not see her.

As she cleaned the widow's bedroom, she leaned her forehead against the window and thought of her family, what it would be like to see them again. Hemp had said that even a bad family was better than none at all. Whenever she tried to imagine never seeing her mother again, a well of hurt threatened to drown her. There were things she missed about Tennessee that just weren't the same in Illinois, like the Hatchie and her mama's hotcakes slathered in grease.

Voices floated up from below, and she turned from the window. At the bottom of the stairs she was surprised to see Hemp emerging from the widow's parlor.

"Y'all find her?"

He stared at her, unable to put into words what Sadie had just accused him of, how she'd asked him not to come back into her house.

"What?"

"I'll let you out," Madge said, avoiding his eyes.

He followed her to the kitchen. She stopped at the wide table and lay her hands flat upon it, as if sensing what would happen next. He pushed against her back and breathed into her neck. She smelled the spirits on his breath. He was drunk.

"Where do you sleep, Miss Tennessee?"

She could barely breathe. The thought of taking him upstairs in Sadie's house terrified her. But she could not stop her feet as they found their way to the back stairs, Hemp following closely. He pushed at her back with his hand as if to keep her from changing her mind. When they reached her room, he closed the door behind them.

The room was cold, and she shivered as he slid her dress from her shoulders.

She turned. "Hemp."

He pushed her onto the bed, his thighbone separating her legs. She made a curring sound as he lunged into her. A frightened horse's yelp carried through the closed window. She listened for the widow's bell, certain it would ring at any moment. He covered her mouth with his. She felt a wetness on his cheek and tasted the salt.

"Hemp," she said again when she could open her mouth.

He did not say her name, did not say one word before he left. She lay there, inhaling the scent of his spilling and wondering if he had been thinking of Annie again.

Without him, a cavern opened inside her. She needed something from him that he could not give. Maybe the only love she could try to make some kind of claim to was back in Tennessee. Maybe it was worth a try to return there, even if it meant leaving behind the business she had begun to carefully build out of Sadie's kitchen.

Tennessee. Tennessee. She formed her lips to make the sounds.

Chicago was an ugly, dirty city. She hated it, and she hated him, too.

"I WANT TO SEE him."

Michael sat across from Sadie in the drawing room. Just the day before, she'd had to kick Hemp out of her parlor. Or perhaps James had kicked him out. The sessions with the spirit had begun to blur the lines of her reality.

"Sadie, for God's sake. This is no time to abandon me. I need to tell my brother something." He leaned forward and spoke into her ear. "James! James! Can he hear me? Does he have to be summoned?"

"Michael, stop it. Please." She said it as though he were a child.

"You don't understand. I need to tell him what happened. I need to show him something."

"It's over. I don't want to do it anymore."

"You don't want to do what anymore?"

"Talk with your brother. I'm tired."

"Look." He pulled a folded piece of paper from his inner pocket. She took it from him.

"I don't deserve my brother's compassion. I bought my way out of the war. I must confess."

She barely looked down at his commutation papers. "You weren't the only one."

"I am a coward."

"Look at how many we lost." She stood and walked to the fireplace, pulling at the new hairs sprouting from her knuckles.

"That man, my driver, was freed by the war. And he still can't find his family. I should have done it. Fighting was the right thing, Sadie."

"The right thing for whom?"

"My brother died in my place. My younger brother. I should have bought his exemption, not my own."

She threw the papers into the fire.

"What did you just do?"

"You don't need those."

He lunged for the poker and tried to retrieve the papers. A few pieces fluttered out. He picked up a piece and dropped it, sucking his fingers. Its brown edges crumbled. He grabbed her as if to hurt her and kissed her instead. She stiffened and pushed him away. He reached for her again, and she slapped him. A spot of blood appeared on his lip.

"What's wrong with us?" he cried in a hollow voice.

"We've lost sight of right and wrong, that's what."

"What has happened to me?"

"Michael, you must listen. Your brother isn't here."

Clouds passed above the house and the room shadowed. His arms hung loosely at his side like flippers. She patted her forehead with a handkerchief. He began to sob and she tried not to listen, turning from him. Too much grief. The whole country in flames.

His ankle throbbed. He thought briefly again of the driver and his missing family. "I've been thinking about your proposition."

The room began to close in on Sadie, as if it were a tomb. She had lied. The spirit was right there, listening to everything. And he was making it difficult for her to breathe.

"Don't answer," she said. "Not yet."

19

MADGE HAD WORKED HARD TO RID THE house of its smell: boiled cabbage, brined meat, and the lingering scent of cigar in the front parlor. Instead, she filled the house with the fragrance of herbs heaped in porcelain bowls. Madge's idea to scent the rooms. Madge's idea to draw back the curtains. Olga did not appear to enjoy the changes at first, but Sadie approved, inexplicably drawn to this proud woman who had quickly picked up how to run a house.

It was also Madge's idea to invite the mediums to dinner.

Madge wiped the railing leading to the second floor and dusted the crevices of the carved sofa in the parlor, while Olga roasted a mallard in the kitchen, preparing for a table of four.

When the mediums finally arrived, they said: "I was not expecting such an invitation" and "My business is doing poorly because of her."

"Please wait, ma'am," said Madge.

Upstairs, in her room, Sadie seethed. A visitor had asked if the colored woman was still selling roots out of her kitchen. Then she'd seen with her very own eyes one of her visitors exiting the front door and making her way around to the kitchen at the back of the house. A few hours later, Sadie peeked into the food storage closet and found shelves of containers, jars, sacks. From floor to ceiling, the colored woman had hoarded enough to fill a store. The air inside the closet breathed. Sadie glanced down at her feet, afraid something might scurry over them. She rarely ventured into the kitchen, and she was taken aback. The woman was running some kind of herb business from her kitchen.

She took the back stairs to Madge's room. The room smelled odd, too. She stuck a hand beneath the mattress, her fingers closing around a cloth sack the size of an apple. She pulled it out and held it to her nose: the bitter of garlic. What kinds of beliefs did the woman attach to it? Madge readily accepted Sadie's contact with spirits, and Sadie was grateful for that. But the fact that each woman secreted her own lore did not excuse this behavior.

As Sadie sat at her dressing table pinning her hair, she could not decide what to do. When Madge entered the room, Sadie was still thinking about it.

"They waiting for you downstairs, Mrs. Walker. Them women," Madge said in a rhythm that still carried more than a touch of Tennessee in it.

Sadie turned to look at her. "What are you selling out of my kitchen?"

The colored woman's face did not register fear at the blunt question, and her posture dared Sadie to make something of the discovery. Sadie had tried to tone down her anger, keep the hint of a threat out of her tone. Still, she was thinking that this breach was serious enough to ruin the arrangement and send Madge back out into the streets.

"Whatever they need."

Sadie studied Madge's face. Long and narrow, eyes set close together, cheekbones angled wide and then down in a dramatic slant,
brown eyes that sparkled hazel in the light. A crowning of thick hair
bundled into two braids. Madge's body was a foreign country, as
strange to Sadie as Samuel's corpse had been. Sadie wanted to know
what and how she was healing, but she was not even sure she should
keep the woman around as she tried to comprehend exactly what kind
of person she had brought into her home. Madge was some kind of
witch doctor, a charlatan. Sadie had read about these cunning slaves
who lived on plantations, weaving spells, telling fortunes, calling upon
evil spirits to do their bidding. They claimed the power to heal, but
they more readily used their knowledge to harm. They carried charms,
amulets, and other fetishes, summoning spirits and ghosts to aid them.
They threatened their foes, and people feared them. Some were known
to be religious, devout even, but these claims to Christianity did not
negate their practice of a dark art.

"What exactly did you think I was doing when I made them teas
for you? Healed that thing on your shoulder? Made that touch of fluid
in your chest go away?"

The maid's voice was unapologetic and loud. What if she had been
putting something in her tea at night?

"Those women have done nothing wrong. Why would you cheat
them?"

"I ain't no cheat."

"You were sticking your hand in fire when I met you."

Madge rubbed her arm, keeping the elbow straight. "That was different."

Sadie felt a spark of recognition. She was fairly certain the colored
woman could not read. Yet there was undeniable depth in those fur-
rowed brows and bright eyes. This ironic coupling of the two women
was not lost on Sadie. Her job was to speak to the dead, to assure the

grieving of a smooth transition between this side and the next, the connection of the spiritual and physical. Madge's work also dealt in death, the delay of it. If the transition were as smooth as Sadie claimed, the door as wide open as James promised, the fear of death was eliminated, was it not? That was the problem. Madge's work was not based in hope. Engaging Madge was to trade an illuminated belief in the other side with a vain search for earthly immortality.

Sadie considered the pomp of death's revelry, the yearning for a hallowed version of life. The cortege, bier, hearse, coffin, pall, marching horses. The tolling bells and solemn firing of cannons. All of it proved little more than attempts to make sense of the end. Sadie had sat beside Samuel's body for hours, a one-woman wake long after the visitors were gone. There had been no doubt about his lifelessness.

"When Samuel died, people came to the house to see him. Olga put out whiskey, and they drank while speaking of business, the city, the war. They mentioned everything but him. Then the undertakers came to take him to the cemetery. I didn't go. I waved good-bye to my dead husband from the front door. That's the kind of wife he bought."

The natural light fell. Neither woman moved to light a lamp.

"My mother died before I could say to her what I needed to say."

"Mine's still living but she couldn't hear me if I shouted."

Sadie looked away, thinking of the lives cut short by war. Madge believed this life was worth saving, and the mourners who visited Sadie's parlor proved the woman right.

"Everyone has to go eventually."

"Passing in my natural sleep will suit me just fine," Madge said.

"I wonder, after I am gone, who will knock at that door hoping to hear my voice. If anyone will knock at all."

"You surely won't know who do and who don't."

"I ought to fire you," Sadie said, hardening again.

"I can save you the trouble."

"You are not to sell anything out of my house, do you understand?"

Sadie pushed a curl behind her ear. She would go down and talk to the mediums, hear their stories, pretend she did not know how much they hated her. She would show them the portrait of her husband, discuss the wonders of James Heil, share her table. Perhaps they might even share a secret or two of their own. She had never felt more alone.

"Tell the ladies I will be right down."

"Yes, Mrs. Walker," Madge said.

"THIS CITY AIN'T NO PLACE for me."

"What are you saying?"

"I'm saying I'm going home. Back to Tennessee."

"Tennessee?" Sadie patted the sweat from her brow. It had been over a week since her discovery, and she'd decided to keep Madge on. But now the woman was telling her that she had made a decision to leave.

"Leaving for good?"

"Yes, ma'am."

Madge poured coffee into a porcelain cup. She stood back and watched as the widow sipped. A weighted silence hung between the two women.

"Why?"

Madge started toward the door but decided to turn around. Her mouth opened, and before she could change her mind, she was telling Sadie about the dream. This dream story was the kind of tale that would have perplexed most people, but the widow, diviner of spirits, understood a dreamer's intuition. Madge told how the house had motioned, the door flapping open and closed like a mouth, the windows blinking like eyes. Madge didn't know why she had dreamed about the house, but she knew that ever since she'd taken advantage of Hemp's weakened state of mind, she'd been missing her mother. Perhaps that was why the house beckoned her home. It was time to return and make amends, get right with the Lord. She could not shake what the widow had said about her own mother's death.

In the two years she'd been in Chicago, she had not thought much about the sisters, but it was 1866, and she had heard of how the war left the South. With all the war wounded, surely the sisters had not starved. They knew too much. But Madge needed to know for certain how they'd fared. Now that she'd asked the doctor to help find Hemp's wife, she could go home without regret.

"You're leaving because I stopped you from selling out of my kitchen," Sadie said.

"Forgive me, Mrs. Walker, but the truth is your threats don't disturb my sleep."

"You're leaving with that man."

"What?"

"He's not worth your trouble, Madge."

Madge's face dropped. "Hush your mouth."

"I know things about him. Things you don't know."

"Hush your mouth."

"The spirit showed me. Something happened between him and his wife's daughter."

"Are they alive?"

"I don't know, and I can't figure out what happened exactly. I just know it was something wrong."

"Is his wife alive?"

"Don't you hear me? I don't know who is alive and who isn't. As soon as the spirit came, I didn't want to hear. I've had enough of secrets. What I can tell you is that the man is not worth it."

Madge's voice lowered to a whisper. "You a mean, vile woman. Just like the sisters."

"I'm not too fond of you, either."

"Good enough."

The widow moved from the leather chair to her desk. "I will make all the arrangements for your trip."

"You ain't got to do that."

Sadie pulled a piece of paper from the drawer of an end table. "Consider it your final pay."

Madge was too enraged to thank her. This woman didn't know Hemp at all. How dare she say those things about him? That girl had tried something on him, and he had resisted. Damn them two women for haunting her the way they did.

But maybe the widow had seen something more than he'd told her. Had Hemp been truthful about everything? Madge's hands started to shake.

As she stood there watching the widow scribble something on paper, she thought: I'm tired of doctoring on everybody except my own self. She'd told Hemp to heal himself. And he had lied to her about what happened with that girl. Wasn't it time she looked after herself for a change? When she said the widow had become like family, Hemp had laughed out loud. *Ain't no white woman your family, girl*, he'd said.

Such truth from a liar's mouth.

Madge's feelings about the woman might have been complicated, but one thing was certain: she had to leave. She had to get away from both Sadie and Hemp. Neither one was good for her.

20

STRUCK BY A FEELING THAT THE DOOR TO THE HOUSE on Ontario Street swung both ways, Sadie had not been surprised by the letter from York telling of her father's arrival date. When Samuel died, James and Madge appeared. Her mother's passing brought on Michael. And now her father was due to arrive that very day and Sadie hastened to write a treaty in the back of a carriage.

The nation's war was over, but not the one between father and daughter. As Richard drove her to the train station to meet him, Sadie was thinking of treaties and the complications of peacemaking. First, there was the how. Would it be words and would they be spoken or written? Would it be actions, a change of course? Then there was the what: what to say and do. Inevitably, there would be costs, concessions, sacrifices. Mistakes were made. Lines were drawn. In the end, one would be right, the other wrong.

For God's sake, what could possibly cause a change of heart in that man? And how exactly was she supposed to navigate this pathway of egos? She did not know what to do. She tried to think of what she'd learned from her books. Some wars ended long before the document was signed, before the meetings in Paris or Ghent. Others resolved with a white flag, a throwing up of hands in a temporary cease-fire, or a frustrated sign of surrender. The lingering question of what to do with the captured, the wounded. Where would the treaty be signed? Who would be the first to put away their purse of hurt? Her father, hoping for a son, instead received a daughter with a man inside. A traitorous ventriloquist. And now she, entrusted with the paper on which they would write the next chapter, left to find a single voice and draw up the outline.

She placed a hand over her chest. This was a complicated affair, this peacemaking. Yet reconciliation was necessary. Though he had been the one to betray, she would be the one to end it. He was her only family. She had no choice.

With their husbands dead and gone, many of the widows who visited the parlor had been left destitute or burdened with debt, their faces revealing this: An earthly passing was like the expiration of some essential truth one has always held dear. Things were not as they seemed. You were not who you thought you were. But what did it mean when the truth shifted and there was no death to bear the blame?

The carriage stopped in front of the train depot, but Sadie was still thinking of how to make peace.

A FLOCK OF BIRDS SCATTERED. Hat pulled low, she furtively watched the people around her. Some stood near traveling cases. Others wore expressions cloaked in anticipation. A woman in a lavender mourning dress clutched a fidgeting child's hand. A man perched on a well-worn valise, legs wide as he tipped back and forth, threads swinging loosely from the edge of his jacket. Sadie fanned herself.

The old man emerged first, his hat badly crumpled as if he had spent part of the journey sitting on it. A long face, eyes topped by a pair of trimmed silver eyebrows, a grid of lines around the eyes. Despite the hat and worn expression, the face was shaven, shoes brushed. He wore a long duster over his clothing, and he unfastened the top button of it as he pointed her out to the porter sent to retrieve his things. She started forward, then stopped, unable to close the distance between them, knowing that with each moment she stood rooted, her reception to her father's arrival cooled.

Though she had tried to forgive him, she could not forget. After the war had begun and his business began to falter, he'd sent her out of the bindery to begin the tedious work of embroidery—sheets, pillowcases, tablecloths—all the things she would need in her new household. The bindery had emptied of customers at around the same time that rumors of a Confederate plan to enter the Susquehanna valley reached them, so when the soldier arrived asking about a suitable dining establishment in town, her father did not hesitate to invite the man to his home for supper. She remembered her first impression of Samuel, how old he'd looked. Her mother began work on a new dress for Sadie after his second visit. And at nineteen years old, without issuing a word of objection, Sadie became a wife, marrying in the small Presbyterian church where she first received the sacrament.

The bookbinder strode across the platform. She read on his face a willingness to overlook her ill manners, to pretend she had not failed to welcome him or show even the slightest relief at his safe arrival.

"Father," she said, the closest she could come to a daughter's greeting, "is that all you have?"

"That is all," he said, but the conductor blew the whistle and she had to read his lips.

Richard signaled that the carriage was loaded. Sadie took her father's arm, felt the bones beneath the coat. "Are you hungry? You must be."

"I am fine."

The last time they'd stood together on a train platform, she'd watched her mother's eyes redden and her father press his hat against his chest as if saluting a flag. *Do you remember the peonies I brought back from Philadelphia?* he'd asked. She did. They'd smelled like newly turned earth and had been cinched together in a damp sack like a scrotum. *For years, they have been a great comfort to me*, he said. *Eventually, the plant grew so big and the roots so tangled, I decided to split it. I dug it up, carefully picking around the roots before I planted one a ways off from the others. All of them grew in their own right, brought more joy than a single one ever could.* He paused, and she waited for the final setting of lips. *Yes, sir*, she said. From the train's window, she'd watched her parents walk away, neither touching the other.

Now, as she and her father walked to the carriage, they struggled once more to make small talk. "How was your trip?"

He coughed violently. "Do you live far from here?"

"Just north." He might encourage her to move from the house, take over her life by stepping into the shoes of a dead husband. It would not surprise her if he tried.

He removed his duster before climbing into the carriage, and she saw how thin he'd become, as thin as a woman.

"So this is the great city of the West," he observed as they wound through the city.

"What do you think of it?"

"What I can see of it does not surprise."

She tried to view the city through his eyes. Two grain elevators hunched like bison in the sky. A man swept mud off a walkway. Sadie did not instruct Richard to take a more scenic route. The river's odor surged as they crossed the bridge.

"Good God," he said, covering his mouth.

"You will get used to it. By the way, who will tend Mother's grave?"

"The Youngs have agreed to look after the house, the grave, and everything else while I am away."

She looked back at the single trunk he'd brought. "I'd hoped that you would stay and live here."

He turned to the window. "That may be. And perhaps I may even stay here and die, but should that be the case, I shall return to York to rest beside her."

"Don't speak so grimly, Father."

"We are a nation of death, Sadie. Surely you understand that by now."

Richard slowed the carriage in front of the house. As they entered the front door, her father fingered the large bird Samuel had chosen as a knocker. He stepped into the drawing room, observed the chairs, the tables loaded with books, the twin urns on the mantel. In front of them, the stairs led to the second floor. Straight ahead, the kitchen. His eyes swung left to the drawn portière.

"What is this?" he asked.

She pulled back the drape. Better the sight of the table, the eerie portrait, the shielded windows than her fumbling words. There was no planchette, no hooded cabinet to signal the kinds of things that went on there. Just the table and two chairs sitting opposite one another in the dark. He stepped inside and looked up at the portrait.

"Pity," he whispered.

"Yes, pity."

"Do you come in here much?"

"I do."

"It was intended for your husband."

"It was."

Clearly, her father was making the same assumption as everyone else, that grief motivated her to devote her husband's parlor to a shrine. Even though he knew better than anyone how little she had known the man, he still saw a house of mourning. She watched his eyes take possession of the room: the gentleman's amusements he could reinstate. A table for cards. A cabinet for liquor. A wall of shelving for books. The plans glittered in his eyes, and she had a distasteful thought.

"How do you occupy yourself?" he asked.

"I am a medium."

"It's dark."

"I work in here."

"Better to let in a little light."

"A spiritualist."

"It is unfortunate to be widowed so young."

"I speak with the dead."

"It has been three years, yet you still wear black. It is better to let in a little light." His voice was soft.

"I have a spirit guide. His name is James Heil."

"I hope you have found a meaningful pastime." He looked around.

"I have, Father. I'm a medium."

"A medium."

"I told you of this voice once before when I visited York. It hasn't gone away. Do you know of Spiritualism?"

"Do I know of it."

"I am one."

His eyes connected with hers. "So you rap on tables, blow trumpets and other such nonsense in here?"

She shook her head. She'd hoped to wait until after dinner, insert this news into a stack of frivolous conversation. But here they were.

"A spirit speaks through me. A man."

"A man."

Yes, she should have waited until after dinner. He had not eaten, and surely his hunger affected his temper. As she struggled to stay quiet, her suspicions grew. He had not come to Chicago to spend time with her but to marry her off again. He still thought it improper for her to live alone. Always, it came back to this. It was what a good father did: marry off his daughter. A woman needed protection. It was what a good daughter did: marry a suitable man. He'd only brought one trunk because his task was plain. And as quickly as she knew why he'd come, she understood why she'd welcomed him. Loneliness suffocated. The adoration of the crowds had proven insufficient.

As they walked into her drawing room, she remembered the conversations in which they'd parried like master and pupil. When she was a girl, he had taught her to press pages in the lying press. Carrying bundles of paper—sheet music, periodicals, sermons—she moved easily between the press and the sewing frame, neatly threading the signatures. Often, she did more than what was expected: gluing spines, trimming edges, attaching linings. All that remained for him was to stamp and tool. In those days, when her hips were still narrow and chest flat, he'd treated her like a son. She had looked forward to his Chicago visit because she missed those days before the war upset her life. She did not want her father to die and leave James behind to relay his messages. She wanted to hear what her father had to say from his own mouth. Spirits, contrary to some beliefs, were not cleansed by their transitions. Many held on to grievances, vendettas. The spirit readily admitted how often he uttered false platitudes of devotion to the living. She did not want to become one of those people the spirits lied to.

Olga entered the drawing room to announce dinner.

He gave the cook a hard stare as she turned to leave the room. "You have good help, I take it?"

The question surprised Sadie. Her family had never employed household help, and she wondered exactly how much he knew of Samuel's wealth. She remembered how unprepared she had been for the four waiting servants.

"That is my cook. She takes good care of me."

"Does she?" He cleared his throat. "I don't understand why you partake of this medium business. You don't need the money."

"I don't do it for the money."

"So why?"

For a moment, she pitied him. "To give comfort."

"To a bunch of fools, doubtless."

She looked straight at him. "Many people are fools, I agree. But it is not differences of opinion that make us fools, Father."

21

IN THE MONTHS SINCE HIS ARRIVAL, HE HAD RE-
fused to enter the darkened parlor. Now he sat at the
table, waiting.

"What's wrong?" She removed her bonnet and pulled back the
curtain. A damp breeze blew through the open window.

"I want to talk to your mother," he said.

"It isn't so easy, Father."

"You do it for strangers. Surely you can do it for your own father.
Have you ever even spoken to your mother?"

Her forehead burned. She called for Olga to bring something cool
to drink, but the woman did not answer. Now that Madge was gone,
the house carried the silence of abandonment.

"I would think that if you really have this ability, as you say you
do, you would speak with your mother's spirit, not sell yourself like
some strumpet on the street."

"Strumpet?"

"Tell me about this Heil. He is corrupting you, is he not?"

She sat in the other chair.

"Are you some kind of witch?"

"Good heavens."

"Did you call me to Chicago to assist you in a fraud?"

"Call you to Chicago? I—"

"Don't you realize this city is crime-ridden?" he interrupted. "I've been reading the papers here since I arrived. I'm afraid for your safety."

Sadie had heard that women who sold their bodies to paying men were called "war widows" whether they had actually been widowed or not. The moniker disturbed her.

"Are you beyond salvation?"

"I just want you to accept me." Her voice diminished, and she could feel herself growing younger. Soon, she would be a child again, a baby, retreating into that space before words. Difficult to argue with the dutiful, difficult to argue with the child that went along uncomplainingly. All she had to do was renounce the spirit, marry, return to York. All would be forgiven, and life would be as it was before.

"Are you a mesmerist as well? Will you change me with your touch? I hardly need help, you know. I'm perfectly balanced."

She wanted to explain the loneliness, how the gifts alienated her. She had brought Madge home because anyone who would stick a hand in fire for money had to be a believer. Now she had even lost her. Sadie was torn: he was her family, but she needed to escape him.

"Your mother would turn in her grave."

"My mother nursed a young woman back to health and gave her own in return. That was a sign of her character."

"She provided hope and rest, not lies."

"I, too, provide hope." She thought of Michael, the spilled tea. She had not wanted him to reject her proposal, not yet. So she'd put him off. And now she feared she had lost him, too. Everything was wrong.

Nothing added up any longer. Perhaps James did corrupt her. She had visited Michael's home and asked him to marry her. What kind of woman did that?

"Tell me about this Heil."

"He was a soldier."

"An officer?"

"No."

"A wife? Children?"

"No."

"Carry on." He waved a hand, turning his body to the side, one foot beneath the table, the other pointed in the direction of the doorway. She found herself unconsciously mimicking his position.

Her father was so single-minded that she wondered if, for him, fatherhood was just another book to bind and shelve. She wanted to reclaim what he'd taken from her, but here he was again: directing, ordering. Olga had not answered, so Sadie drew the curtain herself. Even with her back turned, she felt the hardness of her father's eye resting upon her like judgment. She sat opposite him, placed both palms on the table. He looked down, as if he half-expected the table to rise into the air. She closed her eyes, ready to be done with it. She was tired of this spirit. Warmth seeped through the crown of her head. *Come on, James. Hurry.* After a few minutes, she was certain her mother would come.

The spirit's voice began as if in the middle of a thought.

The trains arrived, running with the blood of the dying and wounded. They lay like dolls, their mouths frozen open, necks twisted. Many would not have been recognized by their own mothers. They were young and old, but they were mostly young. They were married and unmarried. Fathers, brothers, nephews, cousins, uncles. They cried like children, begged for God's mercy. And while I nursed them, I became as they—a soul holding on to the hope that my sacrifice had meant something.

There comes a time when we must rise up and meet our humanity, when our personal beliefs no longer matter and the instinct of self-preservation must disappear. At these moments, every narrow debate becomes irrelevant. The moment is bigger than us. There is a higher truth, you see. That's why I went to that hospital. There was no thinking, no decision making involved. It was the right thing to do. Northerners or Southerners, Unionists or Rebels, I would have gone. But it is still a painful kind of heartbreak to realize that your arms are not long enough to wrap around the entire earth. How small we all are. How insignificant, my dear Andrew.

The voice drifted off. Sadie, who had been motionless, stirred. She opened her eyes and sat quietly. This time, James had not served as conduit. It had been direct contact with her mother's spirit. She was certain of it. She could even smell her mother's natural body scent, as if the woman had just worn her dress. Could she access all of the spirits without him? What did this mean?

"So this is what you do for people," he said, taking what seemed to be his first breath in minutes. "You take their money and consort with this spirit, give people a gospel of false prophecy. They march in here like ants, sit at this table under the image of your good husband while you defile his name and home. Your mother was a holy woman, and when you were born we gave you the name of your grandmother, an honor to see you through life. I came here to break bread under God's roof; instead, I find you consorting with demons."

He spoke so low, so quickly, that even if someone had been standing in the hall listening, they would only have heard the sound of *s*'s slipping through his teeth.

"It was her. It was actually her, not the spirit. I—"

"You shame me. You dishonor your mother."

Sadie sweated beneath her dress. Her mouth moistened. They both stood, but she stepped back from the table.

"This is not," he said, "what your mother would have wanted."

Seldom was she given an opportunity to witness what people did with their belief once they left her house. Powerful enough to heal or destroy, the séance claimed a part of a person, and she had learned that sometimes ignorance was a safer space. Now the veil between her new life and old one had been irrevocably lifted. And Sadie could see by the look on her father's face that he believed. Entirely.

"She went to that hospital so she could be of use. I, too, am trying to be useful."

"How dare you compare yourself to her. She was a woman."

His eyes were black orbs, and nothing, not the flicker of candle, not the sparkle of her necklace, not even his rage reflected in them.

"You have to understand."

He thrust a gnarled hand out. "This spirit induces you to do his work. But what comes of speaking to the dead except more grief?"

He turned, his words clipping the air in front of him. She pursued him out of the parlor into the front hall. He threw his coat over his shoulders, took up his cane, and flung open the door. He turned, standing in the frame. Behind him, the fog obscured everything, hung over the street like smoke.

"But I am trying to tell you something. It wasn't him this time. Please come back inside."

"We were good Presbyterians. Good people. We did not follow the faithful into church as often as we should have, but you were taught. You were taught, Sadie."

It had rained earlier and everything was damp and slick. She could barely see five feet ahead. A pedestrian emerged behind him, ghost-like, and disappeared again, leaving behind the echo of his boots striking the cobbled walk.

"You are one of the good widows, Sadie," he said. "You are one of the faithful—Naomi, Ruth, Abigail. Not Jezebel or Tamar."

Wet strings licked his forehead. When he spoke he tipped his head back, aiming his mouth at her. She could see the peel of lip skin, the crooked tie.

"When Naomi lost her husband, she left Moab, returned to Bethlehem. The land of her people," he said.

He was drawing her out, the way he had done when she was young. "Yes, that's right," Sadie replied, remembering the story. "She went back to Bethlehem to start a new life, but—"

"She did not dishonor the memory of her husband."

"I have very few memories of Samuel, Father, and you have fewer."

"Abigail protected her husband, Nabal, by going to David and counseling restraint."

"Abigail?" she said. "Her father married her to Nabal because he was wealthy, but Nabal turned out to be a mean and cruel man."

"Samuel was no Nabal."

"How would you know?" she said. "How would you know anything? You barely knew the man."

He turned, threw his hands up. She thought he threw them up in frustration but suddenly realized he was falling, slipping, his arms beating the air like wings. A shoe scraped the ground. His cane sailed. She moved toward him, saw his eyes widen as he flew into the bank of fog. She heard a crack, and she rushed down the steps, kneeling beside him.

"Help me! Please, someone!"

She screamed until she heard someone approach—a man's voice urgently calling out to her.

Part Three

22

As the train rolled south, Madge could not help but miss her closet in the widow's house. Being in that kitchen closet was like being with the spirits. Buckeye. Jimsonweed. Hollyhock. She planned to teach the sisters new words for old things, like wild arsenic weed for rat's vein. She would sound out the new words until even Baby Sister, who spoke with a whistle, would get it. She would tell them how the prairie was drawn in shades of purple and yellow and orange. She would tell them how, beneath the tall grasses in the moist earth, she had discovered nubs of goodness rich enough to cure the soul.

First, Madge would have to assure them she had not given their secrets away. The practice of herb doctoring had sustained five generations of women, freed three of them. She would have to remind them she remembered those unshackled feet. Madge imagined how their faces would look when she returned. Would they be pleased? Would there still be a place for her? She prayed they had survived the final ugly days of the war.

The widow had bought her a first-class fare all the way to Tennessee, but the journey was long enough to make it trickier than that. At Sadie's suggestion, Madge traveled in widow's garb. When changing trains, she hung back and observed long enough to decide which car to board. Between Centralia and Cairo, a conductor ordered her out of the ladies' car into the men's-only smoking car, and she was so humiliated that she actually looked forward to boarding a steamboat.

She made her way south, junction after junction, avoiding food counters, eating from her well-stocked pouch. She traveled with a trunk packed lightly enough to manage, dragging it onto the boat at Cairo after she tried unsuccessfully to tip a porter. When she reached Tennessee, the hem of her dress had fallen and she was covered in a film of dust. She stepped off the boat where the Hatchie joined the Mississippi, just above the towhead, and met a flurry of activity: men offering rides on rickety carts, women selling bread and fruit. She waved down a colored man attaching a mule to his cart. Scars ran down his arms, the skin keloided and lumpy. He pointed to the seat.

"I ain't going far," she said, speaking through her veil. "But I can't move this here trunk another lick."

"Climb on up."

He took the whip in his left hand, flicked it.

Her head lolled, as if all the blood had collected there. She could still feel the rocking of the ship.

"I got a paper underneath that there box. I reckon it's pretty old by now. But I was hoping you could . . ."

"Not likely."

"Thought you might could," he said, glancing at her dress.

He wanted the news. She could not read black lines on paper, but she had ears. She tried to think of what she had overheard. How some things had changed and some hadn't. Families still searching for one another. A new president. Colored folks running for office. She did not know how much this man knew, and she did not want to insult him.

She told him where to go, and he took off. Groves of cypress trees edged the forest on the other side of the river. A catbird mewled from the roadside brush. She wanted to take it all in, this land of her birth, but what she really needed was sleep.

"Scat!"

The wagon jerked to a stop. She woke and saw a dog lying in the middle of the road, its head against the ground.

The man stepped down to look. He stretched the dog's leg, pulling the bend out of it. It rolled onto its back. Madge lost sight as the man stooped over. He rose, cradling the dog in his arms. A ladder of pink nipples poked out of its belly.

"What happened to it?" Madge asked as he placed the mongrel in the back of the wagon.

"Cut wide open. Likely hit by the wheel of something."

He picked up the reins and tapped the buttock of the mule with his whip. She wanted to know about the man, but he had not even offered his name. She wanted to ask what happened to the slaves she'd known her whole life, if he knew any of them. As she neared home, the path to the house etched into sight, years of wear making it inhospitable to grass. She lifted up so the breeze could dry the back of her damp dress, ducking as the low-hanging branches of a tree grazed the top of her head. They rounded the last bend. She turned her face, catching sight of the listless dog on the back of the cart.

No one can save it, she thought grimly. *No one can save none one of us.*

The house squatted, sinking into the ground, its logs pitted with age. She'd once been so proud of it, but after living in Chicago she couldn't help but think it was not much of a house—the windows needed repair, the porch sank on one side, the eaves were full of nests. But it was theirs. The sisters did not possess beauty or husbands. All they had was this house deeded them by a grateful white man. As Madge looked upon the place of her birth, her love for Chicago began to disappear from memory.

SHE SEARCHED FOR SIGNS OF LIFE. All was quiet, but the house did not look abandoned. Three chairs on the porch. A broom. Everything in its place, just as it had been in the dream. He pulled the cart up in front of a post and stepped down.

"There a creek nearby? It's hot as the devil's den out here." He stroked the head of his mule.

Madge pointed to the back of the house. "You want me to sew her up?"

"Naw. If'n you got a needle, I can do it. Won't be the first time I done stitched."

"Sure, I get it for you. Thank you, hear?"

He tipped his hat.

She turned toward the house: *Howdy. Yall feeling all right? Afternoon, Berta Mae, Sarah Louise. That you, Baby Sister?*

She stepped over fallen fruit in the yard, looked up at the tree. It had dropped all of its peaches, and they lay scattered throughout the yard. Madge could not remember the last time the tree had shed so early. On the porch, she scraped the bottom of her shoes and patted her face. She crossed a soldierly trail of ants carrying specks of white to a hill wedged between porch planks. The door opened before she could finish inspecting. The oldest, Berta Mae, took her in as she glanced around at the cart, a dull expression on her face.

"Your husband brung you?"

"No, ma'am. He just drive me."

"Who died?"

"Nobody. It's just a dress."

Berta made a sound in her throat, looked accusingly at Madge's stomach.

"You here for good?" She paused as if the niece's answer to this question would determine the measure of her welcome.

"Yes, ma'am."

Berta looked around the yard again before turning and going back inside. She left the door open, and Madge knew this was the best welcome the oldest would give her.

From the outside, the house appeared the same. Inside was another story. The sofa had been torn and sewn closed. The quilt was gone. The women had always lived simply, but there had been a few nice things. A dented copper pan Berta Mae had shined up. A handful of dried flowers. A possum skin. It was all gone now, leaving the room with a hollowed-out feeling. Curtains fluttered at the open windows, blocking out the sunlight. The house was too hot for anything walking on two legs, and it smelled of gutted fish.

Baby Sister cleared her throat. It was so dark, Madge had not seen her sitting in the chair.

"That you, Baby Sister?"

"Who else would it be."

"Ain't you a sight."

"Huh." A tooth glinted.

Madge untied her veil. She heard a deep "Ea-sy" spoken outside.

"Where Say-ruh?"

Baby Sister pointed at the bedroom. A few feet away, Berta noisily moved dishes around, clearly upset she would have to set a table for four again. Madge lay the veil on a chair before going in to see her mother. Inside the bedroom, it was cooler.

"Say-ruh? You sleep?" That was what Madge asked, but what she almost said was, *You dead?* She had not expected her mother to be lying down, a hump beneath covers in daylight hours.

"Course not. Come on over here and let me look at you."

Madge stepped closer, glancing at the unlit candle on the table. She moved around to the other side of the bed. Her mother's eyes were wide.

"What's wrong with your eyes?"

"What's wrong with your'n?"

Sarah's hands reached, and she pulled Madge closer before sitting up. She placed a hand on each of Madge's hips, pressed thumbs into her frontside. Madge closed her eyes and tried to let go, but her mind flew back to the memory of Hemp. His hands had found their way beneath her dress, and he had grabbed her hips as firmly as her mother was grabbing her now. She had leaned into his touch like a hungry dog as he made his way up her body, rubbing her arms before rising again to finger each button on the back of her dress until he got to the bones of her collar. Now her mother's rough hands touched her face, brushed her eyelashes. They smelled of fish. The scent had settled on everything in the house.

"I see you eating good."

Voices passed through the window.

"*You new round here?*"

"*Yes, ma'am.*"

"*You look a little weak. Could be your blood thin.*"

"*You reckon?*"

"*Here. Take this here. Drink it 'fore you lay down at night.*"

"*I ain't sick. Got a dog on back of my cart with a nasty cut, though. Could use a needle.*"

"*And you? Take this.*"

"*It's bleeding mighty heavy.*"

"*A dog?*"

"Madge?" Sarah's hands rested on her belly. "Where you been? Why you come back?"

"Had a dream."

"They come and took our stuff."

"Who?"

"Ain't no Yankees make 'em do what they done."

Madge pulled the covers up to her mother's chin. That was why she'd had the dream. Somebody had paid the house a visit.

"They hurt you?"

Her mother's shining eyes rolled toward the ceiling.

"Sister put a trick on 'em. My guess they six feet under by now."

"Y'all don't do tricks."

"Don't ain't can't."

"You rest, Say-ruh. When you wake up, I show you what I brung."

Sarah did not protest, and Madge left the room, unable to stand the sight of her mother's eyes staring up at the ceiling.

MADGE WOKE TO THE SOUND of the sisters murmuring in the other room and knew they had gone through her trunk. She had forgotten the lack of privacy in a house of women. She rubbed sleep from her eyes.

"What that smell like?"

"Ain't sassafras."

"This one here ain't no good. Smell dead."

"Probably picked too late."

"Give it here, no it ain't."

Madge joined them, sitting in the empty chair left at the table. She had not brought anything they knew about. The herbs lay in the middle of the table. Without the whole story, the dealings with the apothecarist would mean nothing, so she started from the beginning and kept talking until she got to the part about how street after street in Chicago filled with throngs of people, swinging bridges stopped traffic allowing ships to pass, buildings crowded upon one another, smoke curled over freighters, grain elevators as tall as mountains painted the sky. She told how she made her way into a rich white woman's house as a maid, only to build up a secret store of plants and a crop of paying customers.

They stared at her, stupefied.

Berta Mae wore a frown, so Madge removed a sack of coins from inside her dress and placed it on the table. Berta's face did not change as she closed a hand over it.

Madge pointed. "This here is called quinine. It help with the digestion."

"Kwi what? Di what?"

"Quinine. You use it in the place of dogwood. And this here"— she revealed the jar of paste sewn into the inside of her dress—"is my new healing balm I made."

Berta Mae turned her face.

"One more thing. The white woman I work for talk to the dead."

"Chiiiillld—"

"That's how I come up with it. This help people get over they grief. I'm telling you, I hear 'em talking and people need miracles. This balm is they miracle."

The sisters did not move, and neither did Madge. She had been so busy talking, she had overlooked the heat of their anger.

Berta Mae spoke through her teeth. "We don't traffic in no lie, and we don't sell no false hope."

The sisters were a single block of wood, a wall pushing against her. In the face of it, she was less than air, and she always would be. Their demand for respect would never allow her to grow tall. And even when her wisdom outstretched theirs, there would be no recognition. The old ways, even the flawed old ways, would come first. In those rare moments when one of them appeared to be taking her side, the alliance ended the moment another sister entered the room. Madge knew the teaming was built on convenience, but it did not matter. First came the Lord King—forget about Adam—and then came Eve. Then came the woman who birthed the woman who birthed the woman who birthed and birthed and birthed until the sisters were delivered. Last in that line was Madge—the girl child.

She tried to speak confidently, like she did when she was demanding someone pay her for teas. But she couldn't. They still unnerved her. With a quivering lip, she told them of the apothecarist, even though she knew all they heard was *white man*. She told how she had started her own business, but all they heard was *white women*. She bolstered the impossibilities with more descriptions of the city: a lake that did not stop, people wearing the coats of animals. After a while she could tell she was repeating herself, so she stopped talking.

"Madge," her mother said, "what you tell that white woman?"

"I ain't tell her nothing."

"You got a mouth, don't you?" Berta Mae added.

"I told you. She talk to the dead. Make her own living."

It was quiet in the house. The sound of their breath overtook hers. They watched her as if she were the hunted, her next step determining their next step.

"What kind of dead?"

"Do y'all know how far Chicago is from here? And besides, ain't the same woods there?"

"Mmm hm."

"It's a prairie."

"A what?"

"Talk to the dead, huh?"

"We ever tell you about our aunt Mary beat to death for not telling?"

"Mmm hm."

That story had worked on Madge her whole life. Nothing else, they'd preached early on, guaranteed their freedom but their ability to heal. The sisters' secrets were more powerful than the papers hidden in the floorboard because only those secrets could procure new papers should the other ones fail.

"I told you I ain't tell her nothing."

"Just 'cause she ain't fishing don't mean she ain't got a taste for some trout."

"Mmm hm."

Middle-of-the-night quiet settled over them as Madge waited for the final cut. But it did not come. Instead, Baby Sister said, "Nothing you can't do about her eyes?"

Baby Sister had moved the conversation, but now she shrank. She rarely talked, but when she did, she had a way of pulling her body back once she'd spoken, as if stepping away from a conversation she'd begun. Madge had changed since going north, and the aunts regarded this newness skeptically. They had studied the forest long enough to know that they did not know the answer to everything, and at any given moment they might witness unknown effects of the same leaves, stems, barks, roots that they had used their entire lives. The sisters did not preach hope, but they knew it existed.

Madge fingered a pouch. "Nothing," she said though she wanted to add, *Not yet, anyway.* Knowledge was out there beyond the woods of Tennessee, some of it in fields of wildflowers where the earth did not stop.

Madge had a thought: "She can come back with me. All y'all can. We can figure it out together. 'Sides, y'all getting too old to be down here by yourself."

"Thought you was here to stay," said Baby Sister.

Berta Mae laughed. "Besides, what some old women like us do up there? Girl, I was born in them woods. And when my time come, I carry my behind right out there and die in them."

"You can't even chop wood," said a sister.

"Come back here after while and tell me you don't see a fire."

"What you eat lately other than what you got out that river?" Madge asked softly.

"You the stick."

"No, she ain't," Sarah said. "She look good."

"Shut up. How you know how she look."

"When the last time y'all healed?"

"You still a child, child."

Madge turned to her mother. "You remember my hands? What they can do?"

"You still think you something special, don't you," they said.

"Mama, listen to me. I can be your eyes."

"We got four eyes right here," said the eldest. "Don't need two more."

Baby Sister poked her head forward. "Now Berta."

A familiar sight: a mother's affection snatched away from a lovesick daughter. Madge thought again of Hemp and how Berta Mae's words had left a pile of dirt on top of Madge's farewell. *Just remember. Ain't no healing brew between your legs.*

23

MADGE HELPED THE SISTERS. STOCKED the pantry. Picked greens. Fattened the chickens. And, gradually, the sisters' distrust of Sadie's spirit work gave way to curiosity. They wanted to know what kinds of things this widow's spirit talked about, and whether the white woman could make a dead body appear. Even though it was clear they expected answers, they still uttered the questions without an asking tone, as if they already knew the answer, and when Madge hesitated, they shot her a look that said, *I knew it was all a lie*. Three weeks turned into four, and, finally, the sisters cracked open the door, no longer sending Madge outside on chores while they talked to one another. They began to continue conversations after Madge entered the room, even asking her opinion about the beetles crawling on the fava leaves. Madge was reminded that in these woods she was one of them while in Chicago she was an uprooted bush planted in somebody else's garden.

As she returned home one day, she caught movement at the window of the house and knew one of the women was watching for her. A finger of smoke scratched at the sky. The fire was already lit. She had not told them she was bringing home meat, but they had known what kind of girl they raised. As she entered the three-room house, built by slaves who belonged to a white man whose life the girls' mother had saved, she considered the sanctity of western Tennessee. A bona fide place. Not still forming like that city of noise she'd left behind. Inside, Baby Sister took the ham from her. Clearly, the sisters were working on what Madge wanted to believe was finally her homecoming feast. If her arrival had not excited them, the prospect of food did. Madge picked up a bowl of peas that needed snapping. Her mother pulled bugs off the leaves of a cabbage, then dunked it in a bowl of water.

The four women sat down to eat, the smell of salted pork in the air, the sound of their teeth grinding the food. Here was the thing she had missed in Chicago. Even during those years when they had not accepted her, she had lived within shouting distance of this feeling. There was sanctity here.

Once all of the women had their fill, they reclined in the rockers on the porch, the dark curtain of trees behind them. Madge brought out a fourth chair. The flame of a candle inside the house cast a dull light over the women's faces as they quietly spat tobacco juice into the cans at their feet.

"Read," her mother said.

"What?"

"You heard her, girl. Read," Berta said.

None of the women knew their letters, so as far back as Madge could remember, they had made their own stories. The sisters watched Madge, waiting to hear what kind of story she could tell after two years of living away.

Madge cleared her throat.

One time, in a place far away, a king's son was given fifty wives, but he didn't love none one of 'em. The poor prince was so sad 'cause he just didn't feel nothing for none of 'em. Then one day, he come up on the daughter of two old turtles. Now this turtle daughter wasn't no ordinary girl. Fact was, she had two faces—one nice and the other evil. That nice face was so beautiful that the prince was struck down by love and he take her right away to the castle and marry her.

Months go by, and the turtle princess start to kill off the other wives one by one with a poison stew. She kill 'em all until only one other wife left. That poor scared woman go to the prince to tell him about the evil side of the turtle princess, but he just can't believe it. When he go to find the two-faced wife, he can't find her, so he go to the turtle parents. Shamed by their daughter, they confess how she was born with two faces and how they hid it from him. The prince's heart was broke right in two.

He go looking for the turtle princess, and he find her in the woods busy cooking a stew to kill off the last wife. He want to tell her how he know all about her two faces, but he can't because he get caught up in that pretty side again. Fact was, one of the faces so beautiful he can't hardly stand it. The princess go off into the woods to remove her dress so he can take her right there on the forest floor. While the prince wait for her, he get hungry and sip from her stew. And it sure was good. He eat until he can't eat no more. When the turtle princess get back, that prince dead on the ground. She lay down beside him crying, distraught over what she done.

When the people of the kingdom find out, they chase the girl out of that place forever. That last wife, the one she never got to kill, marry the prince brother, and the two became king and queen and the turtle princess was never seen or heard from again.

She stopped.

"You ain't planning to marry, is you?" her mother said.

"Don't she need somebody to marry first?"

"Something happen up there in that city, girl? Something you want to share?"

"Oh, Lord, she done killed somebody wife."

"Why you wear that mourning dress, anyway?"

"Maybe she lost a baby."

"But she say she ain't have no husband."

"Yea though I walk."

Madge interrupted. She had done it the way they always did it, spinning around a story she had heard as a child. This story had nothing to do with her life. She had done something bad, but she sure hadn't killed anybody. "Now y'all stop it. I said, it's just a dress."

She caught her breath. Maybe she did have a secret hankering to kill Hemp's wife. It sure would save her a lot of trouble. She had no business wanting him, but she still did. It wasn't fair. She was flesh and bone. Annie was nothing but a ghost memory. Madge wanted to take him over, his hands, his arms, but he was a man who had always been owned, and though she knew better than to conflate the ownership of love with the ownership of greed, she understood that, for Hemp, the first breath of freedom contained the joy of self-possession.

Hemp's body had been so willing when she lay with him. It made her resent Annie, hate her, even though Madge had never set eyes on the woman. Hemp was the one who proved the sisters wrong. He was a good man. She had to believe him when he said he had only kissed the girl. Still, Madge could not have him. Over and over, she'd considered how the very honor that disproved the sisters' ideas about men was the same virtue that kept him from her. What the sisters had left out was that sometimes women were the ones to do the wounding.

"You hear me talking, Madge? What happened up there?"

Sarah did not wait for an answer. She rose and felt for the doorway to her room. Madge looked at her mother's back and started to say, *This story ain't have nothing to do with me*, but nothing came to her lips.

THE BEGINNING OF JULY ARRIVED, the annual time for the sisters to forage for bark. They tied pouches around their waists and took out pickaxes from under the beds. Madge filled their canteens with water, shelled nuts for a midday meal, sharpened their blades, and the four marched through the yard, swatting at flies. Sarah held on to Madge's elbow.

To the sisters, the woods were a sanctuary, and God dwelled upon its grounds. As they walked, they preached to Madge, repeating old lessons: *Wait till the sap done rose before pulling the bark. When you pull it, make sure you strip off the outer part, scrape at the tree's underbelly. A tree bark like skin, so handle it gentle. Never skin a tree all the way 'round its trunk or you kill it. When you can, take bark from the branch and not the trunk. Gather roots in fall. If you pull roots in spring, get ready to wait for 'em to dry out real good. Make sure to wait for the plant's seeds to age. If the plant still growing, let it alone. Pick leaves from plants just as they start to flower. Pick flowers at full bloom. Always pick leaves and flowers in the morning, but wait till the dew dry. Gather seeds when they ripe. You got to know your trees. Know the difference 'tween a beech and a oak, a mulberry and a magnolia. Once you take note of your trees, move on to the smaller stuff: bushes, shrubs, plants. The woods will teach you. In the right weather, on the right day, ain't no other place. See that bark? It's weak, so you need a lot of it. Put some in your pouch. Boil it long and slow, and that tea work a miracle. Headaches, stomachaches, diarrhea, piles. Toss it 'round in your throat when it's sore. Pour it on rashes and burns. If you want a stronger bark, you got to find a white oak rather than a red oak. See that tree? Chew the bark and you get rid of a toothache. Boil it and the tea will empty you out. Here come a tree every healer need to know. This here is gum. You chew on this for all kind of ailments. Rub it in your sores and wounds. Boil it in milk and give it to a baby.*

They talked as they worked, played a game where Sarah tried to recognize trees by smell and touch, laughing when she got it right, teasing when she got it wrong. *You done lost your touch, Say-ruh. Never needed no eyes before.* They filled their pouches. A canopy of green protected them from the worst of the sun, and the rough brush stabbed at their ankles. Later, they lay out their discoveries on the table. Madge boiled a pot of water, then pulled a worm from her mother's hair. Sarah Louise held a piece of bark to her nose, commented on its sweet odor, bit into it, and chewed thoughtfully.

"Now come on, Say-ruh Lou. We ain't done with you yet. Tell us what this is," Baby Sister said, pushing a chip toward her older sister. Baby Sister's chest caved inward, and she sat back as if she had not asked the question.

Sarah rubbed it between her thumb and index finger, pressed it to her nose, and declared, "Child, you got to do better than that. That's mamaroot."

"What about this one."

"I'm gone beat you with a stick."

"We got to keep you going," Berta said.

"You know I can still beat you with no eyes and two hands tied behind my back."

Madge dropped a piece of wood into the boiling water. When she sat down again, she said, "I be heading back soon." The words came out before she'd had a chance to think. She had not known until that moment, listening to the sisters talk, that this was no longer her home.

"Heading to what." The laughter was gone from Berta's voice.

Madge felt something coming her way and blurted, "To a life," when she'd meant to say "to my life." What she had in Tennessee was a life, too, but it was not the one she had made. Occasionally, Baby

Sister's lips moved as if about to say something, but Madge could see the motion was involuntary.

Madge tried to turn the mood. "Read to me. Read to me about the man with the short arm." None of the sisters answered, and Madge knew there would be no more stories. They had shared with her all they could. What she knew already would have to suffice. She looked down at her tea, thinking of the life she would make. She would advertise herself as a "doctor," but she planned to heal more than the body. She wanted to make amulets, healing balms, things that worked because people believed in them.

Madge was clear on her vision for herself, so why did she still feel so bad? She looked over at the women. All their eyes were on her, even the glassy, unseeing eyes of her mother.

THE NIGHT BEFORE SHE LEFT, Madge rubbed the balm onto her mother's neck, shoulders, and arms. She massaged the joints, rubbing out the knots. The house was quiet, and the mother and daughter shared the moment undisturbed. When she was done, Madge lay beside her.

"You know y'all got to heal again. You can't eat if you don't," Madge whispered.

"I lost my sight when nem mens came."

"Buzzards."

"Lord only knows why they come this way to take out they anger on us."

Madge's dream had been unfinished: the sisters were alive, the house still standing. The untold scene was that her mother had lost her eyes. She wished with a sudden, deep longing that her hands had the power to do more than pronounce. She wished they could heal. She placed a hand over her mother's eyes and prayed for something to flow through them.

With Madge's hands still closed over her face, Sarah continued talking: "They bust in here and they bust me, too. Struck me in my eye with a stick. I seen light and then dark."

Madge ran her other hand down the groove of Sarah's neck.

"Hit me right in the eye. Feel like it was knocked clean out of my head. Feel like somebody done set fire to it. The other eye still work, so I pick myself up and see about my sisters."

Madge could not help but think: What would have happened had she been there? Who would her mother have worried over more if forced to choose? Ridiculous—this jealous feeling of aunts. Nothing but the selfish thoughts of a child. Yet her doubt persisted. Had she been there, she knew what she would have done: taken the blow for her mother. Defended her without a second thought.

"I found 'em both up under the bed. Too scared to come out even though the mens was long gone. Ain't never seen my sisters in such a fright, 'specially Berta. She ain't as tough as you think. Us don't work no black magic. Mama said it ain't right. But everybody know what the other thinking."

"What they take?"

"Don't matter. We make out fine in the wash. Excepting me. I lean on that one eye so hard them first few days, I reckon I lean too hard. Pretty soon it start to follow the other one, like neither one wanting to see the world no more. We so foolish thinking they come here to protect us. White folks round here ain't never messed with us none. One of 'em was hurt when they walked up. We could've helped him. 'Fore long, we knowed they wasn't up to no good."

"Why he hit you?"

"He try to take this." She reached under the mattress, held something in her fist, passed it over to Madge. A small picture in a frame hung on a chain that had turned green long ago. Madge remembered that summer; she had been barely fourteen years old when Sarah squeezed ointment in the eye of a man traveling through town with a camera. He had taken Madge's picture in payment.

"That boy yanked it clean off my neck. So I kicked him in the leg. Sure did. That's when everything go dark."

"How you get it back?"

"Now ain't God funny. Nem mens took out from here so fast, they leave it behind. One of the sisters find it out there in the dirt. I got back my Madge, but I lost my sight. Now all I can do is hold it. Can't ever look on your face no more, even when you laying right here beside me. So you might as well head on back up that way and take it with you. I don't need it no more."

"Say-ruh?"

"Hush now, take it."

"What I want with a picture of myself?"

"You got one?"

"No."

"Well, this here remind you what you look like, remind you who you is."

Madge could not speak.

Sarah turned to face her. "What you aims to do with your God-given gift, girl?"

It was the first time her mother had ever acknowledged her hands. Madge blew out through her lips. She opened her mouth to speak, but she couldn't explain it, couldn't translate the kinds of hopes the city gave her. "I aims to heal."

"Good. But I don't understand why you got to live in that city. Plenty to heal right around these parts. Ain't nothing up there that ain't right here."

Yeah there is, Madge wanted to say. *Trains and ships and palace hotels and gas streetlamps. Big churches full of respectable coloreds like Quinn Chapel and Olivet Baptist and the one Hemp belonged to.*

"Stay here. Stay here with me."

She was so busy thinking of Chicago that she did not see it sneaking up on her. The thing she'd always longed for. The childish *gimme* hand-delivered in her mother's bed on a hot July night. At long last. The proof. The asking. First the profile and now this. These words being handed her, this heartache in the strain of Sarah Lou's voice. It had been the absence of this very thing that had pushed her to leave Tennessee in the first place. That disgusted face over a tub of dirty underwear in a muddy front yard had been no kind of image for a daughter to carry.

Now she had something more.

But even with it nestled in her chest, stored where she could always remember it, she knew she would leave again. This time, there was no washing board to take the blame for Madge's sorrow, no hanging dresses needing a hand. Instead, there were just these words, this string tying them together. They lay there—two free women weighing two futures, with and without the other.

This time Madge would not leave because she did not receive a mother's love. She would leave because she had.

24

UNABLE TO REACH THE RIGHTEOUSNESS HE craved, Hemp took the other direction. The theft began soon after Richard reported that Madge had left for Tennessee. His driver's uniform and the stately rockaway lent him an official look, storeowners never suspecting him of wrongdoing. He stashed candies in his coat pocket, and while waiting for the doctor he unwrapped them and placed two on his tongue at a time. When he was done, he washed the sweetness down with a swallow of corn whiskey. He tried to convince himself that the less he thought of Madge, the easier it would be to erase the sin. He was wrong. He could not escape it. So he moved blindly through the days, convinced of his own depravity.

At the end of the month, he went to see the reverend, taking care not to stand too close.

"I hear you been sick," the reverend said after they had settled into two large chairs in the front room of his house. His wife had offered them freshly made applejack and the room smelled cloyingly sweet.

"Yas, sir. I just gone back to work."

"Mighty bad fever, I hear."

"Annie ain't dead," he said suddenly.

The reverend leaned back into his chair. "Ain't God something?"

"But I don't know where she at. Make me crazy."

The reverend sipped.

"White man sin all over me. I ain't got nothing."

"You got something, son. You got a choice now that you free. Time to make your own path."

"I got a wife out there might be waiting on me. Ain't no choice in that."

The reverend stoked the fire from his chair, leaned the poker back against the wall. "These is better times, but they still hard times."

Hemp made excuses to leave. The reverend handed him his coat, and as Hemp left, he pocketed a quill. When he was outside, he faced home, then turned around and walked in the opposite direction.

HE HAD BEEN SEARCHING for a miracle that would set him back on the right path, and it came from the place he least expected. Somehow, the doctor, whose own sad countenance was in need of a lift, got it in his mind that he would be the one to find Annie. At first Hemp thought: impossible. The doctor said the colored maid had told him about Annie, and Hemp knew he meant Madge.

Hemp tried to rein in his hope. This white friend of the doctor said there were millions of freed slaves. What did the word *millions* mean? There had been a lot of coloreds at the camp in Kentucky, and he wondered how many more would make a million. Crowds of people walked the streets of Chicago. Was that a million? He wanted to ask, but he was afraid he'd upset the man's plan. So he began to figure in his head: if there were a million stalks of hemp spread across a field, it would stretch as far as he could see; a million trees would cover the entire state of Kentucky; a million cattle would make a man richer than God. New York. Virginia. Mississippi. Canada and far-off lands across the ocean. There might be a million places on earth where she could be. The number staggered.

The doctor directed Hemp to the office of a man he said could help. The morning sun cast angled shadows on the fronts of build-ings. Hemp drove east on Michigan Avenue, past the Dearborn House, across Lake Street, turning south on Randolph. Michael counted the buildings, trying to remember the exact location of Peter's office. W. H. Taylor Boots & Shoes. *Chicago Times*. B. Mann Apothecaries. D. A. Foote Silver Plater. F. Hudson, Jr. Wigs. The Courthouse. A barber's shop, billiard saloon, tailor. There it was: above the hat store.

"Stop!"

Hemp slowed the carriage in front of a building at the corner of Franklin and Randolph.

The doctor stepped out and waved. "Come inside with me."

"What's that, sir?"

"I said, come with me."

Hemp nodded and put on his hat. "Yas, sir."

They entered an office. Two desks faced each other, their surfaces piled with papers. In the corner a hairless cat scowled at them from inside a cage.

"What is it?" asked a man sitting at one of the desks. He wore an overcoat, despite the day's warmth. He did not look up.

"Now is that any way to greet a man who saved your life?"

"Servus!"

"Hey, *wie geht's?*"

They shook hands.

"May I take a seat?"

"Please."

Hemp stood beside the door.

"I have a discreet matter," Michael began. During the war, Peter had gotten messages to soldiers for a price. If you could not wait for the post, and your intended recipient was on a remote battlefield, Peter could get a message through in mere days. If anyone could find Hemp's wife, Peter could. He had connections all over the country.

"Anything you say will be held in strictest confidence."

"You see that man over there? My driver?"

"You want me to ask him to leave?"

"He was a slave, and he's looking for his wife."

"And I'm looking for one of my missing cats. Now please tell me about your urgent matter. I will do all I can to help."

"I'd like to help him find her."

His eyes traveled over to the big man and then back to Michael. "Aren't there people who do this sort of thing? Churches or relief societies?"

"There may be, Peter, but you know I don't know anything about this. I don't even know how to begin. Perhaps you could reach out to them."

"Do you know how many slaves were separated from their families? It just isn't possible to reunite them. There must be millions."

"I just need to help one. Hemp?"

Hemp tried to anchor himself so he would not faint. Behind him, the front windows were so soiled, he could barely see the street below. The doctor's friend peered at him from behind a hill of papers on his desk. The floor was littered with stacks of books. In a dark corner, the strange cat, wide-eyed and quiet, stared out from its cage. It made a sound, not quite catlike, and the wrinkled folds of its skin stretched as it raised its head.

"Can you come over here and tell this gentleman about your wife?"

Now that Hemp was being called to give what he considered nothing less than a religious testimony, he grew nervous. Suppose they found a Harrison relative who conjured up some unpaid debt owed the family. Hemp might be returned to Kentucky. And what if they discovered Annie was dead after all, and the widow just couldn't find her on the other side. The doctor whispered to him, reassuring him that it would work out. Hemp sank into the offered seat, looked down at his hands. White lines webbed the skin of his palms.

"What's that, sir? My wife?"

"Yes, the one you lost in Kentucky. This man is going to help you find her."

"Help me find her, sir?"

"That's right. He's going to track her down."

"Track her?"

"That's right." Michael smelled liquor on the driver's breath. *A little early for that*, he thought.

"My wife, sir?"

"But first we have to give a description. So he knows what to look for."

Michael nodded at Peter.

"I don't know . . ."

"I saved your life, Peter. Your life." Michael waved his cane in the air, and Peter ducked as if preparing for a blow.

Peter cleared space on the desk, took out a sheet of paper and a quill. He gave Michael a long look before beginning. "Tell me your name."

Hemp did not know whether to give the man the made-up name or the name she would recognize him by. It angered him that the doctor had given him so little time to prepare. Something like this took planning, and he did not want this opportunity to pass him by because he could not think quickly enough. But if they were going to find Annie, he would have to cooperate.

"Truth is, what they called me was Horse."

"That's what who called you?"

Michael considered himself an educated man. Yet it had not oc-curred to him that the colored men he saw walking the streets had stories of their own. They were not unlike Germans who had survived revolutions. This man had been called Horse. And he had renamed himself Hemp because he came from a Kentucky hemp farm. He must have thought it would help her find him. The strategy would never work, but Michael respected the attempt.

Hemp did not want the doctor to see the shame of his past life. He did not want him to look at his hands and see hooves, at his ankles and see hocks. But the name brought it all back.

He spoke softly. "Everybody, sir."

"Horse?"

"Yas, sir."

Even though he was looking at the floor, he saw the two men ex-change a look and he could only guess what they were thinking.

"All right, then. What was your master's name?"

"What was the name of the town where you lived?"

"When was your wife sold?"

"When did you leave the camp?"

"What was your wife's name?"

Hemp readied himself to cross a thicker line. To utter her name in the presence of these men was to soil it.

"Tell you what. Why don't I just stay quiet while you tell me your story."

Hemp looked over at Michael. Even with all the questions, Hemp still did not understand which story the man wanted. Did he want to know how he'd first come to live on the Harrison farm as a boy? The day he gave the preacher the chair? The day the women were sold? Searching for her in the camp? Walking until his feet bled? He looked at the doctor for direction. So this was the price of finding her: letting a white man trample on his memories. He wished he could speak with Annie in his mind, the way the widow spoke with spirits. He wanted to tell her not to worry, that he would protect her with all his might. He would do it this time, though he had failed to save her before.

"Go on," Michael said. "Tell him everything."

Michael saw the distrust in the colored man's eyes. They were asking him to exhume, and Michael understood. He had done the same in his sessions with the widow. Michael reached out and touched the driver on the shoulder.

"Go on," he urged.

"We worked Master's land together, but then they sell her and the girl off. I don't know where she gone to. Then we hear about the camp and I went to go and join the army. I heard the cabins at the Harrison farm done been emptied. So I come here."

"You mentioned a girl. You have a daughter?"

He nodded. "She did. Yas, sir."

"What was her name?"

"Herod. But I do believe she dead."

"How do you know?"

"I just do."

"All right, then," Peter continued. "Did she have any other family?"

"No, sir."

"Any identifying marks or scars?"

"A dog took half her ear once."

"What kind of work is she likely to look for?"

"All we ever work was a hemp farm. That's the work she know."

Michael wondered why helping a former slave had not entered his mind before. Just the act of being there, occupied by this new task, gave him purpose. He had not thought about his brother all day.

"I believe we have everything we need," Peter said.

Hemp stood and hurried out.

"Where do you intend to start?"

"Well." Peter tapped the paper. "I hope you understand the chances of finding this woman are low."

"I understand."

"I'll place an advertisement in some newspapers. It's likely she works for some white family. I'll send someone to that farm in Kentucky to see if she returned. Many of them went back after the war. Harrison is dead, but some other member of the family may have inherited the land and resumed work. This will all be very expensive, you see."

"There is nothing to worry about in that regard." Michael extended a hand. "I do appreciate this, Peter."

Hemp stood outside waiting. The horse stamped its feet, and Hemp fed the beast from his hand. He knocked a clod of mud from his pants.

As they rode off, Michael opened the window. Warm air swept into the carriage. He tried not to look at the driver differently, tried not to picture him carrying stalks of hemp across a field. He looked through the front window and saw the muscles in Hemp's neck flex, the broad back. He closed his eyes. This had begun as a way to make up for his own failings, but now he was really beginning to care about this man.

Dear God, let this work, he prayed.

25

H EMP DID NOT KNOW WHAT TO CALL WHAT happened to him in the middle of the night. Not dreams or visions. He actually traveled in time. Looking down at himself, he considered the wide peak of hip before taking flight and moving over state lines. A snaking river, bean-shaped lake, branches of railroad. The prairie, trees, hills of bluegrass, a red house sitting on the bank of a creek. An old man rocking in a chair on a covered porch.

Stalks that grew tall as trees, men waiting for the cool of fall when they would take up the hooks, hacking as near to the ground as possible, careful not to curl the tools back into their legs. A swift chopping sound. The crack of hemp stems in his fingers, the brush of fiber, the weight of the hackle, dust clogging his eyes and nose, sun scorching his neck. The stalks left in the field to rot long enough for the casing to soften, until the ritual gathering of them into stacks for drying time.

Come daytime, Hemp's two selves merged again into a new world where the shapes of things eluded him. He could not read, was not a learned man, and it unsettled him that the world did not work as predictably as the planting seasons. He knew how long a hemp crop took to mature, how to measure the lift and droop of a leaf. But he was rattled by the tolling courthouse bell, the rails, the telegraph, unnecessary things interrupting God's order, and though he no longer feared being pressed back into slavery or listened out for the fearsome howl of dogs, he still looked over his shoulder, saw things that were not there. He lived in a house not much better than a slave cabin, and thought with dread that, perhaps after all, free and slave were not so different.

Gracefully, he carried the body that reminded a white man of an animal while he listened to men speaking in languages he had not known existed. Omnibuses rattled. A horse urinated, steam from the hot liquid rising into the air. The man nudged the horse with a dusty boot. A paperboy yelled on a corner, waving a crumpled paper. Another child sold coal out of a dirty sack. No one saw Hemp, despite his size. In Kentucky, he would have been stopped by now, a white man calling out to ask his business. In the cupola above, a lookout yelled that a ship was approaching. The street shook, the city bracing for new arrivals. Hemp descended a leaning board, took twenty-five steps, turned left, then right.

As he walked through the city he thought for the umpteenth time of their last meeting, how he had insulted her. When Madge walked inside, wiping the wet snow from her forehead with the back of her arm, Hemp had been tempted to do it for her, still not understanding why this woman meant so much to him. She had not erased the ugly as Annie had done, but she did cause him to skip thoughts. The men he lived with were all out working, so he had cooked for Madge in the small house. He lit the fire and unhooked the frying pan from the wall. While the oil heated, he dredged the gizzards in flour. He took up two ears of corn from a basket in the corner and ripped off the husks. He picked off a worm, dug out the rotten kernels with his fingernails. The bitter smell of frying gizzards filled the house, and he opened a window. Children clucked in the alley, and a rock crashed into the window. Their chatter turned to wailing, and he shut the window to keep out the noise.

When the gizzards were browned, he scooped them out with a spoon and put them on two plates, grease puddling underneath.

"Let me wash up," she said.

He took the bowl outside and refilled it. She rubbed her hands together.

"The corn ain't fresh," he said.

"I've ate worse."

She dried her hands.

"Sit down," he said gently, placing two plates on the table.

"That hotel should've made you waiter 'stead of letting you go."

He poured water out of a pitcher, feeling simple, more at ease than he had in weeks. He knew she was worried about the turn their friendship had taken, and he was hoping to make it up to her by cooking this dinner. But he could not deny his selfish reasons, either. He wanted to taste that feeling Madge gave him—not asking more than he could give, freeing him from the hard love that bound him to his wife. Annie had scraped the ash from his elbows and knees with a rough stone and then rubbed oil on all the raw places. Madge, with her dark eyes and flash of smile, gave something different—a spiritual thing. Their connection began because she lent him an ear, but it was sustained by an easy give-and-take. He had lain with her twice now because it was naturally what a man did, though it had been a sin, as big a sin as he had ever committed.

Madge crunched into her ear of corn, speaking as she chewed. "I think that doctor like you."

"Oh yeah?"

"Driving is good work, Hemp."

He kept his mouth full so he would not have to think of what to say.

"And your cooking ain't bad, either."

"You need something else?" he asked, though little remained.

She shook her head, and as she picked corn from her teeth he resolved to make her a pick. He thought of all he'd taken from women: Annie and the ones he'd bedded before her. Now that he was free and able-bodied, he intended to pay his debts.

She said to him, "I got something to tell you. I'm going back to Tennessee."

"Tennessee?"

"To be with my womenfolks."

A grain of corn threatened to lodge in his throat.

"This thing we got between us ain't right, Hemp, and you know it. You got to look for your wife, and I'm in the way."

"You roped me."

"Now don't talk like that."

"You tricked me. You knew I thought you was Annie."

"You didn't have no fever that night."

"I was sick, and you was supposed to be healing me."

"You lied to me about Annie's girl."

"What?"

"Hemp, what happened between you and that girl?"

"I told you."

"The widow say you and her did something—"

"Goddamn that woman!" He knocked a chair over. "Nothing, I swear it. I kissed her. That's all. I ain't proud of it, but it happened. It ain't my problem that white woman don't believe me."

Her eyes reddened and she looked down. "I'm sorry, Hemp."

His voice was hoarse. "You ask me about the driving work like you ain't come in that door aiming to destroy me tonight."

Their chests rose and fell together.

"You got a man down in Tennessee, don't you?"

"A what?"

She was crying, and he looked up at the ceiling because he could not stand it. Above him, a string of web hung limply as if something had flown by and broken it.

EVEN AS HE WAITED FOR NEWS about Annie, Madge stayed on his mind. One thing was for certain. If he found Annie, he would have to leave that root woman alone for good. As he followed the doctor into the man's office, he could not stop shaking. He believed Annie was alive, but he was beginning to think white men were not miracle workers, that maybe even Jesus was not white. It had been a month since they began their search, and Hemp's belief had waned. He desperately needed to know where the righteous path lay—to the left or to the right. If Annie came to Chicago to join him, he would have to tell her about Madge. He would have to be honest. He had not anticipated how his rising feelings for the girl would affect him, how she confused and muddled his head.

"Do you have news?" the doctor asked as soon as they walked in the door of the man's office.

Peter stood when Michael approached the desk. The cat was no longer caged. It crouched on the edge of the desk, its head turned toward Michael, blue eyes wide with suspicion. It made a sound like a dog's growl in the back of its throat, as if ready to spring.

"Michael, my friend, please have a seat."

Michael looked uneasily at the cat, refusing the offer. "Just tell me. Any news at all?"

"Can he excuse us?"

"I'll be outside, Dr. High-yul." Hemp closed the door softly behind him.

"How are you feeling, Michael? When is the last time you saw a doctor of your own?"

"Peter, I can emphatically tell you there is nothing wrong with me. Now get on with it."

Peter twirled the inkstand on his desk.

"Did you find the woman?"

"I truly don't understand why you feel it necessary to engage in this behavior. This scheme of yours is comical."

"Is she dead?"

"Michael," he said, his tone gentler, "I will repay your money."

"Of course you won't repay my money. You've already extended yourself. Now tell me what you found." Michael's breath was ragged. The cat jumped off the desk and disappeared.

"You have a reputation, and so do I. Surely you won't be marked as one of those radicals."

Peter lowered his voice.

"What on God's earth are you talking about?"

"I hear you are . . . that you have been consorting with . . ."

"Consorting?"

"That woman on Ontario Street. The woman who speaks to the dead."

"Oh, Peter."

"You will lose everything, Michael. You might even have to leave the city if you continue along this path. It's ruinous. Think of your career."

"Good God, man, what business is it of yours?"

Peter was silent, and Michael realized he had done nothing to find her. He slowly buttoned his coat, passed icy respects on to Peter's wife, and left the office.

Hemp searched his face expectantly as he came out into the street.

"Hemp . . ."

He did not know what to say. He realized, sadly, that the relief of the man's burdens lay somewhere out of reach. The poor man would have to settle for this: a silent shaking of the head, a shame-filled and reddened face. Briefly, Michael wondered what his younger brother would have said at that moment.

"We shall try again. Don't give up hope."

The driver turned his back. A cool wind pulsed through the sun's warmth.

"Take the carriage back and stable the horse. I'll walk," Michael said, waving him off.

Hemp turned the horse around and headed toward the bridge leading to the western district of the city. Michael watched him as he drove off. He wiped his brow as he started to walk.

A man called out, selling feather dusters.

Not all the feather dusters in the world can rid us of our dirty past, Michael wanted to say to him.

When Hemp got to the church, the reverend was on the roof. The wind tore at Hemp's jacket as he looked up.

"Give an old man a hand!"

Hemp climbed the ladder, feeling for the ridges on each side. He pulled his body over the edge of the roof. The reverend helped pull him up.

"See that board? The wood ain't no good."

Hemp's hat flew off and when he lunged for it, he almost slipped. The reverend grabbed him by the coat. "You trying to kill the both of us?"

Hemp flapped his arms. He picked up a hammer and pried loose the faulty board.

"You don't need that finger?" the reverend said.

Below them, a fight broke out in the street. They could not see it, but the sounds of a jeering crowd rose.

The reverend moved down the side of the roof and descended the ladder. "Cut it out now. In God's name, cut it out!"

A nail pricked Hemp's finger. He licked the blood. A pigeon perched nearby, watching him. He thought it might want a drop of his blood, too. When its stare did not waver even as a gust picked up, he thought it might be a messenger, Herod returned.

When Hemp finished repairing the board, he left the pigeon on the roof and stored the ladder under the building. Inside the sanctuary, he saw how much the church was thriving under the deacons' care. Fresh paint. Sanded pews. A piano with all its working keys. Even the hole in the roof was now fully patched. But the sight of the freshened sanctuary failed to cheer him.

"Son, you bleeding? I see you really was trying to lose a finger." The reverend swept dead bugs from the windowsill into his palm.

"Here." The reverend passed him a narrow strip of shirt cloth.

Hemp moistened his cracked lips with a swipe of his tongue.

"My wife better with a hammer than you."

Hemp erupted into laughter, tucking the wrapped finger into his chest as he bent over. The emotion folded him in two, and the more he laughed, the more he could not stop. "Oh-hoh!" He broke into another fit. Laughter like cries.

"Son?"

"Oh-hoh!"

Within his laughing fit, he somehow croaked out, "The doctor couldn't find her."

The reverend propped the broom against the wall. Rubbed his hands together. Nodded slowly.

"Go home, son. Go home."

"What now?"

"Just go home and rest. Go on now."

Hemp did as he was told. In front of the rented house, he gazed at the square of swept dirt, the cracked pot of fern, the faded curtains at the window, an empty washtub in the yard. She had not roped him. She had merely picked up what Annie left behind.

26

*H*E PASSED THROUGH A NARROW ALLEY OF shanties, walking toward the noise. Men bellowing. Boots stomping. A rail hanging halfway off the porch of a house. Inside, one man furiously plucked a banjo while another stood over him strumming a fiddle. Hemp tried to sit down, but men danced into his legs. The crowd cleared the floor and formed a circle. Someone drummed on what sounded like a wooden block, and a man emerged and stood in the middle of the circle, tapping his stick on the floor. He bent forward and then backward and then forward again, circling his torso before he lifted a leg high into the air. The dance was dizzying. Hemp swigged whiskey from a dirty cup. In the corner, two men spooned grub into bowls. The room reeked with the vinegary smell of boiling pigs' feet.

It was hard to admit he could stand, a free man chewing a dried piece of beef in a crowded room full of at least a dozen more free men, and still be sad. The smell of urine flushed the air. He loosened his shirt at the neck, felt for his money to make sure it was still there. Lustful men, dead-eyed women, a floor sticky with drink. He stumbled out into the cold. Air clamored into the gap of collar at his neck. He had no sense of direction, ambled aimlessly. He would never be a respectable, even without the yoke of slavery. The ties of unrighteousness bound him. He licked his lips. Spat on the ground. Walking into the wind, shoulders hunched, hands in pockets, he dragged his feet over the dirty road. The drink slowed his thoughts, numbed him, but he could not forget. All he had ever wanted was a house of his own, a chance to love and protect and provide. He had harbored a vain hope that despite slavery's dominion over him, he might one day rule his own household. The reverend preached on it once—used words like *contract* and *legitimate*—and Hemp had struggled to comprehend. But when he boiled it down, it amounted to this: he was married once and that wife was taken from him, his happiness dissolved in one heartless stroke. He did not understand all of these fancy words, but he knew well enough the effects of them, their power over a man's life, this eating away at his heart. If the path had been open to him, he reckoned he might have become one of those men who make the laws. Instead, he was left to suffer at the behest of others.

What, then, was manhood for the colored? And what was freedom if even God did not possess the authority to answer a man's prayer?

A boy glanced at him, hurrying past. Hemp knocked over a cart, the wheel cracking against the sidewalk. The door to an abandoned store swung open and he kicked it, the wood splintering.

"Hey, what you doing over there?" a voice called from across the street.

He threw his head back, barely able to suppress all that threatened to erupt.

A cluster of men were pushing their way through a doorway, and Hemp hemmed his body behind them, driving them through the opening with a grunt. On the other side, a long alley ended where a man collected payment. He glared at Hemp, cast a warning eye at two nearby louts. Hemp dropped a coin on the table and proceeded inside. The room was large, framed by timber walls beneath a beamed ceiling. Two gas lamps hung from ropes suspended over a square pen, eight feet in diameter and five feet deep. The floor of the pen was brushed clear, the dirt packed down. Men handed their bets through a windowed opening, then filed into three rows of staggered benches on all four sides of the pen. The more well-clad gamblers jostled for the closest seats. Hemp climbed into the highest row, his back to the wall. A cock-eyed man, hat askew, clambered up beside him and clapped Hemp's shoulder. Men filed into the room until there was barely air to breathe. Smoke curled upward, fading into the ceiling. Hemp undid another button of his shirt and coughed, a taste of kerosene on his tongue.

Movement at the doorway caught the crowd's attention, and Hemp turned with them. A line of men entered carrying cages. One by one, they lowered the cages over the walls of the pen, and a wave of darkness spread across the floor, the chirps of vermin winding into screams. From far-off, Hemp heard the bark of a dog, a hollow aarfing sound. A man emerged, the dog tucked beneath his arm. He placed it on a high table. The dog was white with brown markings on its face and chest. It wiggled its snout in the air, sniffing. The cur's owner calmly rubbed the dog's head. The timekeeper stepped up into a box and raised a hand. When he lowered the arm, the man dropped the feist inside the box. It landed on its feet, crouching.

The canine took seconds to decide upon its first victim. It pounced, baring its teeth into the neck of the nearest rat, leaped for another, dispensing of each one in a single vicious bite. The rats sensed the feist before they saw it, but it was already too late. One of them fled, pushing into the horde of scrambling rodents. The feist caught it, long tail dangling from one end of its mouth, a tiny triangle of head from the other.

The dog flung its head to the side in one motion. The rat dropped. The cries of the men rose, their teeth bared, balled fists pumping. The dog caught another rat and then another, snapping them as they ran by. In the corner of the pit, the rodents huddled. One of them separated itself from the pack, and the feist went for it, barely missing its neck. The rat turned, planted its teeth into the dog's cheek. The dog yelped, dropping the rat and pinning it beneath his paws before gnashing it. It chewed, eating a piece of the mangled rodent. Loose flesh hung from the dog's face. Hemp leaned over and vomited. No one noticed, the odor of his sickness mixing easily into the foul scent of blood and animal excrement.

Dozens of rats lay still in the pen, and though their colors varied from brown to black, they were indistinguishable in their sameness. Blood stained the floor. The feist leaped leftward, dashed rightward. One rat charged, running straight at the dog. The dog dispensed of it with one quick bite. The other rats ran in circles, unsure what to do. There were still dozens of them alive, and it occurred to Hemp that had they risen up en masse against the feist they might have killed it. The dog was not much larger than the rats, but what it lacked in size it made up in cunning intent. The rats had not figured out they were the hunted until the rug of dead began to spread before them. The animals hushed. The gamblers screamed at the feist, leaned forward lustily over the walls of the pen, urging it on, their envenomed faces a mix of glee and hate. Even from his place in the back, Hemp could see the tiny doomed eyes of the rodents, flitting this way and that.

The dog paused, lifted one paw and then the other, pacing, as if figuring out its path through the muck. The white of its coat had darkened; its muscled haunches shook. It peered wearily over at its owner. Hemp read an obscenity on the man's lips. The feist drew up, turned, pushing on for a final spree, and in one gracile leap, a primordial howl escaping its lips, it pounced again. When there was no more movement, the timekeeper yelled *Time!* and the dog was lifted out of the pen, its owner hugging it.

Men waved their arms fiendishly; others applauded, their coarsened hands making sounds like drumbeats. Hemp moved to escape, pushing his way through the crowd until he was outside. Feeling that he had barely crossed some jagged border, a bluntish pain thundered in his head. His feet lifted, and he ran toward home, tilting his face up to the black, starless sky as he scurried along this bottom, this road of the unblessed. He wiped his forehead with the back of a hand. It would take many washes to cleanse himself of the wretchedness he'd just witnessed.

When he arrived at the little rented house, an unknown man, some stray given shelter, slumbered in his bed, so Hemp reclined in the chair, resting his eyes, praying for the mercy of morning. Yet the vision of that carnal scene haunted him throughout the night, its clamor of baleful cheers, and he barely slept.

IN ONE SMALL SECTION of the timber yards that stretched along the south branch of the river, the third deacon from Hemp's church was in charge of the castoffs. Rotted, infested with worms, or otherwise ruined for use, the deacon salvaged what he could and threw the rest into a pile for burning. Hemp had visited the yard once before when he asked the deacon about a job. He tried to remember his way to the man's section, walking through row after row of identical straw-colored stacks of white pine twice as tall as a man. Lumber wagons rolled by, the fine dust of wood clouding the air. A man swung open the doors to a warehouse, revealing furniture makers at work. Hemp peered inside, not finding a single colored face among them. In a smaller building beside the furniture factory, a half-dozen men hoisted up the lid of a newly built piano. Hemp found his friend not far from those buildings, perched on a stack of unplaned logs, a pair of leather guards over his hands.

"That you, Deacon Harrison?"

"It's me."

"We ain't got no work." The man glanced around.

"I come to see if you got something you can let me take."

"I know you work with wood and have need of it, but I can't give you nothing."

"Just a scrap. Rotted or whatnot. I don't care. It's just for carving. I don't need much."

The deacon hesitated, then pointed. "That there is the pile. Dig out what you need, but be quick about it and get on your way. I got six mouths at home."

"I'm sure grateful. See you on Sunday."

The deacon touched his broad-brimmed hat and went back to work.

Hemp propped a flat piece of hewed wood, the driest he could find, onto his shoulder and walked home. He set the square of wood down in the yard and brought out his leather pack of tools. He took the stone from his pocket and oiled its belly. He picked up a chisel and ran its back against the stone, sliding it back and forth until the edge was flat and smooth. He sharpened the curved edges of his gouges and the long point of a parting tool before stropping them on a length of horsehide. The edges of the tools sliced sharply against his finger, so he lined them all up within arm's reach, wedging the piece of wood between his knees, and went to work. He used a bow saw to carve out four points, measuring out the horizontal arms so they would match. The surface of the wood was not smooth enough yet. Clouds covered the moon, and he lost his light. That was enough for the night. But the next evening, and the next and the next, after driving the doctor all day, Hemp carved the surface of the wood, tapping softly on the tip of a chisel with his mallet. The extra gouges he had bartered into his possession since coming to Chicago granted him more control, and he used a veiner to smooth the delicate edges of flowers. Although Annie had not recognized the shapes of petals the way Madge did, she had always grown ecstatic at the sight of color in an unexpected place. He carved out a narrow point at the bottom and placed the finished cross beneath his bed.

On a late August morning, Hemp rose well before sunrise and began to walk. When he first started driving for the doctor, the man had patiently taught him the layout of the city's center: Water and Lake and Randolph and Washington and Madison and Monroe. In the other direction, Franklin and Wells and La Salle and Clark and Dearborn and State and Wabash. Softly, Hemp had repeated the names to himself as he followed the man's directions. Beyond that, Hemp had learned to chart the river's arm and legs, the lake's gentle curve, the railway's stretch of tracks. That morning, he chanted softly to himself as he walked, an unlit lamp swinging from his right hand, the cross in his left, his hat pulled low. He followed the lake south along its western bank, marking the streets and taking note of anything irregular so that he would be able to find his way back. He walked for three hours, keeping to the side of the road. He had only been to the cemetery once, when a church member died, and he had traveled on the family's wagon. He could not name the street, but he was certain he would recognize the stretch of grassy park. When he found it, he lit the candle inside his lantern, making his way into a remote corner. He put one foot in front of the other carefully, stepping through newly turned dirt. After his eyes adjusted, he found a clear, hard spot beneath a tree, and he was about to thrust the cross into the ground when he had a vision of it being removed from that place. He moved again, settling upon the flat side of a sloping hill. He pushed the cross into the ground, leaning on the back of his hand with the weight of his body. He squatted beside it and placed the lantern on the ground. He could see the petals of the flowers, no particular species, just a spray of wildflowers, not unlike those that glittered on the Illinois prairie. Annie would have loved it. She would have blown the dust off and patted his hand in appreciation. *And Adam said, This is now bone of my bones, and flesh of my flesh.* Hemp rose, one foot sinking into the ground. The clouds passed and a slice of moon peeked out at him as he walked away.

After leaving the cemetery, he went straight to the widow's house, passing the boats on the canal, crossing the bridge into the northern district. He walked straight to the stable where he found Richard working on a lame horse. The deacon looked up and Hemp did not waste words.

"I got to find her."

And somehow, the wiry man, whose hair was growing whiter by the day, knew Hemp was talking about Madge, not Annie.

"Ain't God something? She due back any day."

"Due back?"

All this time, the path of righteousness had lain right in front of him. Past houses, down streets, past the firehouse, the bordellos, Gambler's Row, across a patch of dirt, over a washtub, into a one-room house with three sunken beds, rusted pots, a tub with a slow leak, and an alley that never quieted, God had found him. Hemp walked the streets, his vision clearer than it had been in months. Something flew toward him and he batted it down. A bird. He reached for it to see if it was hurt, but it flew away, its wings fluttering ecstatically. He felt for Annie's comb in his pocket.

Mr. Heil had tried to find Annie, had failed, and Hemp had resigned himself to the fact that if white men couldn't work a miracle, no one could. But Madge was headed back, and he had a feeling this was it—a miracle of his own making. It was about time, too, because he was finally ready to take off his walking shoes and climb into his chariot.

27

THE FALL HAPPENED BEFORE SHE COULD REACH HIM. She rushed down after him, lifted his head, took a moment to figure out it was not the leg or the knee, but the foot. She held him in her arms and yelled for help. Richard called out to her. She struggled to lift him, pleading for caution, but her coachman mumbled something like "Step back. I got him, Mrs. Walker," as he carried the old man inside.

Sadie unlaced the boot, pulled off the shoe and sock. A spear of bloody bone protruded through the skin. She propped the foot onto a pillow while the coachman hurried off to fetch Dr. Heil.

"Wake up, wake up," she said, shaking him. His head fell back into the crook of her arm. She placed a pillow beneath him and touched his cheek. Too warm.

She wheeled. An empty basin sat on the sideboard, and she carried it to the kitchen to fill it with water from the jug. Back in the drawing room, she dabbed water onto his face. He did not awaken. She moved to the end of the sofa and rolled the pants to the knee, moving him as little as possible. She dipped a piece of linen into the water and squeezed it over the wound. The blood pinked as it rolled down the heel of his foot. A flap of flesh hung perilously.

She pulled a chair up beside him and sat. Belts of gray light stretched across the carpet. On the table, his glasses rested atop a stack of books. In the corner, more books perched on the chair. He had been borrowing generously from the library, and although she was curious to know what he read, she did not have the presence of mind to read the spines. She rose and looked out the window for the carriage, but all was silent. She sat back down. His jaw moved.

"Open the window. It's warm in here."

His voice startled her. "Of course, Father."

She poured water into a glass from the ceramic pitcher and placed it to his lips. He lifted his head and drank.

He began to speak softly, his voice breaking. "I took the money from Samuel. I'm sorry."

She had always known, but now she did not know how to respond to his confession.

"Did you ask for it?" she whispered.

"No, no. He offered, but I took it. We would have been ruined."

She returned the glass to the table and opened a second window. The fog was beginning to rise. She stuck her head out. The air cooled her face. His confession did little to unseat her anger. As her father he had always held the rod of morality, and she would not pry it from him, not now. She pressed a hand to her mouth. She would remain the silenced daughter. If they were to move forward, they would have to do it with the rift intact. Although she could not fathom how one carried on a relationship in which both people stubbornly remained at an impasse, she could not stomach the torment of battle any longer.

"HE NEEDS TO GO to a hospital."

"Can you set it?"

"He will need surgery, and I couldn't possibly—"

Michael finished wrapping the foot, pulling the strip of cloth around the bottom of the heel.

The old man opened his eyes. His stare was sharp.

"Is he actually a real doctor?"

"Dr. Heil trained at Rush Medical College."

"He wants to saw off my foot."

"If you get proper care, you will not lose your foot, sir," said Michael.

Michael moved to touch the man's head, feeling through the hair. "Does this hurt?"

"Tender, yes."

"How about here?"

"Yes." He winced.

Michael coughed, and Sadie followed him into the hall.

"You realize I could have called anyone. I called you because I believe in you, Michael. Can you heal him?" Sadie asked.

"He needs a surgeon."

"You are a surgeon."

"You know I haven't had patients in a long time. Do you want him to live?"

"Of course, I want him to live."

"Well, there is something else."

"Something else?"

"Yes. It isn't just the foot."

"What is it?"

"Did your father hit his head when he fell?"

"I don't know. I couldn't see."

"His forehead looks a little swollen. He says it is tender. I can't be sure. I urge you to take him to the hospital. They will take good care of him there."

"Come with us. I'll feel better if you're there."

He hesitated. "Very well. Sadie? About your proposition. We have to talk about it."

"I was being foolish. You know that."

He was silent.

"Michael, I'm just not the marrying kind. It's what my father wants for me, but I don't want marriage. I don't want children. I don't want any of that."

"What do you want?"

"I want to travel. Yes, I want to travel."

He nodded. "I owe you an apology. I shouldn't have kissed you like that."

"That's in the past."

"Is anything really in the past?"

She handed him his hat.

After Michael left, Sadie went back into the drawing room. Her father's eyes were closed and he appeared to be resting. Her resolve strengthened. She would do whatever was necessary, say whatever he needed to hear in order to reconcile. She would be the one to end this.

SADIE SAT ON A WOODEN BENCH in the hospital ward waiting for Michael to deliver a report on her father. She had hastily pinned on a hat, and no one stopped to look long enough to recognize her beneath it. She was grateful for the quiet.

Allow me to introduce myself. My name is James Heil and I was a soldier in the Fourth Illinois Cavalry of the United States Army. I died during a victorious battle at Shiloh led by General Grant.

She shook her head, trying to rid her thoughts of him. She was tired of this spirit. His grief drained her, and she wished he would leave her alone. She did not know what it would take to shake him from her mind permanently, but she was prepared to do anything. She couldn't move forward with him in tow. She drifted into a light sleep.

Each one of us must bear the burden of our time. My time called upon me to shoulder a great duty.

Do not despair. Every family has their trials.

Mama, you must cast off that dust of misery.

Your old bones shall turn to dust, too, and your grief shall end as all things end.

On all sides, the cost of battle has been borne.

"Sadie?"

She woke with a start.

"He's not awake, but you can see him if you'd like."

Sadie followed Michael through the corridor. Her father lay on a cot, his foot bandaged, head wrapped. She touched his forehead.

"We gave him something to sleep."

She nodded.

"Sadie, the foot will heal. However, as I guessed, he also injured his head."

"Injured?"

"We just don't know how it will affect him, if at all. He has quite a large lump on his cranium. I believe he may have been unconscious immediately following the fall."

"Unconscious?" So the broken foot was just the visible injury. The real wound, the lasting one, remained unseen.

After the bindery failed, the creditor had given her father barely a year to repay his debts. She'd overhead the conversation between her parents. Four visits, two on the porch, two in the parlor, and the deal with Samuel was done. Her parents had taken the money, but did it matter anymore? Although it was clear they had committed the misdeed, she had to forgive and move on.

So why did she feel this overwhelming shame? And why should she feel shame when nothing was her fault?

She needed to tell her father that she did not need James. She was the medium. She'd found a stage through the spirit because his was a man's voice, his presence allowing her to speak. But the words and that small, high-pitched vocal were her own. She knew something of botany, Latin, even politics. She had read enough to understand the substance of her lectures. If there was an act, it was of her own making. She was not a woman possessed by a spirit. She was a woman.

"He will be fine. You'll see. Everything will be the same as before," Michael whispered.

Sadie shook her head. She knew this was not true. In fact, nothing could be further from the truth.

He took her by the arm. "Let's go."

Michael walked slowly, still thrilling from how the hospital's doctors had accepted him. No one inquired of his wartime service, and no one assumed he was a veteran. He led Sadie out into the street, the two of them walking aimlessly. They did not call Richard or the carriage, deciding to walk instead. The duo neared Bryan Hall where so many of the enlistment rallies had been held and Michael stopped to peer into the doorway. He could hear an organ and the harmony of a men's chorus singing inside. He strained to make out the words, recognizing the German sounds. On impulse, he entered, taking Sadie with him. She did not protest as they walked through the wide hall. He peeked inside a room. The men were seated closely together, and there were at least a hundred of them. Old men. Young. Men in suits and worker's clothes, all holding music sheets. Two women stood beside a table, ready to serve the meal.

The director stopped, gave a few notes in a mix of English and German.

"*Sie sind zu spät,*" the director said.

"I apologize," Michael said. An empty chair screeched across the floor. He started toward it, pushing Sadie gently toward the women standing beside the table. They spoke rapidly to her in German and tied an apron around her waist. Michael took a seat and leaned over to squint at a sheet of music. The organ started, and he was glad he could barely hear his own voice, certain he sang off-key. He could not remember the last time he sang. He sight-read the music, focused on pronouncing the correct sounds in his triangle of tongue and lips and teeth. The words formed in his mouth.

When Michael opened his mouth to sing, the room expanded: the smooth stone ceiling curved into a womb, the carved stone columns buttressed his spirits. His fellow choristers with their wrinkled necks, wide shoulders, sun-chapped cheeks, delighted. He did not know anyone there. The director wore a wig, and it tickled Michael, a fitting stroke to the scene. He had never been one to sing. Not even a whistle. This awakened love stunned him, like admiring for the first time the beauty of a pear tree he had walked past since boyhood. Out of the box in his throat came a miraculous sound. Whose sweet tenor was this? This warming of the throat, bellowing of the diaphragm, framing of lips, fluttering tongue, trilling uvula.

At first, he thought: religion has found me. And the more he thought about it, the more confident he was of the idea. But there was something more. Singing hymn after hymn was nothing less than a healing. The act of singing mended. A suturing closed of his heart, a snuffing of his self-doubt. He dawdled in a space where both history and future vanished and he did not know the next note coming from his lips.

The director ended rehearsal. This constant sewing of himself aroused his appetite, and Michael was one of the first to reach the tables of potato salad, bread, sausages, spaetzle. Sadie heaped the food on his plate, but neither of them spoke. He sat in a chair near the window eating his food, his back to her. Windowpanes squared off the light in blocks on the floor. He thought of Heinrich Heine, the poet his father used to read to him—*Life's made me tired enough to drop / I'd like to relax on a silken throne.* Did his faith exist among these men?

The rehearsal went on for some time until the director dismissed them. The men shook hands, and no one asked Michael any questions, even though he was not quite German in the way of some of them. He put Sadie in a hack and began to walk toward his flat, holding fast to his jubilance. In that small interval of time he'd sung with the chorus, he'd felt heroic, his soul elevated, some dead part of him awakened. And as he moved through the city's center, he was not thinking of his brother or Hemp or the widow or even the injured old man. He was busy translating the chorus into English:

That word above all earthly powers, no thanks to them, abideth;
The Spirit and the gifts are ours through Him Who with us sideth:
Let goods and kindred go, this mortal life also;
The body they may kill: God's truth abideth still,
His kingdom is forever.

He wandered into a small apothecary, discovered a jar of ointment on a shelf, and brought it to the front for purchase. The clerk nodded courteously. Scales, mortars, and spoons covered the counter. Michael handed over a note, thinking of all that money could achieve. Feed orphans. Shelter the ill. He remembered the work the Sanitary Commission had done during the war. He placed the jar in his trouser pocket.

He walked outside. Someone held a sign that read: IGNES FATUI. He turned a corner, and a man gave him a bill advertising a gala to support the Soldiers' Home. He read it over, remembering that the place had been home to convalescing soldiers. He rolled the bill up and stuck it in his pocket alongside the jar.

Michael continued walking, turning this corner and that, melodies churning in his head. He did not see Peter hurrying toward him until they had almost bumped into each other.

"Michael. Didn't you hear me calling your name? I found her. God help us all, but I did it Michael. I found that colored man's family."

Michael held fast to Peter's arm to make sure the man was real.

28

SADIE WAITED PATIENTLY WITH THE WOMEN, HER MOUTH
dry. She longed to drink some water from the pitcher, but
she dared not touch it. The organist was a shaggy-looking
man whose fingers danced over the keys. She watched him, thinking of
what it must take to coordinate such independence between the hands.
She felt the music cut through her loneliness, and though these were
not her people, she felt as though she were among family. Could family
be sketched out of such uncommon elements? Ever since her mother's
death, she had felt the loneliness of an orphan. After the music ended,
Sadie served the meal along with the other women. The men filed by,
taking their plates as they chatted in German and English.

When she arrived home, she was in a lightened mood. She climbed
the stairs to her father's bedroom, going through his clothes, refold-
ing and straightening. She smoothed the bedcovers and swiped a hand
over the dusty bedside table before returning to her library.

She opened her drawer and spied unopened mail. On top was a

letter addressed to her in a shaky handwriting. She opened it, her eyes scanning the single line of misshapen and incongruent letters. Someone must have written it for Madge. The woman planned to return to Chicago. The letter was dated weeks earlier and gave a date of her return. Madge had moved about the kitchen so easily as she mixed her strange potions. Finally, Sadie had come to understand the kinship between the two of them. Both trying to make a difference in their own way. Both searching for independence. In the beginning, Sadie had been drawn to the Tennessee woman because she had seen something special in those hands. So she'd given the woman a job. But even the noblest intentions could be tinged with selfishness.

Had it been that long since she'd wandered her own house with pleasure? It struck her that, yes, this was her house, not Samuel's. She thought she might remove his picture from the parlor. She opened the door to Madge's old closet. It had been thoroughly cleaned, but a trace of the woman's scent remained. Sadie had to admit: she missed her. She had only heard bits here and there of the strict aunts who ruled Madge's home in Tennessee. How different Madge's life down there must be. Sadie had never been south. What kind of place was it where men would rather die than release human beings to their own destiny?

When she closed the closet door, Olga met her with a worried frown. "Is something the matter, Mrs. Walker?"

"No, nothing."

"Sit," Olga commanded.

Olga placed a bowl of stew on the table. Sadie never ate in the kitchen, but the offer did not ruffle her. She calmly took her place. The beef stew was a little heavy for the time of day, but she was hungry. She picked up the spoon. She had not eaten at the choir rehearsal.

"This is all my fault, Mrs. Walker. Madge and I called your father here for a visit. We were worried about you."

"What do you mean you called him?"

"We sent for him. Madge charged the ticket to your account. I'm so, so sorry."

Sadie looked at the cook for a moment. Did it really matter? Was anyone to blame? Everything had happened the way it had to. She continued eating. When she was finished, she thanked the woman before moving on to the parlor. It had been several weeks since she'd accepted visitors in the home. The spirit had taken to appearing unexpectedly even when she had not summoned him, and she didn't want to encourage this kind of contact. Madge had been right about being wary of his power, but Sadie did not know how to stop him. The dead man's spirit was too strong.

She closed her eyes and concentrated. She had brought forth her mother without him. Surely she could do it with the other spirits. How did she do it without him interfering? She thought she might have heard directly from the spirits while dozing in the hospital, but she was unsure how to call them on her own. She heard James's voice and quickly opened her eyes. No, she would not allow it this time. She stood and walked around the room, then sat again. This time, a cacophony of voices rose, his among them. She willed herself to stay awake, to not lose consciousness as she often did.

She sat down again. The table began to shake. Her skin cooled. She felt she might be sick. She tasted the remains of the stew at the back of her throat. She placed a hand on each side of her face. *I will not allow him to own me. I will not allow any man to own me.* She pushed him away. He pushed back.

I'm sorry, he said. *I shouldn't have come back. You don't deserve to carry me around like a piece of luggage. I just needed to feel that we died for something.*

Later, Olga found Sadie sprawled across the floor, vomit on her dress. She gently picked her up and carried her upstairs to her bedroom.

A FEW DAYS LATER, Sadie's father came home. Richard helped him into the drawing room. Since he could not navigate the stairs yet, they set up a bed downstairs. Richard propped up the injured foot. Sadie put an extra pillow behind his back.

"Are you comfortable?" she asked.

"I am. Thank you."

"It appears they have taken good care of you."

"I've managed to avoid losing a foot. That's always a good thing."

He tapped his leg, as if to wake it up. The foot was tightly bandaged. Through Michael's heroic efforts, the old man had somehow avoided infection. She had spoken with Michael just the day before. He had told her he no longer needed to speak with his brother. That was good news since James had already released her.

"Yes, the doctor tells me there is no infection."

"That Heil turned out to be a very good doctor, though I will admit I do not like that he encourages your proclivities."

"I brought you some more books," she said, pointing to the stack on the table next to the bed.

"Sadie, I must tell you something. After I heal, I will return to York."

"Yes."

"This city is no place for an old man like me. I miss my garden."

"But what will you do there? Who will look after you?"

"I will look after myself. And there are the neighbors."

"Neighbors?" Sadie thought of the widow who lived across the street from him. The woman would gladly usurp her mother's place. Perhaps she had already been eyeing the neat little house. Sadie did not like the thought of another woman in her mother's bed. But she also knew this was the way things were now. Families shifting. Upheaval. Reconstruction.

"Will you write?" she asked in a pleading tone that almost sounded like *Will you still love me?*

"Of course I will," he answered, then added, "As necessary." He drank from a cup of water beside his stack of books.

He will not change, she thought. Still, she could not shake her need for his approval. This was, she thought, the curse of the dutiful child. "The spirits," she began, "I can speak to them without James Heil now."

"Sadie . . ."

"They need my help. So many people have questions. I can help them."

"I have thought about your viewpoint on this."

"You have?"

"Yes. And I have tried to understand it." He took another sip of water.

"And?"

"You are my child, my family, but we are different. Our truths differ. There is no harm in that, I suppose. It is just . . . what it is."

"This isn't so great a difference as to . . ."

"I'm afraid it's fundamental, Sadie. There are certain irreparable rifts. That is a fact."

"I don't agree."

"It is true," he said, his voice soft.

"In your way of thinking," she said, "there is only death, not life."

"Don't be so dark, Sadie."

"I'm not the one who is dark."

The wife dead. The daughter depraved. The son-in-law killed. In his mind, the war had all but destroyed his family. Yet there was always a space for love to reappear between the cracks, wasn't there? His view lacked faith. Hers kept it. Sadie had hated the war. What sense did it make to place lofty ideals in the hands of men with guns? Yet here was the real hurt—the rupture of father and daughter, a rupture he'd called irreparable. There was no reason to get up in the morning if what he said were true.

The light fell. She pulled the curtains in the parlor and turned up the lamp. She did not look over at him, but she heard him pick up a book. She sat at her desk, cornered a set of calling cards in her fingers. She considered her mediumship over the past year, straining to remember the details of her lectures. There was still so much to learn. How could she speak to married women if she barely knew life as one? How could she speak to unmarried women if she had been widowed so quickly? She had never given birth to a child, never even spent much time with children. It would be difficult to speak to women about the choices ahead of them. Still, she felt she must. Perhaps she was a woman preacher, after all. She glanced over at her father. How peaceful he looked sitting up in the narrow bed, his eyes trained on the page. How easy it must have been for him to live in an empty house, take up with another wife only if he chose. Such independent moves were nothing less than acts of rebellion for her. Each step a leap. Each turn a renunciation of another direction.

She felt the sharp pain of a child realizing the imperfection of a parent. Her father was wrong. She placed the cards back in the drawer. She slid the drawer closed, exhaling in one long breath. On the other side of the room, he quietly turned a page.

She reached for a map on the corner of her desk, unfolded it. She traced a finger from south to north, Tennessee to Illinois, Illinois to Indiana, through Ohio, until it rested on Manhattan City. She had never been there and longed to see the infamous city. She wondered what the crowds would be like, if they would sound a bell of doubt or quietly listen with belief as she stood before them, spreading whatever news passed through her lips.

29

ADGE WORE THE SAME TRAVELING dress she'd worn going home. When it grew too hot, she pulled the veil back, but as soon as the car cooled, she pulled it forward again. The widow had been right. The costume granted her privacy, but any perception of respectability for a colored woman was still tenuous. Each time the railway worker walked through the car, she clutched her travel satchel, her nerves frayed. This constant vigilance during the trip exhausted her.

She napped for a short time, but soon she gave up trying to rest. The wind rattled the train car. She remembered the long walk up from Tennessee, the first time she'd laid eyes on this vast grassland, the mystifying sight of it. She'd listened to the brush, thinking: how knowledgeable the sisters were among the Tennessee hardwoods, how there wasn't a plant or a tree or a bush or a fruit they could not put to work, how their pickaxes probed like Moses's magical rod and fished plants into coarse bags tied to their waists. This prairie, with its lack of trees and waves of willowy flowers, spoke of something beyond Tennessee, beyond her life, perhaps even beyond God. She had never even heard the word *prairie* before coming here. Even the word sounded like the name of a flower. She had a hard time pronouncing it. *Pair-ree*, she said. *The Pair-ree State.*

She touched her fingers to the window. She tried to recall her first enchantment with the North. Although she had never set foot in such a place, she'd known from the very beginning that she would, at least, try to rise and meet it. Everything was so much faster—the people talked and walked and drove their carriages more quickly than any she'd ever seen. Each day she bore witness to something new. The range of her choices was not as boundless as this land, but surely there was room to hope.

First, she had to find a place to brew and store. She could not continue to work out of the widow's kitchen. This healing balm was already working on her ambitions, propelling her to think of the future. *I can do it*, she told herself, rallying her courage. She caught a piece of scrambling paper beneath her foot, picked it up, peering at its indecipherable markings. The edge was ragged, torn from a booklet of some kind. In order to cross this valley, she would have to cross this barrier of deciphering letters, too. She let the paper go, watching as it flew through the car.

She wiped the window with the sleeve of her dress. The prairie glowed with the subtler hues of late summer. She was grateful for the empty car and tried to relax. The conductor walked through and announced the last stop before Chicago. She gathered her things. The train slowed, and she looked longingly at the ugly city, thought of her drafty little room in the widow's house. She could taste the first nip of fall. She had lived in the city long enough to guess how many more days she could go without a shawl. She waited until the platform cleared.

There was no one there to meet her. She had asked a literate woman to write the note, copy the widow's address down. But she did not trust the postal system, and she did not believe they had ever gotten it. If Richard had known, he would have been there to meet her. A kindly man.

A hack driver slowed. She asked for Ontario Street as he loaded her trunk. She settled into the ride, looking onto the city. *Hemp*. Now he was a man. Not some transient stopping through town long enough to flirt with an innocent healing girl. Madge had not known such pain until she'd left him behind, ostensibly for good. She had not been able to bring herself to tell her mother about him, though she'd wanted to. There was no future, no chance for anything serious. She'd always wondered about the stories she'd heard about love, the way it shook the sense out of a woman. Perhaps this new freedom had something to do with abandon, a reckless notion to follow a scent in the wind. Back home in Tennessee, such feelings were dangerous. When each step spelled potential peril, there was no place for such nonsense. A woman's passion had to be measured by the teaspoon.

What on earth could she do with this tender tree of a man anyway? She wished her hands were larger, wished she could wrap her palms and fingers around his entire body, feel out all his insides. This love needed room to grow and roam, but with that other woman's ghost haunting him, there was little space left.

Madge did not know what she would say when she saw him. All she knew was that she could not leave things as they'd been.

When she opened her eyes, they were crossing the bridge into the northern district of the city.

SHE ENTERED THE HOUSE through the kitchen. Olga was sitting at the table peeling potatoes. She barely looked up.

"Thought you were gone for good."

"Thought I was, too."

"She expecting you?"

"Don't know."

"Well, she hasn't hired anyone else, so I suppose you better get out of those traveling clothes and get back to work."

Madge picked up the trunk and carried it to the bottom of the back stairwell. She stopped. She could not help herself. She peeked into her herb cupboard. The cook had been filling it with jars and foodstuffs. It did not smell the same.

Upstairs, she scooted the trunk into a corner and began to undress. When she had changed into a suitable dress, she went looking for the widow. She heard a man's cough coming from the drawing room. The widow's father must have arrived while she was gone.

She climbed the stairs, knocked softly on the widow's bedroom. No answer. She found the widow napping in the library.

"Mrs. Walker, you need anything?"

Sadie's eyes flew open and she sat up. "Madge. You're back."

"That old dream about the house in Tennessee wasn't much of nothing."

"When I saw you standing there, I thought I was dreaming."

"I brought you some tea back."

"My father had a fall. He can't make it up the stairs, so he's sleeping in the drawing room for now."

"Want me to bring it up?"

"You said the dream didn't mean anything. How was your mother?"

Madge took a breath, then allowed the flap inside her to open. "My mother lost her eyes, but she's making it."

"The war left its mark on everyone."

"Yes, ma'am. But if it wasn't for the war, I wouldn't be standing here."

"Please sit, Madge."

"What for?"

"My father says he is returning to York. He doesn't approve of my speaking with spirits."

"I don't blame him," Madge said, then softened her tone. "But that decision is yours. Long as you feel you helping people."

"I can talk to the dead without him, you know."

"Without who?"

"James."

"Ain't that something. Never knew your own strength."

"And what about your strength? What will you do with those hands? Surely you can do more than mix up plants in my kitchen."

"I can make that tea for you and your daddy if you like."

"Thank you, Madge. That would be nice."

Madge turned to leave.

"And Madge? I'm sorry for what I said about Hemp."

"We all got our regrets, Mrs. Walker."

When Madge returned to the kitchen, Richard was sitting at the table drinking a bowl of soup.

"What's new, old man?" She smiled at him.

"Didn't know you were getting back today. I would have met you at the station."

"No need."

"Hemp been around here looking for you."

She froze. "Where is he?"

"Don't know. You could try the church."

She could not help herself. "Did the doctor find Annie?"

"I reckon that's a conversation you need to have with him."

She didn't dare hope. "I got to work right now. Can you take me over there in a little while?"

"I can walk you."

"That'll do. I'll holler when I'm ready."

A couple of hours later, the two of them stopped in front of the church.

"Is he all right?"

"He fine, he fine. But I think the two of you got business to settle," said Richard, opening the door for her. "I see you back at the house."

Inside, Madge saw a man she assumed was the reverend sitting in the front pew staring up at the ceiling. She looked up. She could see the outline of where a large hole had been patched. He spoke without turning around.

"It took us quite a while to patch up that hole. Seem like every time we patched it up, the snow and ice made it fall in again. Finally, we got it good and fixed and not a single ray of sun has peeped through."

"Mighty fine work, Reverend."

He turned. "Forgive my manners. I didn't know I was in the presence of a lady. Come on in. What can I do for you today?"

"I'm looking for Deacon Hemp. Any chance he around here?"

"Haven't seen him today. If it's important, I can—"

"Yes, I need to see him."

"All right then, take a seat and I'll send a boy to fetch him. I believe he driving for a doctor man on the west side. The stable ain't too far from here."

"I really appreciate it. I hate to trouble you."

"No trouble at all."

She sat in a front pew, and the reverend disappeared through a door in the back of the church. She remembered the last time she had come inside this church. She had been with the widow, and they had gone into that back room where a small group of anxious people awaited them. But she could not remember the last time she'd gone into a church to worship. She looked at the small seating area for the choir, the minister's lectern. There was a beautifully embroidered cloth draped across it, the most colorful thing in the room. Her brand of religion didn't include the kinds of things that went on inside churches, but it did not mean she didn't respect the healing that went on here. She recognized healing in all its forms, and when people jumped and danced as they sang and prayed, she could almost see the mending stitches run up their bodies. She ran her hand back and forth over the back of the pew in front of her. It was smoothly planed, and she thought of all the care men like the deacons must have put into maintaining the modest little building. She knew Hemp was one of those men.

The reverend came back a few minutes later. He sat a few feet over from her on the same pew. He returned to staring up at the ceiling. His breathing was labored.

"You know Deacon Hemp from Kentucky?"

She winced, wondering if the man thought she was Annie. The woman's shadow would haunt her forever. She wished she could contact the spirit world like Sadie could, talk to the woman herself. *Let go of him*, she would say. *Let the man move on in peace. A ghost love ain't real as mines.*

"No, I met him here. I'm from Tennessee."

"Oh, is that right?"

She wondered how much Hemp had told his reverend of her, if anything at all. She wanted to feel as if she were important enough to make him confide in this elder. But when she looked at the reverend's face, he did not reveal any knowledge of her. The man's face was unreadable.

But she could read something other than his face. The shallow breath. The tightened chest.

"Reverend?" She scooted closer. "Forgive my asking, but you been feeling all right?"

He looked over at her, and she could see that he would not give her a straight answer. He said exactly what she thought he would: "The Lord is good. I can't complain."

She tried to figure out how she would touch him. If he let her put her hands on him, she would be able to see what was going on. She guessed there was something in his chest; something needing to be cleared. The eyes also appeared a bit yellow, and she knew a good tea for that as well.

"Give me your hands, Reverend."

"What?" His eyes clouded, then cleared. "You that root woman, ain't you? Work for the widow? We got one of those in the church. She made me a tea once, and all it did was put me to sleep."

So Hemp had told him about her. Or maybe Richard had. Surely he did not remember her from that one brief séance. She tried to shake off her vanity.

"Please," she said. "Give me your hands."

He looked around the room, as if someone were watching them. Then he calmly placed both hands in her upturned palms.

She closed her eyes. For a moment, there was nothing but light behind her eyelids. They darkened until she saw red. Just as she'd guessed. The chest was full of something nasty. There was a problem next to his stomach, too, on the right side of his body. Something there wasn't functioning properly, and she'd seen it before. It was causing his eyes to yellow. Yes, she knew a couple of things she could make up for him. She released his hands and opened her eyes.

"What did you just do?"

"I can send something over to you by Richard. Something to help." She barely recognized herself. She wasn't healing this man out of the goodness of her heart. She was healing him because he was close to Hemp, and by helping him, she was inching closer to Hemp. *I'm terrible*, she thought.

"Did God speak to you just now?" he whispered, more than a hint of fear in his voice.

The door to the church opened, and the orange hue of sunset flooded the church. Before she looked back, she knew she would see the dark silhouette of Hemp filling the doorway.

She stood up, the reverend forgotten.

"Is that you?" Hemp said.

"In the flesh," she answered just before the reverend repeated, *What did you just do?*

30

HEMP STEPPED INTO THE CHURCH SO HE could see her better. A brown-faced girl with cottony hair tucked into two rows of braids. Dressed finer than expected. Chin higher than was custom. When she looked up at him, he saw the face of Tennessee. He moved toward her, afraid that if he did not lay hands on her, she would disappear. When he reached her, he gripped both of her arms harder than he'd intended. Her face did not register surprise, as if it were normal for him to grab her so roughly.

"When you get here?" he said, though he wanted to say, *Why you take so long to fetch me?*

"Today."

"Richard told me you was coming back. I thought you was gone for good." He let go of her.

"I suppose ain't nothing permanent but death."

The reverend cleared his throat. "I'll go on back yonder. Nice meeting you . . ."

Her eyes did not move from Hemp's face. She touched a pin at her neck, and he saw that the tips of her fingers were scabbed over from cuts.

"Your hands all right?"

Neither of them heard the door click softly behind the reverend.

"We go picking through the woods down there," she said, nodding.

Now that she was here with him, his tongue was tied. She brought him back to boyhood, to a time when he had been unable to calm himself: a game of bogeyman, the promise of new shoes, a newly slaughtered hog, a fresh cup of milk. He trembled as he looked at her, and he could no longer deny it. She made him want to start over, move forward. She was the reason he'd buried a wooden cross with flowers carved into it. Without her, he would not have done it. Not yet. But he felt something for this woman that refused to go away. He did not know how far Tennessee was from Chicago, but there was weariness on her face, etched around her eyes, and he wanted to make it disappear. He wanted to erase those lines on her hands. He did not want her to ever be tired again. He wanted to be the healer for a change.

"You hungry?" he said suddenly.

"No. You?"

"Just ate."

"I got the widow's credit."

"Woman, would you let me be a man?" He looked awkwardly down at her.

She sat down and motioned for him to sit beside her. "I better sit. It's been a long day. I was on that train for twenty years, seem like."

He placed his palms on his knees and slowly sat. The pew creaked beneath his weight. He sank the tips of his fingers into his hair.

She wanted to ask if the doctor had found Annie. She needed to know that before she said anything else. Maybe he was here to tell her that he was back with his wife, but he did not want to upset her. He looked so anxious. Maybe he was just nervous about the news he was about to deliver. She met his eyes. She had something to say, and she would not rest until she said it. There was no way to get past this hump other than to admit her terrible mistake. A growing space inside her, emptied of pride, prepared to admit her wrongdoing. She would say the words that would allow him to settle back with his wife without fearing that Madge would disrupt their matrimony.

She needed to sleep in a bed. Days of travel had worn her down. She sat up straight, thinking of how to form the right words. As large as Chicago was, it was too small to avoid him. As soon as she said what she had to say, they would be free of each other.

"Hemp, I am so sorry how—"

He touched her arm to silence her. Lips that puckered like a flower when she spoke. Ears tucked in close to her head. The woman was a stroke from God's quill, her looks enough to make a grown man trip over his feet. Her personality, on the other hand, was another story. He detected a mystery in the healer that stretched beyond his ken, but he wanted her so badly, he was ready to throw out his caution. A life with her would be more than a life. It would be as thrilling as a man hunting for gold. This constant puzzling out of her thoughts flushed him with pleasure.

"You ain't got to say nothing."

"I want to ask for your forgiveness if you allow it."

He wanted to laugh. She was asking *him* to forgive *her* when he was the one who mistook her for Annie that night in his grief. He was the one who pushed her up those stairs to her room. Whoever started it, the sin was enough to stain them both. The only way to overcome it was to make an honest couple out of the two of them.

She started to cry.

"Oh no, Madge. Now don't cry." She was probably remembering

the words he'd thrown at her that last night. He wished he could take them back, but he couldn't. He tried to open his mouth and say *I forgive* . . . but nothing came. He was not able to protect Annie when the trader came. He had stood silently by as if his hands did not make fists, watched her go while he mourned like a baby, walked back into the field like the draft horse they thought he was. His search for her in Kentucky was too brief: a feeble rifling through the camp and some abandoned farms, a ride too easily accepted from a white missionary, clothes from a preacher, a shared room at a lodging house, a clipping in a paper, a futile gesture from a doctor. These were the thoughts he had to live with. Madge was right. He was the one who had to forgive, close up his wounds, and move on. It was all that was left to do. The coloreds praying. The whites mourning. The trains whistling. The space between him and his old life widening. The healer crying right there in front of him. Everyone, everywhere, doing the only thing left for them to do.

"Marry me," he whispered, the words tumbling out in a rasp. He wished he could speak with his hands, mold his life like a block of wood. He could better show her how he felt with a piece of tree and some tools.

But it was time for him to speak up like a man. His voice strengthened, "Miss Madge. Marry me," he said, gaining volume with each utterance.

"Marry me . . . marry me."

THEY MARRIED IN THE MIDDLE of a winter storm. The reverend blessed the couple in front of nearly every member of the small but growing church. In the back pew, the widow sat next to Michael. A deacon played a march on the piano. Hemp wore a borrowed uniform from a friend who had sneaked it out of the Tremont House. He stood as straight as a soldier while the reverend performed the rites. The wind whipped the small building, rattling it. But the deacons had worked long and hard to secure a strong and steady roof, and no one feared the building's demise.

In the months since he'd proposed to Madge, Hemp had been renewed, and, as he had always done, he looked beyond himself to find the glory. And he was thinking of trees, how they aged. He did not know as much as Madge about God's creations—the woman had brought back a sack of dirty bark!—but he knew something about the heart of a tree. When it dried, it did not bend and warp as the outer, wetter wood might. And he knew what things a tree could provide: a house to keep them warm, a broom handle to clean it, furniture to rest upon, a barn to shelter a cow, a fork to manage the hay, a spinning wheel to make cloth, a box to keep cheese, a canoe to cross a lake. There was no problem a strong piece of wood could not solve.

He could not remember his daddy's face, but if he closed his eyes, those hands appeared before him, whittling. The man had been the first to put a knife in his young son's hands, and from the beginning, Hemp loved the feel of wood beneath his fingers, the run of grain like a stream's current. He had been too young to use the knife, but he gleefully picked stones from the river, and long nights passed with the elder sitting outside the cabin sharpening his knife against the stone, the soft scraping sound sending the boy into a restful sleep.

As he stood before Madge, he vaguely recalled the night his daddy died. He had been just four years old, and the grown-ups had made him leave the cabin when the man began to show signs of his final moments. A woman with five children had gathered him in with her brood, and he ate a bowl of hot meal before falling off to sleep on a crowded pallet. The following week he had been sold off to another farm, to a Mr. Harrison, twenty miles away.

Hemp could smell the flowers Mrs. Walker had sent, and he was grateful they were not hyacinth. Madge smiled, holding fast to his hand as if the wind would whisk into the church and steal him if she let go. It was cold, and her lip quivered. He reached to still it with his finger. The minister took his time, embellishing the lines with as much formality as the scripture allowed. In his pocket, Hemp carried the marriage certificate, the official record of their union. Though they did not have a place to call their own yet—Madge would continue to live at the widow's house and Hemp still lived with the men—their lives were their own, their futures alight. His days no longer ended with exhaustion, as they had during slavery, but with succor. The satisfaction of a mind at rest, the memory of where he had been enough to make him hold on to her a little tighter.

With a start, he recalled the name his daddy had gone by: Thomas. *My daddy's name was Thomas and so was mines.* When he left that farm soon after his father's death, he had left behind his name. He held back a baby's whimper, the hurt threatening to overcome him.

"Do you have some token of your love, Deacon Harrison?"

"Thomas," he whispered.

"What's that?"

"My name is Thomas."

"All right then, Deacon Thomas." The reverend nodded, cleared his throat. "Do you have a token?"

"Yas, sir." He dug in his pocket. He'd measured her finger with a piece of string while she slept and carved a ring out of wood. He held her hand in his. It was the first ring he had ever given a woman.

"You are now, in the eyes of the Lord, and in the eyes of the *law*, husband and wife."

Bone of my bones, he thought, kissing her on the lips.

As Madge looked up at the face of her new husband, she was thinking of what the sisters had taught her about how to store healing plants, what would keep for a time, and what would rot. How this one needed the heat of the open field and that one the cool of the shade, this one the moist dirt after a spring shower, that one the well-drained soil of a sandy loam. Everything on the earth had its instructions. A careless boot step might kill one plant while another leaped right back up in defiance. The truth of it, they said, was that the body did not belong to the name of the person attached to it, any more than the tree on a man's property belonged to him. The body belonged to the earth, its return inevitable, the healer's role nothing beyond a kind of safekeeping.

He turned his face down to hers, and she sensed fragility in that cheek, knew, suddenly, that despite his size, this man was not as sturdy as a tree, but as fragile as a flower. He would need a moist soil to plant himself, and she would have to be gentle with her touch. He would need the sunlight of her love, the warmth of her compassion.

"You two coming? I hear it's a celebration round back," said the reverend.

"Can you give us a minute?" Madge asked.

She had never joined a church, never reached out to anyone. The sisters had preached self-reliance, but the real thing was community. Now she had gained both a husband and a church. She was not much for churchgoing, but in the next room the congregation waited for them, a hot meal spread out on a wooden table. She could not help but feel love for them in return.

"I want to give you something." She pulled out the locket.

"What's this?" he said.

"Something from my ma. It belong to you now."

He opened it and looked at the image for a long time.

"Now listen. I got something to say, and I don't want you interrupting. I'm giving you this here chain to represent our new life."

"New life."

"That wife is long gone and we belongs to one another now."

"You my wife now. And the devil himself couldn't tear me away from you."

"We can't wipe out the past like it didn't happen. And we sure can't change it. But we can lay some things to rest."

"Yas, suh. We sure can."

Then she stood on her toes, put her lips to his ear, and whispered his name.

31

THE REVEREND REPORTED THAT THEY WERE LINED up to see her, each person holding some token they would exchange for a touch, a pronouncement. Madge told him to report that she did not have her balm with her. He responded that they knew that—all they wanted was relief. Why the devil did this toe hurt? Why can't I move my bowels? Later, she promised she would bring a healing balm. But for now, the reverend reported that all they wanted were her hands. She had already decided she would not accept payment. Not now. These were her people, many of them newly arrived from their nightmarish pasts, many still suffering the hurts of slavery. She had already glimpsed them. Some were missing fingers, ears. Others bore scars across their faces. Their hair was knotted, their scalps bumped with infection, fingers gnarled from long-ago traumas. These were not just the humbled people brought to their knees while tilling American land. These were her kinfolk, and she loved them too much to not give freely of her gift.

A couple of nights before, she'd had a dream. A snowstorm in the winter of 1864. She'd been out on some forgotten errand when the light snowfall turned violent, white flakes as big as walnuts dumping out of the sky. As she turned to go back home, a white man stopped her.

"Where are your papers?" the man demanded.

She looked about her in fright, realizing she had become so accustomed to being in the new city, she had taken to leaving her free papers behind in the rooming house. The man wore neither uniform nor insignia, but his tone was authoritative.

"I don't got none. I mean—"

"No papers?"

"I mean, I didn't bring 'em."

"Well, have you paid your bond? Even if you are free, you cannot remain in the city without paying a bond."

"A what?" Her voice was lost in the wind.

"Come on," he said, yanking her. He led her down a street, and she thought of the orange sash tucked inside her waistband. The man cared nothing about her story, and she was struck with a fear that she would be sent into slavery for the first time in her life. She searched for a friendly face, but the people averted their eyes, emerging out of the snow and disappearing right back into it.

"Hurry it up," he growled.

He led her through an alley that led to Wells Street. A team of runaway horses charged out of the whiteness, pulling a bed of lumber behind them. The man twisted her arm to pull the two of them out of the way, but Madge wrenched free, running through an alley as fast as she could. She did not look back, her heels sinking into the rising snow. She was running for her life, running the way the sisters had taught her to do should someone come after her. She kept going, not pausing for a breath until she was safely in the colored district, her dress soaked, hair

herself more than once. In a land so devastated by death, the best healing balm was hope. The sisters had taught her that even if they did not
claim the lesson. She was one of them after all.

And look what hope had gotten her? A man who loved her enough
to put his ghosts to rest and marry her. She smiled at him, and the look
he returned to her was enough to break her down.

"Come on in," she called out to the young mother leading a tiny
boy by the hand. Madge took in his sightless eyes and thought of her
mother. She suddenly did not feel well herself.

Madge placed her hands on the boy's head. She did not feel anything. Perfectly healthy other than the eyes. A smile turned up his lips
as he ran a finger down her arm. Little angel. She heard a commotion
at the door.

"Excuse me, excuse me."

She recognized the doctor's voice before she saw his face. What
could he possibly want? It couldn't have to do with that old ankle injury again.

But when the crowd cleared she saw that he led a young woman by
the hand. Was she the sick one? Madge's eyes went from the woman
to the doctor and back to the woman again. A short mass of hair. A
prominent nose standing guard over tiny lips. It all came to a point in a
sharp chin, the irregularity of it creating an unforgettable face.

"What can I do for you, Doctor?" Madge asked before glancing
over at her husband. But his look was enough to sink her. She looked
back at the girl. It couldn't be. Her promises to honor the memory of
Hemp's family faded, and she was ashamed to admit the lesser thoughts
that threatened her.

Michael whispered something in the woman's ear. It had taken
some time, but he had finally been able to bring Hemp's daughter to
Chicago. Peter had found her, but it had been up to Michael to bring
her there. It had taken a while. In the meantime, he'd heard from Sadie

stuck to her face, fingers numb with cold. In Tennessee, th
knowledge had protected them, but Madge's close brush wit
taught her that in Chicago, she would have to fight to surv
city was no safe place for any colored person, let alone a singl
without family.

The dream had awakened her and she could not get back
That was when she'd decided to accept the reverend's invitati
she was wondering if she'd made the right decision.

Hemp patted her shoulder and stepped back to let her w
reverend led the first to her, a woman bent over in pain. Mad
this was a back problem that she would not be able to fix. Only
ing oil rubbed on her back by a loved one would give her so
porary relief. The woman was so young. Too young for such t
When Madge laid hands on her, she saw the women attempt to
straighten, so fervently did she want to believe.

"They think I can work miracles," Madge whispered to
erend after the woman left. "You got to tell them that I can't d

"That's why they're here, Miss Madge. These people nee
lieve. You giving that to them."

"Yeah, but Reverend, you of all people ought to know it air
to play God."

"You not playing God, but you got to admit your hands a
cial. What if you can help somebody?"

"I can't lay hands on them and heal them. I didn't bring no
with me, and besides, that woman can't be helped with no tea
back is near about broke."

"That's all right. Can't you see? If medicine can't help her,
her faith is all she got."

Madge did not like it, but as person after person came in to se
she began to understand the reverend's argument. She had sai

about the wedding, about Hemp's attempts to start over. He hoped he wasn't too late. Maybe bringing the girl to them would bring about some closure. Even though his agents delivered the sad news that Annie was dead, surely Hemp would welcome her daughter. Michael vaguely remembered that she was not Hemp's blood relative, but he assumed a measure of paternalism existed between the two given the often unusual circumstances of slave families.

Here was the story Peter had delivered to him several months before. In 1863, the group of women from Harrison's hemp farm were sold to another farmer who lived a hundred miles east. After the war ended, the girl and her mother made their way to Indiana. Eventually, they ended up working together as domestics in a house. The family who hired them happened to be the cousins of a man who'd worked as a missionary at Camp Nelson during the war. When he read in the newspaper of a man named Hemp "Horse" Harrison looking for his family, he remembered the ragged man asking everyone around the camp about a woman and girl. Annie was long gone, but her daughter still worked for his cousin.

As Michael watched the confusion on Madge's face turn to concern, he wondered if he had done this the right way. Perhaps he should have warned them he was coming. A part of him had not believed the woman would actually show up until she stepped onto the train platform. And he'd assumed that since he wasn't bringing the man's previous wife, it would not disrupt the new marriage.

One look at Madge, and he recognized his misjudgment.

"That'll be all for today," the reverend said. He spread his arms as if to sweep everyone out of the room. They did not move at first, still hoping for Madge's touch. But none dared challenge the reverend.

Hemp stepped forward, then stopped, his emotions in a tangle. During that first church séance, he had heard from the girl, hadn't he? She was supposed to be dead. She was the one who told the widow's spirit man that something happened between them that night in the cabin, not Annie. Annie didn't know anything about that. Right? Right?

Relief. He had been wrong to assume that the spirit at the church that night was Herod. The girl was alive. Panic. Annie wasn't with her. Astonishment. How much she had grown! Shame. She was still beautiful.

"Dr. Heil? I don't believe you and I have met. Might I interest you in some coffee? I believe I got some pie to go with it."

"I would be honored." Michael followed the reverend out of the room.

Herod looked at Madge, as if to ask why she was staying when everyone else had cleared out.

"I heard you got a new wife. This her?"

Hemp nodded slowly.

Herod narrowed her eyes. "Mama never could make a fresh start."

"Where is she?" Hemp whispered.

"She didn't make it."

"Couldn't?"

"She passed on not long after the war ended. Her heart was broke." Herod dropped her head, wiped at her eyes. Then she looked back up at him. "There was a time I would have blamed you for that."

Hemp thought of his attempt at a grave, wondered what Herod would think of him burying her mother before he knew for sure the woman was dead. He wanted to know everything that had happened to them after they left. There was so much to say. Too much. But he knew the stories this girl might tell him had the power to take away everything. The wedding had been a chance. Now here was the past, knocking on his door again and threatening his very survival.

"You took her away from me, you know. They said I was cursed, but I ain't never done nothing to nobody."

"Nothing?"

"What I done to you?"

They both turned to Madge who was looking down at her hands as if wondering who they belonged to.

"I ought to leave," Madge said, not looking at the two.

"I don't have no secrets from you, Madge," Hemp said.

"I didn't come here to make trouble."

"Well then, what did you come here for?" Hemp wanted to walk over to Madge and take her hand, let her know he was still with her. But he felt that to do so was to turn his back on Herod. Though he spoke harshly, he couldn't bring himself to turn his back on the girl. Not again. So he just stood there, stuck in the middle of his past and his present.

"I come to close the door on it. Let you know I was sorry for what happened. I'm glad my mama found you. Gave her a little bit of sunshine for a while."

Hemp said nothing.

"I'll be going now. The doctor said he find a place for me to stay the night."

"Herod?" Madge rose. She walked over to the girl and put her arms around her. The girl stood stiffly, not returning the embrace. Madge did not need her to. She felt all the hurt rising through the girl's body, pain that was not the physical kind but the kind that took years and years to root in a person's soul. It was not just the girl's pain but that of a thousand women—wronged women, unloved women, sad women—that rose up through Herod. Madge wished she could will it all away, pull it out of Herod with this inexplicable rush of love she was feeling for the girl. Then Madge felt the hurt settle back down into the girl's trunk. It would take more than a hug from a root doctor to set this girl right again.

"We ain't got no home yet. He still living in a room full of men and I'm sleeping in a white woman's house. But you stay here in Chicago and once we do get a home, you got a place in it. You hear me?"

"I don't need it."

"Hush," Madge said. "Yes, you do. Your body tell me everything I need to know about you. You need it more than any of us."

32

SADIE'S CARRIAGE MOVED SLOWLY OVER THE SNOWY road. Even in the storm, men walked in the streets, hats pulled down over their faces, heads angled forward. The wheels ran over something, and Richard apologized as the carriage righted itself again, continuing on through the city, over the bridge into the North Division, the tall buildings fading into the white sky behind them.

In the house, Sadie removed her cloak, hat, gloves, and wet boots. The snow had started to mix with rain, and her outerwear was drenched. Olga brought her slippers, then stoked the fire. Sadie heard the front door open, and though she knew it was her father, she started abruptly as if it were an intruder. She wanted to move out into the hall, say something, but she hesitated as she heard him climbing the steps, the slow thud of cane on the wooden floor as he fussed with his foot.

"Mrs. Walker, your father is upstairs. Shall I have Olga serve dinner?"

"Yes, that will be fine, Richard. Thank you."

The driver had become both butler and coachman. She thought it might be scandalous, a widowed woman allowing a colored man access into the private recesses of her home, but there were so few people to lean on, so few she could trust. Her father needed help while he convalesced, and Richard served the man faithfully.

Her father remained in Chicago for the time being, and she did not mind it. She was still hoping for some kind of truce before his departure. She had not sat down with him again since he'd first arrived back from the hospital, but she knew it would happen before long. There would come a night when they would sit together in that dark parlor and she would tell her truth and he would tell his, and they would struggle to acknowledge each other's sides. She did not care how long it took. She was willing to wait. He was her family.

She sat in her drawing room and removed her gloves, thinking of the war once again. She could remember the end of it as if it were yesterday. Once news reached Chicago that Richmond had been taken, businesses closed, flags waved, pistols reported, crowds rushed the streets. In the street, spontaneous parades had formed as songs rang out. She had been there, on the steps of the palace hotel. A hundred-gun salute erupted, the smell of gunpowder filling her nose. A brass band marched. Sadie had raised a black cotton umbrella to shield her face from the dust.

Six days later the end of the war was declared, and the wheels of the city halted. Olga asked for two days off, and Sadie stayed in the house away from the commotion of the celebrations across the bridge. She sat in her drawing room embroidering newly arrived fabric from New York, finding comfort in her needle. They said it was an end to the country's dark. But she had not believed that, had needed to see that document of surrender with her own eyes. One wild cannon fired and the war would be on again, men suited and rearmed, sacks slung over shoulders. Hemmed by doubt, a thickness in her throat, her vision waned with each stitch. Sadie hated the clangor of war. Men locked fist to fist, a cranny growing, year by year, into a fissure. When she was nineteen years old, a battle in faraway South Carolina had changed her life, and she still resented the intrusion even though it was over. She'd clipped the loose threads on the surface of the fabric as she struggled to interpret all that had happened.

Then news of the president's death had turned the city's mood again. The neighbor's son, eyes reddened, stood on her doorstep carrying the message at ten o'clock at night near the end of Good Friday. When Lincoln's body arrived by train on the first of May, thousands of mourners lined the streets in cold, driving rain as the procession made its way through the city. Sadie watched from her carriage as ten black horses pulled the hearse carrying the man who had inspired a nation. A band played, but she could not hear it. She could not believe the man was actually dead. She'd thought of her father, comparing the two. Both men tall, thin, one rugged with the hands of a farmer, the other pale with the hands of an artisan. Her father cleared his throat when he was nervous. His ears protruded. His hair grayed early, and on his chin he wore a trimmed silver bush. He could not sing, but he always did so when he was in his garden. He avoided their coarser neighbors, detested gossips. He was short-tempered, but he hid it with deep swallows, a calculated turning of the back when someone's news tested his limits. His favorite poets were Keats and Browning, and she wondered about this sign of a latent sentimental side. He'd built a bindery in the basement of their home, where he worked for hours amid the dust and scent of pulp. He was widely admired. Young men sought him for advice. He was everyone's father, a voice of reason even during more panic-stricken moments in time, a man rigid in belief, stalwart in character, monumental enough to capture rooms when he entered. When she heard the president had died, all she could do was think of her father, the litany of traits that had led him to thrust her into the clutches of a man he barely knew, and she wondered at the two of them, daughter and father, fellow survivors ineluctably riven by war.

Now as she sat in her parlor waiting for the call of dinner, she remembered the delicate, sallow faces of the returning soldiers, how the country had wheeled into a new grief. The damage had sullied everyone around her, yet in that tall house on Ontario Street, she had somehow survived.

MADGE MADE HER WAY toward the bridge that crossed into the northern district of the city. Businessmen rushed about, couples strolled, vendors hawked their wares. It was a bright Chicago day, and although heaps of snow lined the road, it was the kind of day that made her forget the harshness of winter. One of the city's new steam-run streetcars rattled past her, smoke clouding the air. She turned her face and coughed as she considered a quieter street she could take. Her step was light, the morning sun bright on her face.

Once she crossed the bridge, she walked until she reached Ontario Street, a few blocks from the widow's house. She thought of the wedding dress Sadie had given her, the feel of the silk against her skin. When she'd first met her, the widow had worn only black. Now there was a rainbow in her closet. Time sure did change things. Each night, she and Hemp—no, Thomas—considered their strange new world as they discussed the future with fear and uncertainty. At least they had each other. And Herod.

Inside the widow's kitchen, Madge was more than a healer and a wife. Chopping and steeping, brewing and tasting, she felt transformed into a person set to do something remarkable in the world. As she walked toward the widow's house she thought, *I am sure enough American. This what Americans do. Make something out of nothing. Start over and make a new self.*

"You're late. It's work to be done," Olga said, swishing a broom across the floor. "Seems like I'm the only one around here without a paying customer."

"I can teach you a few things if you like."

"I'd like to teach you a few things," Olga muttered as she leaned the broom against the wall.

Olga's foul humor could not disturb Madge's joy, but as Madge took the empty jars from her sack and spread them out on the table a bolt of sadness ran through her. She was thinking of how she'd left her family behind twice. The first time, on the walk up from Tennessee, she had dreamed of them as she slept on the prairie floor, the moist ground sinking beneath her. The second time, she had dreamed of them as she leaned her face against a train car window. Now the memories flooded her, triggered by the start of a ritual that would always tie her to the sisters. Thomas had been right. She had known love, and the past was real. Designing a life of her own making would not be easy, and though she was finally freer than free, it had cost her. Sometimes it seemed like everyone, everywhere, had sacrificed something to get to something better.

She shook her head, thinking if she just kept moving, she could momentarily rid herself of the memories. She mashed ginger root in a bowl.

She felt someone looking over her shoulder, and she stiffened, thinking it was that worrisome spirit again. When she saw it was Olga, she relaxed and began mixing again.

"It sure does take a lot of different ingredients to make a healing balm," Olga said.

"Ain't that the truth," Madge said.

Olga lit the fire in the oven, and the kitchen warmed. The two women worked beside each other, the clamor of pots and bowls filling the room.

Acknowledgments

My agent, Stephanie Cabot, has gone above and beyond to make this book happen. Thank you. It has been an honor to work with Terry Karten, my editor. This manuscript also benefitted from the sharp editorial eyes of Dawn Davis and Tracy Sherrod. I am immensely grateful to both of you.

The DC Commission on the Arts generously provided an Individual Artist grant in support of *Balm*. With those funds, I traveled to archives, libraries, battlefields, and museums. I could not have done it without their support.

During the course of my research, I encountered many generous people eager to lend a hand. Matt Rutherford and Lauren Reno at the Newberry Library in Chicago. Tim James at Bookbinders Museum in San Francisco. Jenna Entwistle at the York County Archives and Library. Barby Morland at Library of Congress. Thanks to the many nameless people who directed or assisted me at the University of Chicago Regenstein Library, the Chicago History Museum, and the Boston Public Library. I am also thankful to the security guards who asked about my research and encouraged me to continue.

I have always said fiction writers have a lot of ground to cover if we want to catch up with the scholars. I am deeply indebted to the brilliant work of Sharla Fett, Frances Smith Foster, Yvonne Chireau, Ann

Braude, Heather Andrea Williams, Donald Miller, Leon Litwack, Ann Taves, Molly McGarry, and Pier Gabrielle Foreman. Christopher Robert Reed graciously spent an afternoon talking black Chicago history with me. *Balm* was originally inspired by Drew Gilpin Faust's *The Republic of Suffering*.

My sister-in-law Maria Aparicio helped answer medical questions. My classmate, Dr. Manuel Saint-Victor, first told me about sympathetic blindness.

Special thanks to my writer mentors: Tina McElroy Ansa, Pearl Cleage, Terry McMillan, and Marita Golden. My dear mentor and friend James A. Miller: you are always a light in my heart. My colleagues at the Stonecoast MFA program are supportive and kind.

Fortunately, my mother's sisters are nothing like the sisters in this book. I am forever grateful for the love of my aunts: Beverly Fitzpatrick, Agnes Epps, Carole Thornton, and the late Rosemary Hughes.

Special thanks to my two nieces Helen Aparicio and Barbara McClure for helping with my little ones. My dearest Mrs. Della Jones has become family. Thanks to my beloved sister and brother: Jeanna and Harry. Thanks to my parents, Barbara and James, for the awesome PR machine, also known as parental bragging.

Special thanks to the Pen/Faulkner Foundation Writers-in-Schools program and the students at District of Columbia high schools, especially Ballou, Coolidge, The Seed School, Chavez, Banneker, Bell, McKinley, and Anacostia. You are all exceptional. Go out and change the world.

Finally, I am humbled by the continued support of my little familia—David, Emilia, and Elena, who keeps asking me to write a book about her. Everything is about you, my darling.

About the Author

DOLEN PERKINS-VALDEZ is the author of the *New York Times* bestselling novel *Wench*. *USA Today* called the book "deeply moving" and "beautifully written." *People* called it "a devastatingly beautiful account of a cruel past." *O, The Oprah Magazine* chose it as a Top Ten Pick of the Month, and NPR named it a Top 5 Book Club Pick of 2010. Dolen's fiction has appeared in *The Kenyon Review, StoryQuarterly, StorySouth,* and elsewhere. In 2011, she was a finalist for two NAACP Image Awards and the Hurston-Wright Legacy Award for fiction. She was also awarded the First Novelist Award by the Black Caucus of the American Library Association and has received a DC Commission on the Arts Grant. Dolen teaches in the Stonecoast MFA program. A graduate of Harvard and a former University of California President's Postdoctoral Fellow at UCLA, Dolen lives in Washington, D.C., with her family.